Blackpool Rock Bloodshed

Albert Smith's Culinary Capers

Recipe 10

Steve Higgs

Publisher: Steve Higgs

Table of Contents:

The Wolfman

'I think that went rather well tonight, don't you, Wolf?'

Wolf held little opinion on the subject. His human's odd magic act was not something he could understand. It was sufficient that he knew when to move and where to appear and that his human would have left a tasty piece of meat for him to find when he got to the right place.

His human was counting their takings, not that money was a concept Wolf fully understood either.

Tethered to the railings on the promenade, Wolf waited for his human to finish packing up their stage. It all went into a small hand cart which his human would then drag back to the van they lived in. It was a simple life and thus the wolf found it most agreeable.

His human continued to jabber as he so often did, Wolf paying him little attention as he watched out to sea. The waves kept on rolling, unconcerned about whether anyone thought they should or not.

It was late now, the beach area devoid of life, and the customers the wolfman act attracted each night dwindled with each passing week. Fridays and Saturdays were not too bad even this late into the season, but things were looking bleak for the winter unless he could find some paid work.

That had been easier when he was younger. Now in his sixties, no one wanted to employ him. Not even for menial labour. Thankfully, his wolfman act always drew a good crowd and he'd been saving over the summer. On good days he was able to put proper folding money into his little saving jar. They would make it through the winter this year. He could worry about next year when it was a little closer.

'The crocodile nearest the canoe,' he remarked to Wolf.

Wolf turned his head, unsure what the old man was saying.

Pausing before he disconnected the next piece of his stage, the wolf's human paused to get his breath and explained what he was saying.

'You see it's no good worrying about the crocodiles on the bank, Wolf. The one you need to whack on the head is the one that is nearest. Deal with the one that is about to eat your canoe and worry about the other ones if and when they decide to get into the water.'

'I'm a bit peckish,' the wolfman admitted to the wolf. It had been hours since the meagre dinner he allowed himself. 'Perhaps we can find something worthwhile behind the bins,' he suggested hopefully.

Freegan eating was one of his favourite pastimes. With money as tight as it could possibly be, and winter coming, anything he could get without needing to pay was the right way to go. With the last item loaded, he flipped a mental coin and decided to leave the handcart where it was.

'Guard it for me, Wolf.' He ruffled the Wolf's fur, scratching his ears and giving the big animal a hug before heading across the road to explore the wheelie bins behind the parade of restaurants and shops there.

Wolf tried to follow, reaching the full extent of his lead, and stopping when he could go no further. The leather collar and lead were another thing his human had picked up for free while marvelling that someone would throw them away.

Watching intently until his human went into the dark and was lost to sight, Wolf stayed on his feet, stressing and quietly whining. They were together all day every day. The only time they were ever apart was when his human used the public toilets to clean himself each day. When that happened, Wolf was tied up outside and knew where the man was the whole time.

A car went by, momentarily blocking his view of the other side of the street and the dark side road that led behind a parade of shops. There was a loading area and bins back there, Wolf knew, they frequented them quite often to forage for leftovers.

'He'll be back in a minute,' Wolf told himself. 'He won't be long, and he'll have an armful of sandwiches or pastries when he returns.' The bins behind this particular strip of shops were one of his human's favourites. The bakery always had food to throw out at the end of the day and it was almost always on top, making it easy to get to.

However, a minute ticked by without his human emerging from the dark.

Becoming ever more uneasy, when he heard a shout, Wolf strained against his lead and collar once more. The shout came again. It was not his human's voice, but it had come from the same loading area entrance on the opposite side of the street, and it had been the sound of someone getting agitated.

Wolf bucked, yanking against the leash holding him to the steel railings. It hurt his throat, but he did it again anyway. His human might be in trouble, and he was going to find out for sure.

Twisting around to try getting the collar off over his head, he paused when he heard fast footsteps. They were coming from the dark side street, and they were his human's feet – he would know the sound of the wolfman's shoes anywhere.

Now attempting the impossible task of backing out of his collar while also looking across the road, a feat that demanded he face two different and opposite directions at the same time, Wolf had to look through the side of his eyes when he heard yet another shout.

His human burst from the shadows. Moving faster than Wolf thought he had ever seen him go, the man was running for his life.

Wolf's heart trebled its speed, but just when he was about to thrash to his right in another bid to rid himself of the stupid collar, his human stopped running.

His arms went into the air, thrown skyward as an expression of terrible pain filled his face. The hands clawed at the night for a second as if trying to grip it and hold on before the man stumbled and fell flat on his face.

Wolf could only stare. Turned side on to the street opposite, and with his collar digging painfully into his ears, he watched to see if his human would get up. At this distance, Wolf could not see the knife protruding from his human's back, but he did see another human when he emerged from the shadow.

Walking nonchalantly up to the man now prostrate on the dirty ground, he grinned down at his victim.

'Don't poke your nose in. It's a simple enough instruction,' he remarked. Then he crouched to retrieve his knife, gripping the handle while being sure not to touch the body. With a yank, the blade came free, sealing the fate of the wolfman as his lifeblood spilled ever more freely into the street.

Wolf snapped.

A final lunge tore the flesh of his ears, but he barely felt the sting as his head came free and his paws exploded into action.

Across the road, the man was putting his knife away.

'Come along, Muldoon, I feel we ought to vacate this vicinity,' he commented to an unseen third party still lurking in the shadows.

'Who was that, Jimmy?' asked Muldoon.

Jimmy shrugged. 'Who cares? He stands as a useful lesson. I mean business, Muldoon and no one will disrespect me.'

Spotting movement, Muldoon squinting at the fast-moving object streaking across the road in the direction of his boss.

'Ooh, doggy!' he cooed.

Frowning, Jimmy followed Muldoon's gaze, curious to see what the dopey giant was talking about.

He did so just as a car's horn blasted a warning and tried to avoid the flash of fur that had shot in front of it.

With his eyes flaring in panic, Jimmy reached for his knife again, but he did so as he started running.

'Quick, get to the car!' he barked an order.

His car was just around the corner, no more than a few yards away as they ran back into the darkness behind the shops, but he was not going to get there before the wolf caught up.

Fortunately for Jimmy, he knew he could easily outpace Muldoon. Friends since school, Jimmy knew how slowly the lumbering ox moved. Jimmy didn't need to outrun the dog, he just needed to outrun Muldoon and leave the snarling hound with an easy target.

In the road, the car had clipped Wolf's right rear flank, the blow only glancing yet still enough to stun his thigh muscles and cause bruising. It ought to have slowed him down, but he could smell his human's blood, and nothing was going to stop him from bringing down the wolfman's attacker.

Now coming into the dark behind the fleeing man, he could see his partner. The giant man presented an easy target, but Wolf had no interest in Muldoon. He wanted the one who hurt his human.

Jimmy reached the back of his car, and threw himself over the boot, sliding across the polished paintwork to land on the passenger's side. He was going to be inside the car long before the dog or whatever it was got anywhere near him. He grabbed the doorhandle with a satisfied gasp. A gasp that quickly changed into a yell when he discovered the doors were locked.

Wolf leapt onto the back end of the car where he skidded on the polished surface and could not find purchase even when he tried to dig his claws in.

Falling to the ground on the other side, he landed on the same piece of flesh the car had struck and let out an involuntary yelp of pain.

Jimmy screamed for Muldoon to open the car, employing insults and curse words to get across the urgency of the situation.

The giant henchman started patting his pockets but for Jimmy it was all far too late. He could see the dog was getting back to its feet. It was a massive brute of an animal, and it was mad. Heck, was it even a dog? It looked more like a wolf!

Leaping to get onto the roof of his car, Jimmy almost made it.

Wolf saw what the human was trying to do. He planned to tear the human apart, every thought passing through his brain clouded by the fog of rage. As the man went vertical, Wolf leapt, snagging a leg just above the ankle.

'Arrrrghhhh!' Jimmy screamed, the pain searing through his flesh, creating a torrent of torment as he flailed and tried to get away.

Muldoon finally got the car open, the lights flashing once when the central locking reacted to the remote he held.

From the boot of the car, a muffled shout reminded both men of their need to vacate the area. Their captive had come around and would become a problem if they didn't dispose of him soon. It was poor timing on the part of the wolfman that he interrupted Muldoon stuffing their victim into the boot of their car when he did. He'd seen their faces and that sealed his fate in an instant.

Hanging from Jimmy's leg, his teeth digging into the flesh, the wolf was trying to drag his prize back down to the ground on his side of the car. Hanging on for dear life, he shook his head from side to side, eliciting a fresh set of tortured screams. However, too focused on the human between his teeth, he failed to see or hear Muldoon coming.

Struck on his ribs with a handy piece of broken pallet Muldoon found lying next to the car, Wolf yelped as the air was knocked from his lungs. Scrambling to get away from the pain, he lost his prize and simply wasn't able to get back in the fight as his vision swam. A piece of blood-soaked material was stuck in his teeth, hanging from one side of his mouth like an extra tongue though he was only dimly aware of it.

Muldoon wrapped a meaty arm around his boss and threw him onto the passenger's seat.

The big dog was getting back to his paws, but Muldoon didn't think the animal represented any further danger. Generally, when he hit things, they stayed hit. Most often they just didn't get up again. The fact that the big dog was back on its feet made it tough, but Muldoon didn't bother to hurry his pace as he settled into the driver's seat and gunned the engine.

Wolf tried to run, wincing and faltering. His back right leg hurt where the car hit it, but that was nothing compared to the pain in his chest. He tried to run again, chasing after the car as his human's attacker got away. It was no use though. He knew well enough that cars move faster than he could run, and right now he couldn't manage anything faster than a limp.

Huffing a rage-filled breath as the humans escaped, he turned around and hobbled back to where his human still lay.

Half in and half out of the moonlight, the old man hadn't moved since he hit the ground. Wolf licked his face, encouraging him to move. Getting no response, he tried again, and again.

The human's face felt cold to the touch.

When he accepted what he already knew, he tipped his head back and filled the night air with a mournful howl. The police received no fewer than fifteen calls in a ten-minute period, pinpointing a likely area to search while jokers in the station suggested taking silver bullets – just in case.

Wolf laid across his human's back, doing his best to keep him warm even though he knew there was no point. It was an instinctual thing to do, his body responding automatically because his brain was doing other things.

Wolf knew the sound, the smell, and the taste of the human he needed to find. He was going to avenge his human if it was the last thing he ever did.

Crime Scene

The cool breeze filled Rex's nose as the bus pulled away behind him. He tilted his snout upwards, sampling the air and holding it in his nostrils for a few moments to decipher the scents it held. The smell of the sea, a mixture of salt and many other things was easy to detect. A trace of fish, a small wad of recently chewed spearmint gum stuck to a bench a few yards away, a kebab shop less than fifty yards to his right, and something else, something ... primal. All these scents and more filtered into Rex's nose to be listed, catalogued, and stored in the space of a heartbeat.

Holding his lead, Rex's human, a man not too far from his eightieth birthday called Albert Smith, also sniffed the air. For Albert, the visit to Blackpool was one of nostalgia. He had been here some seven decades earlier on a holiday with his parents. He remembered little of the trip, other than the wide strips of beach, the impression of long, hot summer days, and of playing in the surf.

Those things were largely intangible and could be obtained on many beaches on a warm summer's day not only in England but in many other countries around the planet. What made Blackpool special, and was the focus of his reason for visiting, was the opportunity to buy a stick of Blackpool Rock.

Not that Albert thought there was anything particularly special about Blackpool Rock. It was a sugary confection that as a man he had loathed to let his children eat for fear of what it might do to their teeth. Now that concern was for his children to pass on to his grandchildren.

Nevertheless, Albert was going to buy a stick of Rock, probably a small one, and would consume it while watching the waves lapping gently at the shore.

They were here for just one night, the plan being to then push onward towards Kendal for some mint cake. He had zigged and zagged a bit on his tour of the country, his intended order of visits getting scrapped as he responded to what he believed to be a master criminal at work. He still hadn't entirely given up on that investigation, but the trail had gone cold more than a week ago, and until he found a fresh lead, there appeared to be little he could do to advance the case.

A grey sky threatened rain, not unusual at this time of year, and prompted Albert to get moving. From his pocket, he pulled a scrap of paper on which he had written the name and address of the B&B he'd booked for the night. It was on the seafront, but that was about all he knew.

Rex glanced up as his human started walking, checking which direction they were heading before setting off himself.

Albert flagged down the first person he saw. It was evening in the late autumn and the sun had retired for the day many hours ago. Tourist season was on its last legs and there were very few people about.

'I say, could you help an old boy find his way?' he hallooed a man out walking his dog.

The dog, a Basset Hound, gave Rex a doleful look. He didn't mean to, it was just the way his face was.

While the two humans conversed above their heads, Rex sniffed the air again meaningfully.

'Can you smell it?' he asked.

The Basset sniggered. 'It always smells like that here. It's a wolf,' he supplied.

Rex's face registered his surprise.

'A wolf?'

'Yup. Live and in the fur. It performs an act down here with its human.' He turned away from Rex to look one way along the promenade and then swivelled around to look the other. 'Hmm, he's usually here, actually.' The Basset Hound looked perplexed. 'You know, I can't remember the last time he wasn't here. This is sort of where his human hangs out.'

Rex felt a light tug on his lead. His human was thanking the Basset's human and picking up his small suitcase again.

'Come along, Rex, we've got quite the walk it would seem,' chirped Albert, sounding happy.

Trotting along at the old man's side, Rex thought about the presence of a wolf and how he felt about it. It was the wolf's scent he'd picked up the moment they got off the bus, he just hadn't known that was what it was.

It was like smelling dog plus. Like somehow all dog scents had been shoved into a giant cooking pot and boiled down to a concentrated smell. To Rex's nose it was unrefined nature, the primordial soup from which all dog species evolved.

Distracted by a discarded doughnut, which he snagged and swallowed without Albert even noticing, Rex let his mind drift, savouring the many smells assailing his olfactory system.

Albert kept his eyes out for road signs, squinting to make them out by the dim light cast from the overhead streetlamps. They walked for almost a mile, faint rain coming in on the breeze.

'Where is it?' Albert muttered to himself, wondering if he had somehow passed it. 'Can you sniff it out, Rex?' he asked, though it was not a serious question.

Rex found himself thoroughly distracted by the food smells wafting on the air - there were altogether too many of them. Had he been paying attention to his human, he might have offered him a curious expression. It was not within his skill set to find their destination when he had no smell reference for it. This was one of those rare occasions when a human's eyesight actually proved to be an advantage over a dog's nose.

'Ah, here we are, boy. I guess we should have got off at the next bus stop, not the one before. Still, a brisk walk never did anybody any harm,' Albert chattered contently to himself.

Rex looked up at his human. He understood most of what the old man had said. Combining what he heard with the fact that they were crossing the road, he was able to deduce that they were finally nearing the end of today's journey.

Across the road the pair turned left to close the final thirty yards to their destination, a sign for which Albert could see illuminated ahead of them. It was at the end of a parade of shops and restaurants; small independently owned businesses as one often finds in seaside resorts.

However, just a few yards later Albert's feet came unexpectedly to a halt. Unexpectedly for Rex, that is.

The dog turned his head and sniffed, a kaleidoscope of images cascading in his mind to tell him exactly why his human was staring into the dark side road.

Albert was staring at the crime scene tape. It was something he'd seen altogether too many times in his professional life, and he knew a murder scene when he saw one. There was no chalk outline on the floor - that is something from the movies, however there were other tell-tale signs.

The gutters all around were filled with dirt and detritus, except here where they were washed clean. The clean-up team had washed blood off the tarmac and into the gutter, cleaning away everything else at the same time. He could also spot the marks where the forensic team had placed their equipment as they attempted to ascertain what had happened.

The thought dominating Albert's mind was how fresh the site had to be.

The ageing detective remained rock still, his eyes darting about as his brain worked overtime. Adding up the clues, Albert estimated that a singular victim had died. It was near the mouth of a side street that appeared to lead to a loading yard behind the parade of shops. It was a lonely place to die.

Snapping out of it a moment later, he questioned why he was studying the scene - morbid curiosity was the only answer his brain could supply.

Shrugging his neck when a fresh gust of wind gave him a chill, Albert shrunk deeper inside his coat, turned to the left, and moved on.

Rex had been able to smell the blood. Even the forensic team's cleaning attempts could not disguise the coppery stench enough to hide it from his nose. His canine brain couldn't assess the visual clues to fully understand that he was looking at a murder scene, but he suspected that was what it was anyway. Not only that, but the whole area also stank of wolf.

Albert pushed the crime scene out of his mind and pressed on directly to his hotel. It was already evening, and he wanted a cup of tea and perhaps a biscuit after his journey. His lodgings for the night would provide both.

He got five yards before his feet came to a stop again.

On the corner of the side street where it met the seafront, an old sweet shop boasted 'Traditional Blackpool Rock, The Way It's Been Made for Over One Hundred Years'. Albert considered that it might just be a silly boast. But he also acknowledged that it was good enough to get him inside the shop.

As he pushed through the door, a small bell tinkled above his head. The old worldliness of it brought the smile to his face. He had encountered many such small shops on this tour of the country as if all the destinations he'd visited were from another era. The shop was full to the brim. Every shelf was piled high, every wall was covered in shelves. Even the floor had box upon box stacked to display their wares. Behind the counter at the far end, Albert could see a shopkeeper moving about.

Turning his attention back to the shelves, Albert perused the various sweet offerings on display. Much of it was standard seaside fare that one might find in any resort.

The honeycomb caught his eye - he could not remember the last time he had eaten any. It wasn't just the honeycomb though. The shelves were lined with delicacies he hadn't seen in many years. In fact, he estimated it might have been decades since he had last seen some of the items on display. Black Jacks, a chewy liquorice sweet, were an item from his youth when one used to be able to buy multiples for a ha'penny.

The memories the shop evoked tweaked the corners of his mouth into a smile that stayed in place.

The little bell above the door tinkled again, and though Albert didn't turn his head to look, he noticed two men enter the shop - one with a limp and one who was so big and tall he had to duck to get through the door.

Interrupting a Crime in Progress

The selection of Rock was underneath the glass counter at the other end of the shop where the shopkeepers were gathered. Deciding he had spent enough time needlessly nosing at items he had no intention of buying, Albert gave Rex's lead a gentle tug and moved through the shop to purchase the item he'd come in for.

Rex sniffed the air, checking the scent of the two men out of habit rather than for any other reason.

The men who entered the shop after him were blocking his view of the shopkeepers. They were conversing about something, so being polite, Albert inspected a display of buckets and spades, pretending it was of interest. However, it did not take him long to overhear the tone in which the two parties were conversing.

Behind the counter, the shopkeepers, a man and woman, sounded nervous or afraid. In contrast, the two men facing them, the one with the limp and the giant, were keeping their voices low which made it difficult for Albert to hear precisely what they were saying.

Opting to move closer and listen for a few seconds, Albert wanted to be absolutely sure he understood the situation before he acted.

'It's like I said,' the smaller of the two men calmly explained to the people behind the counter. 'Fat Bernhard is no longer providing your protection. You saw what happened to his collector last night, yes?'

Albert heard an audible gulp from behind the counter.

The smaller of the two men, the one with the limp, continued speaking, 'It would be most unfortunate if your protection were to lapse. That is why I am here. Muldoon and I will see to it that nothing happens to you or to your premises. Your weekly premium will not increase. That's good news, isn't it?' The man was trying to make it sound as if it was something to be joyful about.

In an instant, Albert knew what he was listening to. The two men in front of him where hoodlums setting up a protection racket, and if he understood correctly, they were moving into somebody else's turf.

The ageing detective's heart was beating at twice its usual speed, adrenalin and nerves driving his pulse upwards. He licked his lips, lifted his left hand to his mouth, and coughed politely.

It was obvious that no one else knew he was in the shop. The shopkeepers must have heard him enter, but had forgotten about him in the excitement of the events unfolding.

Both men facing the counter turned around, their faces set to look mean.

It was the smaller of them, clearly the one in charge, who spoke, 'I think you ought to make yourself scarce, old man. Otherwise, something nasty might happen to you.'

The giant, whose name was Muldoon if Albert had heard right, took a pace forward, his hands twitching as if getting ready to perform some vile act.

Rex, whose backside had been firmly planted on the ground, rose to all four paws, his hackles rising.

Forcing his voice to remain strong - the giant henchman was about as frightening as any man he had ever seen - Albert locked eyes with the man who had spoken.

'This is hardly twenty first century behaviour, sir. I think perhaps you ought to leave these premises and these good people to go about their business unmolested. Otherwise, I fear the authorities may need to get involved.' Ultimatum delivered, Albert refused to avert his eyes.

What he noticed throughout the exchange was that the man with the limp kept flicking his eyes downward to check on Rex. Was the dog making him feel uneasy?

If that were the case, then it worked in Albert's favour, for the only weapon he had was Rex.

With a twitch of his head, the man with the limp sent his giant henchman forward.

'You can't say I didn't warn you,' Jimmy said with a shrug.

Albert was thinking the same thing. He hadn't seen a weapon displayed by either man. That of course did not mean that they were not armed. But it was too late now to change his course of action.

Dropping Rex's lead, he issued a single command, 'Rex, guard!'

Rex had been waiting for this. From the first moment his human spoke to the two men at the counter, he had assumed this was going to end in a game of chase and bite or something similar. Since leaving home several weeks ago now, he'd had more opportunity to chase and bite humans than ever before in his life. It was almost as if he were back in police dog training. The big difference was that the humans back then had been padded and wanted him to chase them. It was much more fun doing it for real.

Rex lunged, barking loudly and continuously. The command given was different from the one to attack, and he knew it meant that he was not to inflict harm unless threatened. Whether anyone got bitten or not was down to the two humans who were already backing away.

From behind the counter the man shouted, 'No!'

The man's shout surprised Albert, but only for a moment. Dealing with gangsters, the type of men who ran protection rackets, had not been Albert's job in the police. He had crossed them and their victims once or twice, nevertheless. So he knew that he was witnessing the shopkeeper's belief that trying to improve their situation was only going to make it worse.

Ignoring what anyone else said, Albert took out his phone, his hands shaking slightly from the effect of adrenaline in his blood stream. Ignoring that too, he pressed the nine button three times and waited to be connected.

The two hoodlums were shouting obscenities, swearing and screaming at the dog now pinning them in the corner. Each time one of them attempted to move Rex lunged and nipped at them.

Just as the voice of the police dispatcher echoed in Albert's ear, he heard the male shopkeeper shout once more.

'Please, you're just making things worse! Please leave!'

Shouting to make himself heard, Albert swiftly relayed his location and what was happening, including a quick description of the two men.

'Both IC1 males, late twenties,' he gave the police descriptor for a Caucasian man. 'One approximately six feet and one inch tall with brown hair cut short and parted to the right side. He walks with a marked limp. The other, approximately seven feet and two inches,' Albert doubted he had ever met a taller man, 'with ash blonde hair. He must be four hundred pounds and it looks like it's all muscle.' He ended the call by demanding a fast response, then held the phone at arm's length so the dispatcher could hear the bedlam inside the shop.

The two men had taken to throwing things at Rex, ripping boxes of sweets from the shelves. However, they were having little luck in hitting him and even less when it came to deterring him from his course of action.

Behind the counter, the woman was sobbing. She held onto the man next to her in such a way that Albert assumed they were husband and wife - a married team running a business together.

Jimmy tried to make a break for it, darting forward to get to the door and narrowly avoiding getting bitten by Rex as he changed his mind.

Rex had them well and truly pinned. He was rather enjoying himself.

Despite that, it was a blessing when they heard a siren outside. It approached at speed. A squad car then skidded to a halt right in front of the shop.

Two men in uniform bailed out, one from each side as they rushed to get into the premises.

Albert moved to intercept them, but the man with the limp was already demanding that the officers restrain the dog, or perhaps shoot it, and insisting the old man, though he employed a less polite term, be arrested.

The first officer through the door shouted for everyone to be calm and quiet.

'Settle down all of you!' he commanded. 'I am Constable Gordon,' he indicated his colleague, 'And this is Constable Jones.' Facing Albert he asked, 'Are you the person who placed the call, Sir?'

Constable Jones had a radio in his hand. He was calling for animal control.

Albert cocked an eyebrow, surprised the police officer would assume the dog was even a problem.

Ignoring Constable Gordon's question, he focused on Constable Jones.

'There's no need for that,' he said. 'Rex is my dog. He is quite well trained. At this moment he's ensuring that two men intent on running a protection racket cannot escape the premises.'

'That's utter nonsense!' the man with a limp insisted. 'We are confectionary wholesalers,' he lied, fumbling in a jacket pocket to then produce a business card. Though clearly fake, Albert had to give the man a nod of acknowledgement for having a cover story prepared. 'We were just in here conversing with the owners when this man set his dog on us.' The man with the limp continued, 'Ask the owners, please. I am certain they will agree with everything I say.' The man with the limp then turned his eyes towards the two shopkeepers and though no one could see his expression, Albert had no doubt his eyes were threatening, daring them to disagree.

Jones went around the back of Gordon, heading towards the counter at the rear of the shop while keeping everyone in sight.

'Is that true?' he asked the shopkeepers.

'You don't have to be afraid,' Albert urged the terrified couple. 'The police can arrest these men and charge them if you are prepared to speak up.'

'Arrest us for what?' challenged a man with a limp. 'For attempting to conduct business? We were offering them a better deal than their current supplier. Isn't that true?' he prompted the couple behind the counter to answer.

All eyes turned towards the couple. They looked nervous and were standing as close to each other as they could get, holding hands for support and comfort.

The man mumbled something Albert wasn't able to hear. Apparently, neither of the cops heard it either, for the Constable Jones asked him to repeat what he had said.

'I said, that is correct,' the male shopkeeper confirmed, speaking more clearly, his eyes nervously watching the man with the limp. Shifting his focus to address Constable Jones, he said, 'These men were in here talking to us about confectionary when the other gentleman misunderstood what he was hearing and ordered his dog to attack them.'

Albert sagged a little, disappointed that they were not brave enough to fight for themselves. Worse yet, they had chosen to point the finger at him, and now he was the criminal.

Rex, still standing and facing the two men he had been told to guard, was now confused about what was happening. He recognised the two new men as police officers. Their uniforms made it easy to see what they were. Regardless, they did not seem to be taking over from him as he expected.

Addressing them directly, he said, 'Are your noses malfunctioning completely? Surely you can smell the bad on these two clowns?'

Unfortunately, the man with the limp reacted to Rex's odd noises, further turning the table against him and his human.

'Arrrghh! He's at it again!' exclaimed the man with the limp, backing as far into the corner as he could get while attempting to hide behind his larger associate.

Muldoon's brow furrowed. 'Nah, Jimmy, he's just being friendly now,' he remarked, wondering if it was an appropriate time to try to pet the dog and make friends.

Jimmy was about to slap Muldoon around the back of the head for being so stupid. He had the cops on his side, they were eating out of his hand. All he needed now was his pet ape to make the dog seem friendly.

Rex saw the giant's hand coming for him, Muldoon reaching out to stroke his head while Rex's attention was on the two stupid cops. He took the move as one of subtle attack and whipped around, narrowly missing Muldoon's fingers as he hastily yanked his arm back.

'See!' yelled Jimmy. 'He's dangerous!'

'Ok,' said Constable Gordon, the first cop to enter the shop and the one positioned closest to Albert. 'I've seen enough.' Aiming his gaze at the old man, he said, 'I need you to get your dog under control now, Sir.'

Albert blinked, struggling to believe the two uniformed officers were this dumb.

To prove a point he said, 'Rex, to me,' in a calm voice.

Hearing his human's command, and hoping the old man had a better grasp on what was happening, he instantly dropped his guard stance and loped to the front of the shop where he took up post sitting next to Albert's left foot.

'See?' questioned Albert, hooking an eyebrow at Constable Gordon. 'Not even slightly dangerous unless one happens to be a criminal enforcing a protection racket.'

'That's slander!' shouted Jimmy. He was yet to move from his spot by the counter and now bore a confident grin he couldn't be bothered to hide.

Constable Gordon held out an arm, indicating for Albert to leave the shop. 'If you please, Sir.' He made it clear it was time for Albert to leave.

Managing to keep a frustrated breath inside, Albert gave a gentle tug of Rex's lead. Outside in the street he had one last go at making the young constable see sense.

'I can assure you that I am not mistaken about what I saw and heard. Those two men are running a protection racket. You are going to tell me that they are not known to you and that you are aware of the local organised criminals. However, I learned within just a few seconds of listening to them that they are new to this area and attempting to move in. Can you tell me if something happened in this area last night? They mentioned something about it.'

Constable Gordon had been watching Albert's face, glancing at the dog occasionally with an air of curiosity. He had to admit that the dog did seem completely placid and under control.

The call to animal control had already been placed and though he could radio dispatch and have them turned around, he'd only wanted to call them out because Claire and Ann were on shift tonight and he hoped it might be them on their way to his location.

The lads at the station had several crude terms for the all-female animal control crew, but really they were just two hot women and Constable Gordon knew they were both single.

Taking out his notebook, he flicked to a new page and looked up at the old man's eyes. 'Your name, Sir?'

Albert sighed. 'Albert Smith.'

'Your address, Sir?'

Albert explained that he was on a tour of the British Isles, doing so before he provided his address in Kent because he knew the officer would immediately question why he was in Blackpool by himself. In Albert's opinion very few men travelled alone.

Nevertheless, Constable Gordon made him go through the rigmarole of explaining his reason for being in Blackpool and obtained the address for Albert's hotel – just a few yards farther along the seafront. He listened to Albert's version of events, noting key details, but Albert could tell the cop wasn't going to act upon it.

With little choice in the matter, Albert answered Constable Gordon's questions. He was certain the young officer was going to do nothing further than give him a verbal warning though even that seemed ridiculous.

Now physically separated from the shopkeepers and the men who had been threatening them, Albert was unable to see or hear what might be happening inside the shop. He doubted the couple, who seemed terrified in the presence of the two men, would be willing to change their tune now or later.

When the young officer finished and closed his notebook, Albert once again posed the question he wanted to hear an answer to.

'Can you tell me what happened here last night, please? Is it something to do with the murder that took place in that side street back there?' He indicated back towards the gap between the businesses with his head.

Watching Constable Gordon intently, Albert saw it when surprise registered on the cop's face.

'What do you know about that, Sir?' Constable Gordon asked in an accusatory manner. In truth, he suspected the old man was probably telling the truth about what he had seen and heard in the sweet shop. However, there was no evidence to back up his claims.

Shortly, he would check with Jones, but if the shopkeepers wouldn't change their story, there really wasn't anything he could do.

Constable Jones would of course record the two men's names, checking their IDs to make sure they were not giving false ones, but it was an unfortunate truth the police resources in Blackpool were stretched thin, too thin to worry too much about protection rackets.

Every few years a task force would attempt to tackle that particular crime, yet even though a few arrests might be made, and they knew who was behind organised crime in the area, the police had been unable to get to the people at the top. Despite hard effort and many, many manhours, obtaining sufficient evidence to build a case continued to evade the local constabulary.

Albert wanted to explain that he knew all sorts of things about the murder last night. All he had needed was a few seconds to examine the crime scene. The fact that the crime scene tape was still there told him that the crime itself was quite fresh. No more than a day, he would guess. The crime scene team could not have been gone much longer than that because the tape was still present.

Instead, what he said was, 'I used to be a senior detective. Of course that was a few years ago now, but it's easy to see the clues even for my old eyes.'

Humouring the old man, Constable Gordon said, 'Very good, Sir. If you were indeed a senior detective, you will know that I can make no comment about an ongoing investigation.'

'Do you at least plan to question those two men?' Albert asked, beginning to show his exasperation. 'When they were threatening the couple inside that shop, they mentioned the thing that happened last night as a means to motivate them.'

Constable Gordon was no longer listening. He had spotted the animal control truck passing on the other side of the road and looking for a place to turn round. Specifically, what he noticed was that Claire was in the driving seat and Ann, who was every bit as delicious, was in the passenger seat.

He lifted an arm, waving to the two women, and gave them what he hoped was a dazzling smile. The effect, though he didn't know it, was for the two women to question whether he needed to go to the toilet.

They parked directly behind his squad car, pausing only to gather their bits and pieces before joining him on the pavement.

The presence of animal control made Albert nervous. He knew Rex wasn't dangerous, unless commanded to act in a dangerous manner. Such was his training. However, Rex was also a very large dog, and Albert couldn't be sure what was going to happen now.

'My, he's a big one,' commented Ann, taking in the size of the German Shepherd dog. He was indeed a large example of the breed, but she and Claire were old hands at this game. In the first five seconds, they assessed that the dog they were looking at was not one they were going to have to deal with.

It was not the first time in the last few weeks that they had been called out unnecessarily by Constable Gordon. None of the other officers seemed to need their help so regularly. In fact, there was a pool running in the animal control department that Constable Gordon had a thing for one of the guys and called out animal control in the hope that whoever it was he fancied would turn up. Neither Claire nor Ann realised that he was not, in fact, gay.

All in all, it was a further thirty minutes before Albert was given his verbal caution and permitted to go on his way.

Rex didn't mind waiting. The two ladies from the animal control department fussed around Rex, telling him what a beautiful doggy he was and admiring his excellent manners.

While that was happening, Jimmy and Muldoon were having their story checked out. Constable Jones took the time to check addresses and phone numbers. Both men were Blackpool residents and were able to show Constable Jones their wholesale business website. It was a real website for a fake firm that Jimmy was using as a cover. He'd been planning his takeover operation for years, watching and learning so that he would be able to strike swiftly and cleanly.

He had a big plan. A glorious plan. A plan that he considered to be his birthright to enact. It was his destiny to take over the criminal underworld in Blackpool and had recruited a team to help make that happen.

The police could check all they wanted. His name was real, but would not lead them to find any reason to suspect him – neither he nor Muldoon, nor any of the members of his team had a criminal record. His address was also real though it was not where he lived. If they checked it, they would find a terraced house that appeared to be lived in, but they would not find him.

Inevitably, Constable Jones could only conclude that the two men were exactly what they claimed. They were wholesalers and they could prove it. With the shopkeepers supporting their story, he had no choice but to let them go on their way.

Watching them walk, or limp in Jimmy's case, along the seafront and out of sight, Albert had to accept the shopkeepers had chosen to keep quiet about what was really happening.

Dismissed by Constable Gordon, Albert had half a mind to go back into the shop so that he could buy his stick of Rock. He knew it would be a contrary thing to do, and he would have to walk past the two police constables in order to get to the shop.

Acknowledging that it simply wasn't worth the trouble it would bring, he chose instead to pick up his small suitcase. Once he'd adjusted Rex's lead from his left hand to his right, he continued along the road toward tonight's hotel.

Albert did his best to put the incident behind him. He was in Blackpool for just one night, and it was supposed to be a fun occasion where he got to reminisce about his childhood and his parents, for whom he had nothing but fond memories.

The Clarence Hotel, which was a small, family-run business right on the seafront was slightly different to his usual. Albert generally favoured bed and breakfasts for the simple fact that they were always family-run and therefore paid far greater attention to the individual customers coming in.

During his life, he had found that hotels, especially chains, saw customers as numbers rather than individuals. However, he wanted a place on the seafront and when he tried to book a bed and breakfast at short notice, he found them all to be fully booked. To his surprise, when he called the Clarence Hotel, they had rooms available.

He was met at reception by a man in his fifties who introduced himself as Tony, the owner and manager of the hotel. Once he confirmed Albert's booking, he dinged a call bell on the front desk. Moments later, a much younger version of Tony appeared through a door to his rear.

Introduced as his son, Tony then instructed Spencer to collect Albert's bags and take them up to his room.

'Oh, there's no need for that,' Albert said. 'They don't weigh anything really.'

'Is it just the one night, Sir?' Tony wished to confirm. 'We have space at the moment if you do choose to stay an extra day.'

Unneeded, Spencer chose to withdraw, closing the door behind him to leave the two gentlemen sorting out business.

Albert was about to say that he planned to move on and had other places to go, but something held him back. He knew what it was, of course. It was the temptation of an investigation. Though he tried to ignore it, thoughts of the couple in the sweet shop filled his head.

What he really wanted to do was go back to the sweet shop and talk to them about what had happened. But telling himself there was no good reason to get involved, even if he caved and went back there later, he had other needs right now. It was dinnertime, and his stomach was already rumbling its emptiness. First item on his agenda was to set out his things in his room and feed Rex. Going in search of sustenance would follow shortly thereafter.

He could have paid to have half board at the Clarence Hotel, but that would mean he ate two thirds of his meals in the same place. It seemed criminal given the number of venues on offer. Still in Lancashire after travelling a very short leg from his previous destination, he'd already seen several signs boasting Blackpool's best hotpot.

He'd already had his fill of that particular dish and was looking forward to finding something different to eat. With sausage and mash on his mind, he left the hotel with Rex in tow and set out to find a public house.

It didn't take him long. One street back from the seafront, less than two hundred yards from his accommodation, Albert found the Prince's Head, a public house without giant television screens in it. He could not abide pubs where people went to watch television.

With a pint of ale and half pint of Guinness in his hands, Albert found an empty table where he could inspect the menu.

Just as he was sitting down, his phone rang.

It took him longer than it ought to retrieve his phone from his jacket pocket. It was stuffed underneath a handkerchief, and he feared that yanking it free might result in the delicate device tumbling to the floor. He had already killed one phone recently when he dropped it from a height.

The name displayed on the screen was that of his daughter, Selina. Just seeing her name bought a smile to his face.

'Good evening, darling. How are things in Kent? How's my darling granddaughter?'

Selina's voice echoed in his ear, 'Hello, Dad, everything's fine here. What are you up to at the moment? Where are you, in fact?'

Albert took a sip of his ale, refreshing his palate before answering, 'I'm in Blackpool, my dear. Rex and I have a room at a nice hotel on the seafront. We're not going to be here for long, just today, I think. Did I ever mention that I came here with my parents when I was a boy?'

Selina chuckled. 'Yes, dad. I think we've all heard that story many, many times. I hope you're staying out of trouble.'

A spike of guilt shot through him as he remembered once again the two hoodlums in the sweet shop. He did not feel, however, that his daughter needed to know about that. It wasn't as if he created the situation.

To avoid answering her question, he asked, 'Is there a specific reason you called, darling? Not that you need a reason to call me, of course. It's always lovely to hear your voice.'

'No, Dad, I was just checking in really. It seems that you've been gone for ages now. I know I saw you just a few days ago but it's been a long time for your grandchildren. I hope you get the chance to come home and see them soon. I think they're all missing their grandfather.'

Albert suspected his daughter was applying guilt to get him to do that which everybody in the family seemed to want him to do - to come home. He'd been resisting for weeks, but the tug to return to his home county was growing. He missed his grandchildren; they were all gifts to be cherished in his opinion.

Thoughtfully, he replied, 'I have a few more places to visit, Selina. I promise though that I plan to come home before too long. This trip has been something of a revelation. Honestly, I know I've said this before, but I think I would have faded away had I stayed in that empty house.'

It was a slightly cruel tactic to remind Selina of her dead mother. But it was also true that Albert had left home because he felt he really needed to. Were it not for Rex, Albert wondered what might have become of him by now. The dog gave him purpose and responsibility, plus a live creature to talk to even if he didn't get much conversation from him.

They chatted for a few minutes, talking about this and that. What the weather was like in Kent, what was happening in her job at the moment, and how his granddaughter Apple-Blossom had done at her recent piano recital.

Selina needed to excuse herself so that she could finish putting the kids to bed, which suited Albert just fine because his stomach was only getting emptier, and he really wanted to order some food.

They said goodnight with the promise to talk again soon and as he pulled the phone away from his ear, he lifted a hand to wave to a waitress. The waitress in question didn't see him, so he looked for another, and got a wet nose against his leg to remind him that Rex's drink was still sitting in its glass on the table.

Albert chuckled, ruffling the dog's fur and scratching his ear.

'Sorry, Rex.' Albert stopped stroking the dog's head to fish around in the backpack he always carried. Inside was a travel bowl and a bottle of water so that Rex need never be thirsty. That same bowl was employed again now so he could fill it with the dark black liquid.

Gripping the side of the table, Albert bent down with his free hand to place the bowl on the floor. Rex's nose was in it before Albert could get his hands out of the way, and his phone was ringing again before we could get himself back to upright.

This time, the name displayed was that of his eldest son, Gary. He was always pleased to hear from his children - he loved them dearly, but right now what he wanted to do was order some sausage and mash.

Ignoring the phone, and feeling a little guilty about it, he flagged down a waitress and placed a hasty order. The phone rang off before he could answer it and started ringing again before he could pick it up to return his son's call.

'Dad!' Gary started speaking before Albert could even say hello. 'Where are you? How soon can you get back to Kent? There's been a development.' Albert was about to ask what Gary was talking about when the answer was supplied without prompting. 'A development in that Gastrothief case, I mean.'

Suddenly, Albert was sitting upright in his chair. He'd been thinking about this just an hour or so ago. It had proven to be a most intriguing case for a short while, diverting his route around the British Isles as he visited places where he believed a crime at the hands of the Gastrothief had been committed.

'What is it, son? What has happened? What development are you talking about?' Albert rattled out questions in quick fire succession before falling silent so that he could hear an answer. His son was a Detective Superintendent for the Metropolitan Police in London. Indeed, all his children were senior detectives in the Met.

It had taken some convincing to get his children on board with the concept that there might be somebody out there behind the random crimes he'd identified. The fact is, they were not random at all if one looked at them from a particular perspective. Albert believed they were all linked, and could all be traced back to an as yet unidentified person.

He was holding his breath in anticipation for what Gary might say.

'Well, Dad, something happened in Kent not that many miles from your house. Three people have gone missing from a single vineyard. Not only that, but also the vineyard's wine-tasting expert was found dead at the scene. He'd fallen from the roof of one of the buildings, which would not normally lead anyone to believe that there was foul play, but I have to question what he was doing up there. With the missing persons to add to the unexplained death, I genuinely think we have another example of a crime related to your Gastrothief.'

Albert's mind was reeling. Gary was right, thus far the instances of crimes which Albert had been able to trace back to his supposed Gastrothief were all to do with obtaining food, drink, or equipment with which one would make food, or experts in the field of making a particular dish.

He travelled all the way to Arbroath hoping to intercept agents of the Gastrothief attempting to do ... something. In truth, he wasn't sure what that was or what it might be. There had been a single clue, found when Gary dispatched officers to inspect the accommodation of a man Albert was certain worked for the Gastrothief. That man had died during an abortive kidnapping in Biggleswade, but left a trail Albert was able to follow for a time.

Thoughts of Arbroath reminded him of Argyll who went missing right before Albert left the town. There had been no sign the agents of the Gastrothief were in the area or had any intention of ever having been there. That was where the trail went cold. It occurred to Albert though that Argyll's disappearance might not be accidental.

'Dad? Dad, are you still there?'

Gary's questions interrupted Albert's train of thought, giving him a nudge because he hadn't spoken for several seconds.

Rex lifted his head, his jowls dripping Guinness onto Albert's trousers. He was looking for the rest of his drink because his human would only give him a portion at a time rather than the whole thing at once. He was quite partial to the odd black liquid, but held the opinion that it would go down far better if one added a packet of crisps.

He'd eaten his dinner of course, his human insisting on feeding him before they left the hotel. He also had a chance to run along the beach before they came looking for food, but there was always room in his belly for more.

Shoving Rex's head away with one hand, Albert tried to focus on several things at once. Negotiating Rex's tongue as the daft dog tried to lick the liquid from the glass, Albert attempted to empty it into his bowl. He was also trying not to lose his train of thought while simultaneously answering Gary's question.

'Yes, Gary, I'm still here. This does indeed sound like it could be another case of the Gastrothief striking. I still cannot fathom out or even hazard a wild guess what this is all about. He's kidnapping people from the food industry, we know that much, so he must be taking them somewhere. Why else would there be no bodies? How recently did this happen?' Albert posed a pertinent question.

Gary made a noise as he sucked on his cheek in disappointment. 'It was three days ago, Dad,' he admitted. They both knew that this meant the trail was already going cold.

Albert sucked in a deep breath through his nose, absorbing the information and giving himself a few seconds to consider what he wanted to do about it. Had Gary revealed it happened a number of hours ago, he might have looked for a night train back to London so he could arrive in Kent first thing in the morning. He was only in Blackpool on a whim after all.

The lure to investigate this particular case was too great to resist. It wasn't pride driving him, nor was it desire to prove himself that he still had what it took. Actually, he wasn't really sure he could articulate why he wanted to catch this particular criminal, but it had something to do with the fact that he had been the first one to identify him. He alone had spotted the pattern of crimes and made the connection between them. As much for his own satisfaction as anything else, he wanted to see the case through to its conclusion.

'Okay, Son. Thank you for letting me know. I'm going to come home, I think. I'll probably travel in the morning.' It was a snap decision on his part, but not entirely because of his interest in the case. The phone conversation with Selina continued to echo in his head. If he left in the morning, he could see his grandchildren before the sun set again.

A few days back home would do him no harm at all. He wasn't going home for good; he was certain of that. Even if the Gastrothief case suddenly ended, which he didn't think it was about to, he would want to continue his journey around the British Isles. He simply wasn't done exploring yet.

He could refresh his suitcase, check on his house, and spend a little time with his family before he and Rex got on their way once more. To his mind, the decision was made.

He talked with Gary for another couple of minutes, confirming his plan that he would be home sometime the following afternoon. Gary offered to collect him from the station, but Albert assured him that there was really no need. Once he was settled at home, his family could visit him, or he would go to them. That would tick an important box, but once that was done, he fully planned to investigate what happened at the vineyard in Kent.

His sausage and mash came, lifting his mood and his opinion of Blackpool because it was quite delightful. Served with a jug of thick onion gravy, and with mash laced with wholegrain mustard seeds, the entire dish was a symphony of delight.

Albert finished his ale and stayed for a small gin and tonic, sipping it at the bar while Rex snoozed at his feet. Considering his evening complete, even though it was still early, Albert left the public house with his feet aimed towards the seafront and the Clarence Hotel.

He was looking forward to a bath and an opportunity to read his book for an hour before bed. In the morning, he would find somewhere to buy a stick of Blackpool Rock and then get a taxi to the train station.

Little did he know, just a short distance away, events were conspiring to ruin his plans.

Can You Outrun Your Own Smell?

Ryan hadn’t run this fast in years, and the effort of it was proving too much. He wasn't even sure what was chasing him, other than it was a giant dog of some kind. He could hear it now snarling and growling as it continued to track him down.

The fear it instilled was sufficient to keep him running even though he felt as if his heart was going to burst from his chest or his lungs would simply explode from the work they were being forced to do.

Was it the same animal that bit Jimmy last night? Ryan thought it had to be, but how could that be true? How could an animal have a vendetta against them? That was what it sounded like. That was what it felt like.

The giant beast had already chased down Drew. Ryan heard his partner screaming in terror as they both ran in opposite directions to get away. Now it was coming for him. It had his scent, and it didn't matter which way he went, he didn't seem to be able to lose it. Was the hell beast somehow employed by Fat Bernhard?

Don’t be so ridiculous. Ryan told himself off for thinking such stupid thoughts. But when he heard it howl again, all reason went from his head.

It was closer now. Much closer.

Ryan’s vision was starting to blur and go fuzzy from lack of oxygen. He wasn’t really breathing anymore, just gasping for air like a fish stuck on land. He knew he needed to keep running, but he just didn’t have anything left in him. If he didn’t stop to get his breath back, he was going to collapse.

Just as he thought that, a terrible constricting pain gripped his chest. Ryan knew what it was instantly. He smoked far too many cigarettes, he drank far too much whisky, and he never ever paid attention to what he ate. A special forces veteran, he could still talk the talk – that was what convinced Jimmy to take him on despite being more than a decade older than the next oldest on the team – but the fitness he could once boast was now far in his past.

As the years of unhealthy living caught up to him, he sank to his knees. Pins and needles were shooting into his arms and the tightness in his chest seemed to increase by the second. He knew it was all over for him.

A few seconds later the wolf arrived. Running was necessary if he wanted to catch the man who killed his human, but seeing his quarry lying on the ground, he slowed his pace.

His left hip was a dull aching mass, a numb pain that extended into his leg. He could run, but he would rather not if he didn't have to.

Approaching the man, he sniffed the air more deeply, sampling it and comparing what he could smell to what he remembered of the man from last night.

Grunting his disappointment, Wolf had to accept that this wasn't the man he wanted either. All day he had trailed around the seaside resort, searching for the scent of his human's killer. Raw determination was his ally – he was never going to give up.

His efforts though had been dogged by animal control specialists. They almost nabbed him on one occasion, and he lost the scent he was tracking when he slipped through a broken fence to avoid getting caught.

The two men he'd cornered and chased tonight smelled of his human's killer. That meant they had to know him. Wolf almost caught the first one, but like last night, the man managed to get into a car and escape. So he switched targets, confident he could track and find the second human unless he too found motorised transport.

He nudged Ryan with his nose, but Ryan didn't react. He was never going to react to anything again. The massive heart attack had killed him almost before he collapsed to the floor. Technically, he was still alive, but his heart had already stopped beating, and his scent had changed.

Wolf backed away and sat on his haunches. Then he tipped his head back, closed his eyes, and howled his frustration.

Howl at the Moon

Rex went from asleep to alert and to standing on all four paws in the space of a heartbeat. The howl was still fading to nothingness but the sound of it was forever locked inside Rex's head.

The need for justice, the pain and longing contained within the howl, combined with Rex's own desire to know more about the elemental creature behind it. It created in him a need to respond that he could not have resisted if he tried.

Albert awoke to find Rex scratching at the door and whining. Momentarily confused in the dark and thrown by his unusual surroundings, it took him a moment for his thoughts to align. Remembering that he was staying in a hotel in Blackpool, Albert fumbled around to find the light on the nightstand.

'What is it, boy?' Albert was using his right elbow to prop himself up in bed and fighting the covers to get his feet on the floor. He was not alien to the concept of needing to use the facilities in the night - it was just one of those things that went with age so far as he was concerned.

Nevertheless, it was most unusual for Rex to need to go out at night. Albert checked his memory, confirming that he hadn't omitted to perform the dog's ritual of a last walk before bed. Certain that he had not forgotten, the dog was still clearly in need of an excursion.

'I'm coming, Rex. Just give me a moment to find my shoes and a coat.' As hastily as he could, Albert stuffed his feet into his shoes, omitting to put on socks in his haste.

Rex spun on the spot, his agitated paws dancing with his impatience to get outside. If he didn't get outside soon, the wolf might have moved on and the sea breeze made tracking difficult.

Spurred on by the memory of a rather unfortunate toilet incident at a veterinary surgery in Keswick, Albert was still attempting to pull his coat tight around his body when he opened the door.

Rex shot through the gap, bounding down the corridor towards the stairs and leaving Albert still hopping as he fought to get a shoe on his left foot. Once outside his room, Albert then realised he had omitted to pick up Rex's lead. In a split-second decision, he chose to leave it behind - Rex would return swiftly enough once his business was complete.

Or so Albert believed.

'Hold on, Rex,' Albert called insistently, but quietly, as his dog's tail vanished around the corner and out of sight. He knew the hotel's front door would be shut and that it would create a barrier where he could catch up. He hurried nevertheless, shuffling along the corridor as fast as he could for fear the dog might relieve himself on one of the plants in the hotel's lobby.

Rex was indeed defeated by the closed door which he nudged with his head and scratched at with his right front paw. Frustrated that he could go no further, and had no idea how to open the door, Rex ran back to see how far behind the old man was.

Albert was halfway down the stairs when Rex reappeared. His dog, who ought to be asleep, was full of life and bursting with energy. Was he going to arrive in the lobby to find the dog's joyous exuberance was because his desperate need to go outside was no longer a priority? Was there now a rather unfortunate mess to clean up?

Coming off the stairs, Albert was pleased when the dog ran to the door again, staring at it meaningfully. Rex still needed to go out, and Albert could not see an obvious puddle anywhere.

Rex learned long ago that his human struggled to understand what he was trying to tell him, and did his best to make it easy for him. This was a simple one. All he needed to do was stare at the door, look meaningfully at his human, and then stare at the door again.

Albert all but ran across the lobby, keen to get outside and even more keen to get the task done and get back into bed. He expected it to be cold outside and he was not disappointed.

With his left hand holding Rex's collar tightly, he turned the latch on the lobby front door and shoved it open with a shoulder. The cold, late autumn air instantly bit at his exposed ankles and blew up his sleeves. Where he was crouching slightly, there must have been a funnel created behind his neck because cold air blew straight down his back.

There were three steps down from the hotel's front door to the pavement, no doubt intended to keep the sea out if the tide ever came high enough to wash across the promenade. At the bottom of those, Albert checked left and right for traffic before releasing his hand from Rex's collar.

'Okay, Rex, go do your thing. Be quick about it, please,' Albert begged.

He expected the dog to dash directly across the road where he planned to follow at a more sedate pace. However, Rex took a pace, sniffed the air, and performed what Albert believed in the theatre would be called an exit, stage left.

'Hey!' Albert yelled, no longer keeping his voice down for fear of waking other hotel residents. 'Rex! Where are you going?' There then followed a few seconds of silence as he stared disbelievingly at his dog's back end vanishing into the darkness.

Rex had been able to pick up the scent of the wolf almost the instant he left the hotel. It was strong and distinctive. He had needed only a second to confirm the direction from which it was coming before setting off. With his head down, he ran as fast as he could but not so fast that he would lose the scent trail. He was going to find the wolf and when he did, he had a few questions to ask.

Animal Control

The same howl that drove Rex from his room was heard by forty-seven other people. That included Richard Finney and Andrew Cuxton, two members of the Blackpool animal control team. They were parked in their van with their windows wound down an inch. It meant the interior of their cab was colder than they would want it, something Andy had complained about many times, but it also allowed them to hear whatever noises there might be to hear.

'You heard that, right?' asked Richard.

Andy had a piece of a chicken and stuffing sandwich in his mouth. It was half chewed, but not yet ready to be swallowed - his jaw had stopped working upon hearing the howl. Attempting to restart his mouth so that he might clear the blockage, Andy managed to nod his head.

'That's our wolf,' Richard remarked with a devilish grin.

The news that there was a wolf loose in Blackpool had been received with mild disinterest from most members of the animal control team. They caught animals all the livelong day, so yes, a wolf was something different to your average lost pet, but for their colleagues it was nothing to get excited about.

The police had found the animal defending the body of a murdered human who was later identified as a man who performed a street theatre act on the seafront. The wolf was part of the act, apparently. The wolf ran away when the police tried to catch him, which caused much conversation at the animal control centre as they sagely pointed out to each other that the police ought to have called the professionals.

Now it was on the loose and someone had to catch it. Andy and Richard were not assigned to track it down. Actually, they were supposed to be somewhere else entirely, but Richard had it in his head that they could catch the wolf even though Claire and Ann were supposed to be after it.

Quite why this was a good idea, Andy had yet to establish. He could have asked Richard, but that would have involved showing interest – not something he bothered with very often.

With exaggerated actions that Richard believed would make him look purposeful and determined, he yanked on his gloves and grabbed his control pole.

'Come along, Andy,' Richard grabbed his door handle, shunting the door open to let the cool night air swirl in. 'It's time to be heroes,' he stated in a forced gruff voice.

Sixty yards away, the wolf, unaware that he was being pursued, was looking for somewhere to sleep. He had been awake and on the trail ever since his human died. Unused to such a long period without sleep, now that the adrenaline of chasing Drew and Ryan had left his system, he felt utterly exhausted.

He needed to get some rest, and all he needed was somewhere dark and enclosed to curl up.

Forming a triangle between the animal control men and the wolf's location, Rex was beginning to close in. The scent trail he followed crossed itself several times. Assessing what else he could smell, Rex detected a human in trouble. He did not know whether humans were aware or not, but when they feel panicked or afraid, they secrete a different scent that is subtle but easy to detect if one knows what to smell for.

Distracted by this new smell, he left the wolf's scent trail to investigate.

One hundred and fifty yards behind Rex, Albert was muttering, cursing, and generally threatening violence as he attempted to find his dog. He didn't want to go too far, concerned the dog had run off because he'd smelled an abandoned kebab somewhere and was about to return to the hotel anyway. That being the case, Rex would not find Albert waiting for him and they could wind up chasing each other around all night.

Of course, that would not happen, because in that scenario Rex would simply follow his human's scent trail, one which he could identify almost without needing to use his nose it was so familiar to him.

Albert had his hands stuffed into his coat pockets to keep them warm, but the cold night air was penetrating everywhere else anyway. Wearing cotton pyjamas and no underwear beneath his coat, he was ill prepared for being outside for an extended period. Not that it was cold enough to cause hypothermia or to land him in hospital, but it was going to take him a good while to warm up if he didn't get back inside soon.

He continued to call for his dog, shouting Rex's name as loudly as he could and with as much urgency as he could muster.

Rex could hear his human's voice. Truthfully, he felt quite bad about running away, but his need to find the wolf was absolute. Something in the animal's howl convinced him the wolf was in trouble. Given that he had picked up a strong sense of the wolf scent at the murder scene, which placed him there without any question in Rex's mind, he needed to know how the wolf was involved.

His nose led him to a human lying face down in the street. He was in a back alleyway, wedged between two businesses, and adjacent to a building site surrounded by temporary fencing to keep people out.

That the human was dead could not be questioned. That the wolf's scent was on the man's body was equally easy to be certain of. Rex sniffed and sampled the air, his nose tracking up and down the man's back as he tried to form a picture of what had happened. The man was dead, but Rex was used to discovering bodies that had an obvious cause of death. This one did not.

His initial concern that perhaps the wolf had tracked and killed this victim was dismissed because there were no wounds, nor any trace of the wolf's saliva. Rex decided to push on, retracing his steps to find the wolf's scent trail once more.

A short distance away, Richard was leading his partner in what he believed was the right direction.

'You're just guessing,' argued Andy, rolling his eyes. 'You don't have any idea which way the wolf went.'

'It's instinctual,' Andy. 'You have to think like a wolf and allow your senses to lead you forwards.'

Andy hurried to keep up, though he could not quite work out why he was listening to his partner's nonsense.

'What are you waffling on about, man? How exactly do you know how to think like a wolf?'

Richard chose to ignore Andy's question because it inconveniently exposed that he was talking utter rubbish. Instead, he froze, lifting his left arm in a fist as he had seen soldiers do in action movies. He believed it meant that everyone else in the patrol was to also stop moving, but Andy clearly hadn't seen the same movies.

'What are you doing now?' Andy questioned, arriving at Richard's side.

Exhaling with an exasperated sigh that ruffled his lips on its exit, Richard wondered how he had become shackled to his dopey, short companion. He held the raised fist in front of Andy's face.

'This means you should freeze,' he hissed, keeping quiet because he was pretending to be on the wolf's trail. 'I saw something ahead,' he whispered, dropping his arm again to take full control of his pole. 'I think it's the wolf.'

'I think you're making it up.' Andy pushed past his colleague in the tight alleyway, questioning why he had to be the one out here with Crazy Richard.

The wolf lifted his head, sniffing the air and twisting this way and that as he attempted to capture the sound again. Had he heard a man speaking?

The breeze was pushing the air the wrong way for him to detect Richard and Andy, but as he lowered his head again, he stayed alert.

Rex was closing in - the scent of the wolf getting stronger with each passing yard. It was time to apply caution – the wolf might not respect his intrusion even though Rex's intentions were both good and honourable. How should he announce himself though? Was it best to call out, barking to alert the wolf and let him know there was nothing to fear?

Surely, the wolf would just laugh at him.

Why would a wolf fear a dog?

What then? Bark out, 'Hey, I'm a dog and I heard your howling? Did you murder a couple of humans? Did they deserve it?'

Rex didn't fear an attack by the wolf – he knew how big he was and that any animal, even a wolf, would think twice before taking him on.

It was tricky.

While Rex pondered the complexities of introducing himself to a wild animal lost in the town, Albert continued to hunt for his dog. His muttering included a number of suggestions for what he was going to do to the dog when he finally caught up to him. Most involved Rex's bottom which was either getting hit with something or having an object: a foot, a house brick, a Volvo ... inserted into it at speed.

Now more than a hundred yards from the hotel and one street back from the seafront, Albert was thinking about turning back. Naturally, that was when he spotted something moving in the shadows ahead.

He'd been following Rex as best he could. Without a dog's olfactory system to guide him, Albert stuck to visual clues. There were puddles leftover from the earlier rain, but the rest of the pavement was dry. It meant that where Rex's paws passed through a pool of contained water, there were then prints for Albert to trail until they diminished once more.

He didn't know it, but what he saw moving between two cars as it slunk into an alleyway, was a fox. All Albert saw was a bushy tail disappearing.

'Rex!' he bellowed. 'Rex, stop right there!'

Ahead of him, lights came on in the bedrooms of two houses. Any second now the curtains were going to twitch as the inhabitants looked out to see who was making all the noise.

Feeling guilty and embarrassed, as he imagined his desperate shouts waking small children whose parents had struggled to get them to sleep, he ducked behind a large car where he could hide from sight.

Crouching low, and with his back protesting at the awkward position, his intended methods of reprimand for Rex increased in their inventiveness.

Wolf raised his head again. He hadn't imagined hearing humans coming his way. It was probably nothing to worry about, but he'd already had one run in with the animal control idiots today and believed throwing caution to the wind was a great way to get caught.

Backed into an alcove underneath a set of concrete steps, if they found him he had nowhere to go but into their nets. With no choice that he could see, but risking exposing himself when they could easily pass right by without ever seeing him, Wolf crept out of his hiding space.

'What exactly is it you think you saw?' Andy demanded, at least speaking at a hushed volume this time.

Continuing with his pretence, Richard crept forward, his eyes locked on a dark patch beneath a set of concrete steps that led to a loading dock behind one of the businesses. He knew he was going to discover that nothing was there and was hastily attempting to come up with something to say that would stop Andy from mocking him.

'I caught a scent of something on the breeze,' he claimed, attempting to make it sound like he possessed a supernatural ability. He wanted to stand out from his colleagues at the animal control centre and hoped that by catching the wolf and displaying skills the others did not possess he would be revered by his peers – and most especially the girls.

Hearing Richard's latest comment, Andy found his face forming a disgusted frown. It was not unusual for his partner to talk nonsense, but now he was acting as if he was some kind of super soldier. Watching Richard advance, Andy got to see his colleague urgently waving with his left hand. Clearly, he wanted Andy to move to his left to take up a flanking position.

At precisely the moment when he was going to announce his intention to go back to the van and, if Richard didn't come with him, to drive off without him, a large wolf emerged from the black space they were both staring at.

Albert heard two strangled cries of panic. He had no idea what might have caused them, but late at night and in the dark, he imagined it had to be Rex surprising someone. Making a wild guess, Albert assumed it was a couple of chaps staggering home from the pub and stopping to relieve themselves somewhere they imagined to be handy.

Getting a fix on the position of the squeals he heard, Albert hurried in that direction and turned off the pavement to enter a dark alley.

Rex also heard the startled cries of alarm. He was still trying to work out how to announce himself to the wolf. He knew that he was downwind, which was how he could smell where the wolf was and felt confident the wolf was unlikely to smell him. Propelled into motion by the sound of humans in trouble, Rex started running once more. The sound of the shouts and the location of the wolf were one and the same. Rex's concern that the wolf might be harming people came to the fore once more.

Andy was embarrassed by the yelp he gave upon seeing the wolf. It had been reported to them as dangerous, though he knew it to be as tame as a wolf ever could be. It was a registered animal and the property of a man who performed a street theatre act each night on the Blackpool promenade. He'd even seen the act himself once.

What embarrassed Andy most was that when he yelped in surprise, Richard had responded to the shock with the war cry, darting forward to intercept the dangerous canine.

What he didn't know, was that Richard had done no such thing. Richard had been about to cough when the wolf appeared, and so his own cry of panic came out as a deep growling noise. At the same time, he had tripped on something unseen in the dark and that made it look like he was lunging forward.

Wolf had been startled to find two humans in such close range. It hadn't been deliberate on their part, but they had approached him from a downwind location, and he had not been able to smell them. They were both armed with control poles, the loops at the end open and loose, ready to slip over his neck.

Instantly energised by the need to escape, Wolf thrust off with his back legs. He was aiming for a gap between the two humans, certain all he needed to do was get past the reach of their arms. Once he was moving, he believed it would be very difficult for them to catch him.

The question of how they found him in the first place was one he could ponder later.

Unfortunately, and in a bizarre twist of fate, as Richard backpedalled, fear and shock driving his feet to get away as the wolf came forward, he slipped, fell, and whipped the control pole down right in front of Wolf's head.

To Andy, the only person present to observe it, it appeared to him as if Richard were mimicking *Neo* from the *Matrix*. The manner and speed in which he moved to angle his body and get the control pole to snag the wolf in one fluid movement was nothing short of inhuman. With wide eyes and an open jaw, Andy gawped at his partner.

Wolf bucked against the restraint around his neck, feeling it tighten to restrict his breathing. How on earth had the human managed to catch him?

Richard was hanging on for dear life. Lying in the dirt and dampness on the floor of the alleyway, he had no idea he'd caught the wolf until it nearly yanked the control pole out of his hands.

'That was the most amazing thing I've ever seen,' Andy gasped in awe. 'How did you do that?'

Suddenly realising Andy thought his actions were deliberate, Richard tried desperately to think of a cool line to deliver. He was getting to his feet, no easy feat with the wolf fighting like billyo to get away.

Allowing a confident and jubilant smile to spread across his lips, Richard almost got to say, 'Some of us are just natural hunters.'

However, before he could get the first word out, Rex hit him from behind. It was a move Rex liked to refer to as cat-flapping. One moment the man pinning the wolf in place was standing vertically, the next he was horizontal, his body parallel to the ground beneath him.

'Arrrrggghhhh!' screamed Andy. 'There're two of them! There're two wolves!'

Richard heard what was said, but couldn't give comment. All he could see were the stars above him. That he had lost his grip on the control pole was a fact he was vaguely conscious of. More present in his mind was the pain coming from the back of his legs and the knowledge that he was very soon to crash back to the hard concrete below.

Barking to the wolf, Rex said, 'Quick! Come with me!'

With the control pole still trapped tightly around his neck, Wolf was nevertheless free from restraint, and he did not need to be invited twice to make good his escape.

The long metal pole trailed and scraped as he bounded along the alleyway, running for all he was worth. He had no idea who the large German Shepherd dog was, where he had come from, or why he was helping. There was no mistaking the stench of humanity on the dog's fur, which made him a domesticated animal and not a stray, yet there would be time for asking questions later. Now the only thing Wolf wanted to do was get some distance between him and the two men from animal control.

Not so very far away, Albert heard the kerfuffle and the very recognisable sound of Rex barking. He wanted to push on, worrying that the longer it took him to find his dog, the more difficult or less likely their reunion would become.

Going after Rex was not an option though, for at his feet was something that had to take priority.

It was not the first time that Albert had seen a dead body, not by a long stroke. Nor was it the first time he had ever been the person to find the corpse in question. Tonight though, he was feeling rather put upon that it had to be his turn again.

In hindsight, Albert wished he'd thrown a pillow at Rex and ordered him to return to bed instead of letting him out. Since wishing wouldn't get him anywhere, he needed to deal with the current situation. Of course, he hadn't thought to pick up his phone when he left his room. Why would he? So now he was rather stuck.

It wouldn't do to leave the body where it was, though Albert accepted he might have to if he was unable to attract anyone's attention. He walked to the end of the alley and into the pale streetlight.

It was only just after midnight, but there was no one in sight in either direction. Albert considered shouting again, less worried now about waking anyone since the circumstances had changed and he could justify doing so. He found that he didn't have to, the sound of muted conversation drifting to his ears through the labyrinth of alleyways.

When seconds later, two men appeared, he recognised their uniforms. He couldn't have known it, but less than twenty yards from his current location, when he was carefully examining the body, Andy from the town's animal control unit had been helping his colleague back to his feet.

Richard had done his best to play down how much his head was pounding. It was his skull that hit the concrete first, followed by the rest of him and much of it was bruised.

Lying on the ground, Richard had been feverishly wracking his brain to come up with a cool line he might deploy. He thought he'd done a good job of covering up the fact that he'd fallen and only snagged the wolf by chance, but Andy had interrupted him before he could speak.

'That was amazing!' gasped Andy, discovering a newfound respect for his partner. He wasn't sure even how to describe what he had seen.

Richard had caught the wolf, no one could take that away from him, but what happened afterwards was difficult to explain. Making their way back to their truck, Andy did his best to describe the large dog seemingly bursting onto the scene from out of nowhere and was gesticulating wildly when he suddenly froze.

Ahead of him, as they reached a junction between alleyways as they wound through the houses, was a man standing over what looked like a body.

Momentarily taken aback, Richard soon felt the need to fulfil his new hero status role.

'Hey, what do you think you're doing there?' he demanded to know. Then for good show, he pushed his way in front of Andy who was rooted to the spot.

Albert heard the men coming - they made enough noise - and was pleasantly surprised to see two men in a uniform he recognised. He'd seen the same uniform on two women just a number of hours ago outside the sweet shop. It was vastly superior to attracting the attention of two drunks on their way home after a late night bender.

'Do you chaps have a phone?' Albert asked. 'This man is dead. I need you to call the police.'

Andy asked, 'What did you do to him?'

Snorting in amazement at the ridiculous question, Albert said, 'I didn't do anything to him. I just found him like this.'

Richard laughed, scoffing at the old man.

'Yeah, okay. Pull the other one, it's got bells on it. Andy do the eyebrow thing.'

Before Albert could question what an earth they were talking about, the smaller, more rotund of the two men, hiked his right eyebrow as high up his forehead as it would go.

'See that?' Richard asked. 'That's Andy's are-you-being-serious eyebrow. It's famous about these parts. I think maybe you killed him.' Richard accused.

Albert took his hands from his pockets and crossed them over his chest. In his many years in the police force he'd met a lot of idiots. Mostly they were the criminals he was attempting to chase as they foolishly believed they could somehow evade the law. Although, on occasion, the idiots were those he worked with.

'If I were guilty of harming this man, what would I gain by requesting that you call the police?' Albert inquired. 'Do you have a phone?' he posed his first question again. 'I really think it would be helpful if one of you were to call for the police, please.'

'He's got a point, Richard,' Andy pointed out.

He couldn't think of a suitable answer, but still hoping he could turn things to his advantage, and make himself look like the hero, Richard took it upon himself to make the call to the emergency services.

When the cops arrived, twelve minutes later, the flashing blue lights of their squad car illuminating the dark alleyway as they pulled up to the nearest entrance, Albert was disappointed to see that the two officers were those he'd already met.

Constable Gordon took one look at the old man and allowed a deep frown to darken his features. Dredging the pensioner's name from the recesses of his skull, he exited his car.

'Mr. Smith? Well, aren't you having quite the visit to Blackpool? One case of disturbing the peace for which I very generously gave you a pass. And now I find you just a few hours later standing over a body.'

Unlike last night, when he had given constable Gordon the benefit of the doubt, Albert accepted that he was dealing with yet another idiot. Choosing to ignore the young man's statement, since he hadn't asked a question - a fundamental error for a policeman so far as he was concerned - Albert posed one of his own.

'Did you identify the two men in the sweet shop?' Albert fixed the young officer with a hard stare. Before Constable Gordon could answer, Albert continued talking, 'I shall assume that you did, and that you are now feverishly attempting to follow up on your error in judgement in letting them go.'

Constable Gordon was not used to being spoken to in such a manner. Accepting that Mr Smith claimed to be a retired senior police officer explained why he thought that he could, but that was not enough to convince him to allow the old man to continue.

Ignoring the question, since he believed it held no relevance to the current situation, he asked, 'Would you care to explain what you are doing in a dark alleyway standing over a body after midnight, Sir?'

Albert fielded the simple question with one of his own. Constable Gordon really wasn't up to the mark.

‘I was looking for my dog. I'm sure you remember him. He's a large German Shepherd. He insisted that he needed to be let out of our hotel room. However, I lost control of him once we were outside, and he ran off. In searching for him, I came across what appears to be a body. I employ the term ‘appears to be’ correctly at this time because no medical examiner has been here to confirm the status of the man we are discussing. Do you have any other silly questions?’ Albert goaded.

He knew he wasn’t doing himself any favours, but no longer cared. If they chose to arrest him on suspicion of murder, his one phone call would bring trouble down on the heads of the local police in a manner they would not believe.

‘A German Shepherd?’ questioned Andy. ‘We saw one of those just a couple of minutes ago. It hit Richard just as he was catching the wolf. It was amazing. You should have seen it,’ he began to gush, unable to hold his hero-worship in check.

‘Wolf?’ questioned Constable Jones, arriving next to his partner. ‘The one owned by the man who was murdered last night?’

Albert noted the detail about the identity of the man who was murdered the previous evening, but was far more focused on hearing more about his dog.

‘Which way did he go, please?’ Albert begged. ‘He’ll be lost already. We've only been in Blackpool a few hours.’ Albert made to move away, getting his feet ready so that he could go in whatever direction the two animal control men suggested.

Constable Gordon grabbed Albert’s arm. Hooking a hand around his left bicep.

'You're not going anywhere, Sir.' Constable Gordon promised. 'Not until I've got this situation cleared up.'

Richard cut in above everyone else, diverting the attention back to a more pertinent topic.

'Um, Andy was just telling you about my amazing catch. You really should listen to him; he will describe it in glorious detail.' He slapped his partner on the back for good measure, making it seem as if they had performed the task together because he was going to rely on Andy to tell everyone else how amazing he'd been.

Constable Jones was on his radio, having stepped away. He was organising all the additional services they now needed. While the others had been arguing, he performed the task of checking the pulse of the man lying on the ground and confirmed there was no need to attempt any form of resuscitation.

Getting angry, Albert poked a finger in the air, aiming it very clearly at Constable Gordon.

'I need to find my dog.' He spoke the words clearly and precisely to make sure they could not be misinterpreted. 'He is my assistance dog. Also, it's rather cold out and you might notice that I am not a young man, and I am wearing my bedclothes.'

Neither of the young officers we're going to allow Albert to push them around. However, in deference to his age, Constable Gordon agreed to allow Albert to sit in the back of his squad car. It would be warm in there, but he was not going to let the old man leave the area to search for his dog.

Andy and Richard knew they were getting the task before Constable Gordon even looked their way.

'You're going to ask us to find that missing dog, aren't you?' confirmed Richard in a tone that made it clear he didn't think it was his job.

'Yes, I am,' agreed constable Gordon. 'Off you go, chaps.'

Mumbling and grumbling, both men accepted there was simply no arguing and set off back to their van. They wanted to catch the wolf. There was kudos and status to be gained by doing so. But now that they had lost it once, they doubted it was still in this area.

Thankful to be warm, but concerned about his dog anyway, Albert rested his head against the seat back in the rear of the squad car and waited for the circus to arrive.

Fat Bernhard

'What do you mean, no one can find Brooksy?'

The question was posed by a large man sitting on an inflatable ring which in turn was on a large armchair. The inflatable ring was all to do with a terrible case of haemorrhoids.

His name was Bernhard Grimshaw, though everyone knew him as Fat Bernhard, and he ran all the protection rackets in Blackpool. He used to run almost all organised crime in the town, but foolishly handed power over when his daughter grew to understand what her father was.

She made him feel guilty and that he had somehow failed as a father. However, she eventually shunned him anyway, pushing him out of her life and moving away. When he attempted to retake his crown, he found there was a new criminal overlord.

Raymond 'Razor' Rutheridge was a man of tiny stature, but great power and vision. Less than five feet tall, and weighing under one hundred pounds, he discovered his vicious streak at a young age when the taunting of his classmates caused him to snap.

Now there wasn't a man alive who was brave enough to remark on his size, not if they wanted to see another sunrise anyway.

The big problem for anyone who wanted to challenge for the crown was that Raymond ran his new empire without even being in the country. He lived on a superyacht and never came into British waters. He had gangs running his enterprises for him, and Fat Bernhard was invited to manage the protection end of things.

Others might have baulked at being offered the bottom rung, especially when they had once been at the top. Yet advancing years had mellowed his ambition, and he found the quiet task of extorting money from local businesses kept him largely under the radar - the police took little notice of his gangs' activities.

The other crime syndicates in the area were into prostitution, smuggling, and drugs – all more interesting crimes. By focusing his efforts on what he considered to be an intelligent criminal enterprise, which his competitors took no interest in, he avoided interference from almost all parties.

Until now it seemed.

Brooksy was the fourth of his enforcers to go missing in the last week. Already, Big Dave, Too Tall Taff, and Arnold 'Classic' Braunsweiger had up and vanished while performing their weekly collections.

Fat Bernhard was staring at his four most trusted lieutenants. All looked nervous, none of them wanting to deliver the bad news and having drawn straws to see which of them would be stuck with the task.

He shifted position, the inflatable ring squeaking as he did so. The movement rewarded him with a sharp jolt of pain where he really didn't want it. Cursing loudly, he twisted his bottom back to where it had been.

'I think someone's taking them, boss,' ventured Fat Bernhard's most senior right hand man.

Fat Bernhard threw an arm in the air. 'Of course someone is taking them, you idiot. You didn't think they'd all won lottery tickets and flown off to the Bahamas, did you? The question you morons need to answer,' he poked a pudgy finger at all four of them in turn, 'is who? If there is a new player in town, I want to know who it is.'

The man on the far right of the four in front of him was a man who graced the group by dint of being the longest serving of Fat Bernhard's men. Timidly, he raised a hand.

'Don't raise your hand!' roared the gang boss. 'If you've got a question or something to say spit it out.'

'You don't think it can be the Cypriots, do you, boss?' asked Cyril.

It hadn't actually occurred to Fat Bernhard to question whether it might be one of his rivals choosing to step in on his easy money. They had never done so in the past. The gangs in Blackpool had existed in harmony for many years because the man at the top insisted it be so. They each knew what the other gangs specialised in and would keep clear. Not stepping on each other's toes had ensured prosperity for all.

'He's right, Chief,' remarked Kenny the Snake, so called because he was as thin as a rake handle and possessed a terrible lisp. It was no coincidence that he avoided using the word boss when addressing Fat Bernhard.

'What do you mean he's right?' Fat Bernhard wanted to know. 'What is it that I don't know that you think you do?' he accused.

Now on the spot, Kenny needed to give an answer. 'Well, chief,' Kenny did his best to avoid any word with an 'S' in it if at all possible, 'I overheard two men who work for Giorgio talking about him just a few nights ago. One was regaling the other with an anecdote he claimed to have heard from Giorgio. It was about you chief.'

Fat Bernhard frowned, not entirely sure he wanted to hear what Kenny had to say.

'Go on,' he commanded.

Kenny licked his lips nervously. 'Well, chief, it was to do with your weight.'

'Really?' Fat Bernhard could barely believe his ears. 'Giorgio and I have been friends for years. If he's decided to move in on my turf, I'll have to kill him myself.'

The gang boss took a few seconds to think, cupping his chin and staring at the floor while he tapped an index finger on his jaw line. Looking up, he fixed his lieutenants with a hard glare.

'I want hard evidence. I want you lot out in the streets. I want to know where Brooksy and the others have gone. Whatever else happens, we can't have this getting back to Raymond. If I'm going to move against the Cypriots, we need to be one hundred percent certain that they are behind this.'

He got a lot of 'Yes bosses' in reply and when no one had moved two seconds later, he flared his eyes at them in a meaningful manner, then watched as they all ran for the door.

Teaming Up

It took Rex almost thirty minutes to chew through the cable around the wolf's neck. It was purposefully designed to be almost chew proof. Indeed, when his teeth went easily through the outer plastic sheath, he found there was steel cable inside. Knowing that he would lose that particular battle, he ate the pole instead.

It took some effort, but when he'd reduced it to a sufficiently battered mess, the mechanism inside gave way, releasing the wolf's neck.

Now that they were better able to face one another, Rex and the Wolf sized each other up. They were not much different in height or weight, both animals standing at the top end of the maximum their breed could grow to.

'Why did you do that?' asked Wolf. 'Why did you help me back there?'

Rex sat back on his haunches, studying the wolf. He'd never seen one before, and it was a little like meeting one's hero, as if a fabled creature had somehow come to life.

'I'm sure any other dog would have done the same in my situation. When I saw you, I could not tell if you would get free or overpower the humans by yourself, but I felt certain you would stand a better chance if I assisted.'

Wolf accepted the dog's reply. 'What now then, dog? Surely, you have a human you need to return to. I can smell him on you.'

Thoughts of Albert filled Rex's head with sorrow. He did not like that he had abandoned his human even though he believed that at the time it was the right thing to do. His human, though old, was quite capable and had proven himself worthy of respect on many occasions. However, the sound of his human's voice demanding he return still echoed in Rex's head and he knew that he had been a bad dog.

To answer the wolf's question, Rex said, 'I do. Yet some things must come before our duty to a human. I can smell a human on you too. Though I fear you are going to tell me he is no longer with us.'

The dog was remarkably astute. Wolf had not expected it, but in the short time he'd spent in Rex's company, he had come to learn the dog was far more capable than he would normally expect.

Talk of the wolfman drove an icicle through the wolf's heart and lit a fire once more in his belly.

'He was killed. I saw a man kill him, and I was not able to stop it from happening. That was last night, and I have been tailing him ever since. I am going to find him. And I will have my revenge.' Had Wolf been human, this would have been the point at which he might have thumped a fist on a table.

Dogs and wolves do not do that, yet the emotion carried in his eyes had much the same effect on Rex.

'You have his scent?' Rex sought to confirm.

'I do,' the wolf replied, his voice betraying his deadly intent.

Rex lifted his nose and sniffed the air.

'You are injured,' he remarked. 'You are bleeding.'

The wolf grumbled and settled onto the ground. The place they had stopped was inside an abandoned building. It was dry and it was warm enough out of the breeze. They could rest there for the night.

Ignoring the comment about his health, the wolf said,' I must rest. In the morning I will start my search afresh.'

Rex kept guard for a while. Listening and smelling for anyone who might come near.

Exhausted, the wolf fell quickly into a deep sleep, his dreams filled with chases and horrible images of his human's final moments.

Rex thought of Albert until he accepted they were unlikely to be disturbed in their hiding place. Then he too laid down and slept.

Though he had not planned to, indeed he tried hard to fight it, Albert fell asleep in the back of the squad car. Travelling always made him tired, so when the warmth of the car's heater thawed the cold in his bones, he was unable to prevent the drift into slumber.

He awoke when the rear door on the opposite side opened and cold air wafted in. A woman in her early thirties slid inside, shutting the door behind her.

'Goodness, that's better,' she remarked, blowing on her hands. She had fine auburn hair cut short so it sat an inch above her collar, and green eyes that sparkled like emeralds. She was neither pretty nor unattractive, but possessed a homely look that evoked in Albert a comforting notion that she might be a fine woman for a man to spend a life with.

'You're Albert Smith, yes?' she asked, though Albert was certain she knew the answer. It was posed not as a detail to check, but rather as a conversation starter.

Albert nodded his head. 'I am,' he confirmed. 'And you are?' he left the question hanging for her to fill in the blank.

The young woman twisted in her seat to hold out her right hand.

'Detective Chief Inspector Eliza Benjamin-Mackie.'

Albert shook the offered hand, noting the strength of her grip. She was a woman in what had traditionally been a man's environment and clearly succeeding. Her grip and her success though were secondary factors, it was her name that was going around in his head.

'Benjamin-Mackie?' he questioned. It was a name he had not heard in many years, but it was such an unusual one it triggered a new question.

Anticipating what he was going to say next, Eliza released Albert's hand with a smile.

'You're about to ask if I know or if I'm related to a man called George Benjamin-Mackie, yes?' She had already done her homework and knew precisely who she was talking to. 'He's my father.'

Albert's sleep addled brain was not quite up to speed, his conversation skills lacking. So all he managed to say in reply was, 'Your father?'

Eliza chuckled. 'You are undoubtedly thinking that all of George's children ought to be far older than me and you would be correct. I was, shall we say, a late and unexpected addition.'

Albert was marvelling at the young lady's revelation. He did not doubt what she was saying, he could see his old friend's features reflected in her face. George Benjamin-Mackie had been his Sergeant when Albert was a Chief Inspector.

A memory surfaced of George moving away. It had been towards the end of his career and the two men had not been partnered together for years by then. George had moved upon promotion to work ... somewhere, Albert could not remember where, but he knew it was somewhere north. Clearly, he came to Blackpool.

Hesitant to ask a question he now dearly wanted an answer to, he was once again beaten to the punch by the perceptive young woman.

'Yes, my father is still alive. I think he'll be rather pleased to see you if you are still around later today. He doesn't get out much now, not that I'm suggesting he is too frail. Mum died five years ago, and he moved his sister, my aunt Sylvia, in with him. He tried living alone for a short while, but I think he found it quite a strain, and his brother-in-law had died just twelve months before mum. Dad and auntie annoy the heck out of each other, but I think that keeps them young.'

Albert understood exactly what Eliza was saying. Putting that to one side, interesting though it was, he had other questions to ask.

However, as if sensing that he was about to change the subject, Eliza once again beat him to the punch.

'I'm afraid I have no news as to the whereabouts of your dog. The two men from animal control who were here earlier reported back some time ago. They have since ended their shift but let us know they were unsuccessful in finding any trace of your dog or the wolf they were apparently out here attempting to capture.' Seeing the worry flash across the older man's face, she reached out with a hand which he placed on his arm for comfort. 'I shouldn't worry too much. I believe their success rate in returning lost pets is quite high. He is chipped, yes?'

Rex was indeed chipped which would make it easy to identify who he was when they caught up to him. However, Albert had spent a little time before he fell asleep analysing his dog's behaviour. Having heard what Constable Jones said about the murder the previous evening, the wolf was clearly in some way connected to the man who was killed. That being the case, Rex's out-of-character behaviour had to be something to do with the wolf. The animal control guys claimed they saw Rex when he interrupted them trapping the wolf. In fact, they made it sound as if Rex deliberately got in the way and made sure the wolf escaped.

For a while now Albert had been wondering about his dog. Specifically, about Rex's level of intelligence. He'd grown certain during this trip, where he spent almost every waking hour with Rex, that the dog regularly attempted to communicate with him.

Albert did not think that was normal canine behaviour.

So for his dog to deliberately run away and then find a wolf who was somehow connected to a murder that occurred a little more than twenty-four hours ago ... Albert did not believe in coincidence.

Albert hadn't spoken for more than a minute, Eliza taking his silence as concern for his pet.

'If you give me your number, Mr. Smith, I promise I will stay on top of animal control and alert you the moment I hear anything. Are you planning to be in Blackpool for very long?'

Albert snorted a sad laugh. According to the clock in the front of the car it was now almost three in the morning. Following on from Gary's phone call the previous evening, his amended plan was to travel home as soon as he'd eaten breakfast. With Rex on the lam, Albert could not leave town. Or it might be more accurate to say he was not going to leave town. Not until he was reunited with his dog.

To acknowledge what his old friend's daughter was saying, he replied, 'Thank you. I wasn't planning to stay for very long, but I guess things have changed. Is there any chance I can get a lift back to my hotel? It's the Clarence on the seafront. I know it's not very far, but if it's all the same to you, I'd really rather not walk. It looks quite cold out, and I am hardly dressed for it.'

'Of course, Mr. Smith. There's no need to even get out of the car. I'll have one of my constables deliver you to the door as soon as I can.'

Looking beyond her and out the window to the activity in the alleyway, Albert didn't bother trying to fight his curiosity.

'The man I found ... did he die of natural causes? I ask because I came across what was very clearly the scene of a murder not that many yards from where we are now. I understand, from listening to your police officers, you may wish to brief them on minding what they say around civilians, that it was a local man who was killed.'

DCI Benjamin-Mackie flipped her eyebrows. The news that her officers could not keep their lips sealed was not news at all. Her boss had cause to talk to the entire department on the subject not so very long ago. She would reiterate his words shortly, especially since she knew Albert was referring to constables Gordon and Jones.

Choosing her words carefully, she said, 'Given what you've just said, Mr. Smith, it would be rather remiss of me to say anything on the subject.'

Albert chuckled at his error. Tired, he hadn't thought about the order in which he should have approached the subject. He should have asked her about the dead man first and then talked about her officers' loose lips, he might have achieved an altogether more satisfactory result that way.

A man in a suit and a winter coat rapped his knuckles on the window and crouched slightly to show his face. He didn't say anything and stood up again once he locked eyes with Eliza.

'That's my boss,' she explained. From an inner jacket pocket, she withdrew a business card. It was an unglamorous white thing with black type, issued for the purpose of giving out to potential witnesses and other persons. Using a pen she took from the same pocket, she wrote a phone number on the back of the card before handing it to Albert.

He accepted it graciously, turning it over in his hands to look at both sides.

'That's the home number for my father,' she pointed to it with an unmanicured fingernail. 'If you have the chance, I'm sure he'll be very pleased to hear from you. He doesn't have many friends up here.'

It was her final remark, Albert getting a nod of acknowledgement as she swung her legs around, opened the door, and got out again.

Left alone in the car once more, and now wide awake, Albert thought more about where Rex might be and for what purpose he might have chosen to run off. Was it something to do with the wolf? If so, was it then in turn something to do with the murder last night?

He got to examine what little he knew from several angles for ten minutes, at which point Constable Jones opened the driver's door, poked his head through to offer Albert a smile, and then plonked himself down into the driver's seat.

'I'm your taxi driver home, Sir. Where is it we're going?'

Breakfast for Everyone

Albert was only able to achieve a couple of hours sleep that night. Though tired, his worry for Rex, and where his dog might have got to, kept him awake. It was the longest he'd being separated from Rex since the former police dog first came to stay with him.

Upon waking, Albert checked his phone. There were no messages from anyone, which meant that Rex had not been found yet. Fighting hard against a heavy heart, Albert trudged through the routine of his morning ablutions and went downstairs for breakfast.

Stopping off at the hotel's reception desk, he found a lady in attendance this morning.

'Good morning,' he greeted her with the best smile he could muster.

The lady looked up from the counter, returning a smile with genuine warmth when she said, 'Good morning, Sir. Is there anything I can help you with?'

A sigh escaped Albert's lips when he tried to work out what it was that he actually wanted to say.

'I'm supposed to be checking out this morning, but my dog went missing last night.'

The lady's expression changed immediately.

'Oh, my goodness!'

Sensing she was about to start asking questions regarding how such an event could come to pass, Albert got in first.

'The police and animal control are looking for him. I'm sure he will be found. He's too big to find a hiding place,' Albert used a smile to hide his concern. 'Obviously though, I'll need to stay in Blackpool until he turns up, and I can't tell when that might be. Do you have rooms available still?'

The lady didn't even need to check the computer to provide an answer.

'Oh, yes, we have quite a few rooms available at the moment. I'll put a note on the system,' she said as she moved her hands to grasp the mouse, 'and will keep your room open. You can update us day by day. Is that okay?' she asked.

Albert thanked the lady, relieved that he wasn't going to have to leave the hotel. He hoped that it might be the case that Rex would return of his own volition. The sooner the better, of course.

What he did not know, was that Rex was not very far away at all. Rex was unsettled by not being around to protect his human. Aware of the frequency with which the old man tended to get into trouble, he had insisted that he and the wolf remain in the area until daylight.

However, once awake, Rex's thoughts quickly turned to breakfast. Without Albert around to put kibble into his bowl, he recognised that in order to eat he was going to have to fend for himself. It wasn't just food though. His human always carried a small bowl and a bottle of water wherever they went so neither man nor dog ever went thirsty. Had he been in the hotel room with his human right now, to quench his thirst all he would need do is walk across the room to his water bowl.

Keen to get up and get moving, Rex checked to see if the wolf was awake.

Meanwhile, back in the hotel, Albert discovered there was someone waiting for him. Sitting on one of a pair of chairs arranged around a small table, was a man he had passed on his way to the reception desk. At the time he had paid him no mind; a large broadsheet paper had covered the man's face.

That newspaper was now gone, and the man was rising to his feet as Albert left the reception desk to head towards the hotel's restaurant for his breakfast.

He recognised the man instantly and did not fight the smile that spread across his face.

'George!' Albert's right hand was coming up and moving forward, matching that of the man advancing towards him.

'Albert!'

The two men gripped each other's hands, both attempting to talk at the same time and then both falling silent to let the other speak. Finally, George indicated that Albert should talk first.

'It's so good to see you again, old boy. You're looking well.'

George patted his ample belly which was several inches wider than it had been the last time they were together. Of course, that had been a couple of decades ago.

'Retirement has been good to me,' George acknowledged. 'I've put on a few pounds, but then which of us hasn't?' he asked the rhetorical question with a chuckle.

Albert pointed a hand towards the hotel's restaurant.

'Won't you join me for breakfast? Or have you eaten already?'

Just a few moments later, both men were being escorted to a table in the window which overlooked the seafront.

One street back from the hotel, Wolf was introducing Rex to the concept of freegan eating.

'The trick to it is to get there first,' Wolf explained. Both dogs we're loping at a steady pace along another one of the alleys that ran between the houses. Wolf had been using these passages to move around because they allowed him to stay largely out of sight.

'Where is it that we're going?' asked Rex.

Wolf gave a cryptic answer, 'You'll see.'

Their destination, it transpired, was a kebab house. The business was closed, a steel shutter covering the front windows still - it was not a business that served breakfast. That did not matter to wolf, for he was approaching the premises from the rear.

'I've been coming here for years,' he explained. 'At first, they used to chase me away, but I made myself useful by ensuring that no other animals came begging. They always have leftovers from the previous evening, which they then throw out when they're setting up the following morning.'

Rex's stomach was rumbling its emptiness and his mouth was producing an abundance of saliva as he imagined the tasty meaty treats the wolf was describing.

Entering the yard, Rex could tell they were in the right place - his nose assured him that the rear of the building he was looking at was the one in which he would find his breakfast.

They sat and waited a respectful distance from the rear door.

Impatiently, when nothing happened in the next five minutes, Rex asked, 'Do we need to scratch at the door or something?'

Wolf turned his head slightly, giving the dog a questioning look.

'I don't scratch at doors, I'm a wolf. If I want to get someone's attention, I howl.' To demonstrate, he then closed his eyes and tipped back his head.

'Is that such a good idea?' Rex asked quickly. 'Won't your howling alert animal control to your location?' he pointed out.

Wolf had been about to howl, but stopped himself before the sound could leave his mouth. The dog was absolutely right. By the time his eyes were open again, Rex was already at the back door, his right front paw lifted to scratch at the paint work.

Wolf did not exactly approve, but the dog's method worked all the same. Just a few seconds later, the door rattled and opened.

Framed in the doorway was a Turkish man in his sixties. Short cut white hair framed his balding head and stood in stark contrast to his deeply tanned skin. He took in the sight outside, smiling at the wolf and waggling his eyebrows in a conspiratorial way.

'Got yourself a lady friend I see,' the man chuckled.

Rex checked behind to see who the man was talking about, then realised the dumb human meant him. 'Wait, what?'

The wolf sniggered at his new companion.

'You want some breakfast?' the Turkish man asked, disappearing inside the building for a moment before returning with a plastic platter of cooked meat. 'Here you go,' he remarked as he placed it on the ground outside the door.

Rex and Wolf fell upon it, but the man intercepted Wolf, placing a hand in his way to hold him back.

'Ladies first,' he insisted.

This time it was Rex who chuckled, happy to take the gender confusion on the chin if it meant he got to eat.

Wolf was only held back for half a second, but that was long enough for Rex to devour a fair chunk of the available food. There was more than either needed, but they filled their bellies, licking the platter clean, their rough tongues rasping at the surface of the plastic to leave nothing behind.

The Turkish man had ducked back inside the building as they ate, but only so he could collect a bowl into which he had poured milk.

'This is great,' mumbled Rex as he slopped the white liquid into his mouth.

'Yeah,' agreed Wolf, sucking at the refreshing, cold beverage with equal ferocity, 'He's never given me milk before. It must be your influence.'

'He thinks I'm a bitch,' Rex muttered.

Wolf snorted into the bowl, sending a shower of milk over both their heads.

'It's because you're so pretty,' he laughed.

Rex shot the wolf a grumpy frown, but didn't take his focus away from the milk until it was all gone.

The Turkish man picked the empty bowl up when there was nothing left in it but a little bit of lick.

'Well done, lovebirds,' he ruffled the fur on their heads. 'See you again tomorrow.'

'You say you've been coming here for years?' Rex asked conversationally as they walked away.

'How could I possibly resist?'

The wolf made a fair point. It was the best breakfast Rex thought he had ever eaten.

In the hotel, Albert scraped together the last few morsels of his full English breakfast. During the last half hour, the two men had caught up with each other's lives, reminisced about their lost wives, and reminded each other of some of the cases they investigated together all those years ago.

When the waitress took their plates away, George asked a question to lead their conversation in a new direction.

'So what brings you to Blackpool then, Albert?'

Albert finished his cup of tea and checked inside the teapot to see if there was enough left for a third cup before answering.

'I've been on a culinary tour around the country,' he revealed. 'So far, I've stopped in Melton Mowbray to learn how to make a pork pie, Bakewell to learn how to make a Bakewell pudding ...'

'Don't you mean a Bakewell tart?' George challenged.

Albert chuckled. 'No, actually I don't. Calling it a tart in Bakewell can get a person stabbed. Or...' Albert remembered the events that took place when he visited that town, 'perhaps bludgeoned. Anyway, Rex and I have been making our way around the country, taking in some of its finest dishes.'

The mention of Albert's dog brought a sour note, and the twinge of emotion that crossed Albert's face was not missed by his breakfast companion.

'Yes, Eliza told me that your dog had gone missing last night. I take it you've heard nothing since?'

Albert shook his head. 'I'm not sure how worried I should be to tell you the truth. I can't see Rex getting hurt, so my concern really is about how long it takes for them to find him or for him to find me. Either way, I'm going to be hanging around in Blackpool for a while.' To change the subject, for his missing dog was not one he wanted to talk about, Albert brought up the wolf.

'Ah, yes,' George consulted his memory. 'I can't say that I know a lot about this, but I do know of the man in question. I haven't seen his act, but I've heard others talk about it. Often as not, they are questioning where he managed to obtain a real wolf. Eliza said he was murdered just the other night, the wolfman that is, not the wolf.'

Albert agreed, 'That's what I heard too. I think it might be worth me poking my nose in a little bit.' Albert hadn't intended to make an announcement, or for what he said to be taken that way. He was thinking that since Rex had last been seen with the wolf, perhaps knowing where the wolfman lived and worked or where his local hangouts were, might help him to locate his dog. It felt like a longshot, and it probably was. However, with no other avenues to explore, and a desire to leave Blackpool so he could return home to explore the Gastrothief case, Albert figured he might as well fill his time by doing something proactive.

George, though, took Albert's words as an invitation.

'That's a great idea! You and I can investigate together, Albert. It will be just like old times!'

Albert's eyebrows went for a hike up his forehead. He wanted to say that that was not what he had intended, but it was obvious George was enthralled by the idea. Not wanting to dash his enthusiasm and thinking that a local guide could only help, he reached out his hand so the two men could shake on it.

'Do you have a plan to catch your human's killer?' Rex asked. 'You told me that you have his scent, by which I assume you mean you have it recorded in your head. If you had a scent trail to follow, you would of course be following it, so I'm curious to hear what your plan is to find the man in question.'

Wolf regarded the German Shepherd, frowning at him with little scepticism, and not for the first time.

'Tell me again why it is that you were offering to help me. We don't know each other, I can tell by your accent that you're not from around here, and I know that you abandoned your own human so that you could rescue me last night. So I hope you will not find me rude when I ask what's in it for you?'

What was in it for him? Until that moment, Rex hadn't put any thought to what was motivating him. He'd been curious to meet the wolf, but he'd done that already. So why was he now still hanging around when arguably his duty was to return to Albert's side?

He didn't have to think too long to come up with an answer.

'I used to be a police dog,' he revealed. 'And my human was a detective. His pups still are, in fact. He likes to think that humans are better at solving cases than dogs, which is laughable really because they attempt to do so by using their eyes.'

'Yeah, what's with that?' asked the wolf. 'My human barely used his nose at all.'

'Strange, isn't it?' Rex agreed. 'Anyway, there you have it. My human and I have been solving cases sort of side by side with his skills on occasion complementing mine. I am presented with a chance to not only help you, but also to demonstrate how superior a dog is when it comes to sniffing out clues. I would be letting down all canines everywhere if I failed to seize this chance to show off our superiority.'

Rex's explanation was sufficient to satisfy the wolf, who lifted his nose toward the sky and sniffed to see if there might be a scent that he could follow.

Rex did the same, sampling the air to see what it contained.

When Wolf opened his eyes again, it was to admit that he had no scent trail to follow. 'I believe we will find them if we look hard enough. He was in this area just two days ago, and I found men carrying traces of his scent last night. I believe he will return.'

Rex listened to the conviction and determination in the wolf's voice. Carefully, he suggested an alternative method.

'If I might be so bold, I would like to suggest a new strategy. You stated that you bit your human's killer and that he then escaped in a car. I believe that that should be our starting point. If we return to that location, there may be clues to find that will aid us to track down their current whereabouts. Is there anything else you remember about your human's killer?'

Rex fell silent, allowing the wolf some time to think.

Wolf was examining his memory of the event, going over what he saw and heard and smelled.

'Clues,' he repeated Rex's word. 'There was another human inside the car. Is that the sort of thing you mean?'

'What did the human look like? Was it a man or a woman? What did they smell of?' Rex prompted the wolf to give him more information. He doubted it was any kind of clue at all, but this was not the time to put the wolf off.

Wolf blinked. 'It was a man, but I cannot tell you anything other than that. He was not inside the car ... sorry that's confusing, isn't it? What I mean is, he wasn't in the bit that humans usually ride in. He was in the bit at the back.'

'The boot?' Rex attempted to confirm.

Wolf performed the canine equivalent of a shrug. 'Is that what it's called? I've never been in a car.'

Pushing the last comment to one side, Rex considered what the wolf had just told him. The only reason he could come up with for there to be a human in the boot of another human's car was that they were being kidnapped.

'I think we need to go back to where this happened.' Content that they now had a better plan than just wandering around hoping to pick up a scent, and could approach the investigation more methodically, Rex started walking. It wasn't far to get back to the scene of the wolfman's murder.

Little did they know it was the worst place they could go.

The First Real Clue

In the loading yard behind the parade of shops and restaurants, Wolf did his best to explain the events.

'The car was right here.' Wolf was standing in the middle of the spot where the car had been on that fateful night. 'It was facing in this direction,' he indicated with his head, 'and when it moved, that's the direction it went in.'

Had Rex been a human, he would have asked inane questions such as colour, make, and model, or perhaps hoped that the witness had gotten a look at the registration plate. None of these things meant anything to a dog. Instead, he was sniffing all around the area, picking up where feet had been, where different people had touched the walls, where a cat had urinated into the mud.

He dismissed the last scent as unlikely to be relevant.

A voice from above his head caught his attention.

'Oi, pooch, what are you doing down there? This is not your territory. Why don't you run on back to your human?'

Rex did not need to look up to know that he was being addressed by an alley cat. Nevertheless, he paused what he was doing to meet the animal's gaze.

'There was a murder here two nights ago. A human killed another human, did you smell anything?' Rex doubted not only that that the alley cat would have any worthwhile information to provide, but also that it would prove to be deliberately unhelpful even if it did.

The alley cat made a mocking face, not that this surprised Rex. Cats in general are known for being unhelpful, unless you had something with which you could motivate them, or they believed they had something to gain.

Over his shoulder the cat called, 'Hey, Fangs, come and listen to this. There's a cute little puppy dog down here trying to solve a crime.' Addressing Rex again, he asked, 'What are you? Some kind of police dog?'

Accepting that he was going to gain nothing from talking to the cat, Rex turned away, continuing with his inch-by-inch survey of the crime scene.

'Hey! Did you just dismiss me?' the alley cat growled, his tone instantly angry and threatening.

Rex pretended that he had not even heard him, acting as if all his focus was required to analyse the soil and surrounding area. Unfortunately for Rex, there was very little left for him to smell. Too many people had passed through, the human forensic team ruining any chance he had of finding a worthwhile scent. Where Wolf had bitten his human's killer, there would have been blood drops, and that would have been sufficient to give Rex a good scent to work from.

The clean-up crew who came in afterwards to remove the blood had done a good enough job that what was left wasn't enough.

He continued sniffing anyway, not yet ready to give up, but had to stop when cats began landing all around him.

'I think we might have to teach you some respect,' the tomcat said.

'Yeah, teach him some respect, boss,' echoed a voice instantly. The second speaker was Fangs, the tomcat's right hand cat.

Rex glanced around, he was surrounded by perhaps thirty or more stray cats. They looked dirty, many possessed tatty ears or missing eyes -

indications of regular battles though Rex did not know whether they were fighting rival gangs of cats or if Blackpool had an alligator problem.

'I don't think you want to do this,' Rex remarked.

His comment was received with a round of laughter which then abruptly shut off, every cat falling silent except the boss cat. He had his eyes shut, and his head tipped back because Rex's reply had been so amusing.

'Um, boss,' Fangs hissed.

The boss tomcat stopped laughing and opened his eyes.

'What?' Then he noticed that none of his cats were looking at him but at a point two feet above his head. Tilting his head upwards, he was shocked to find a large set of teeth glistening with saliva and thoroughly visible because the owner's lips were pulled back to show them off to the greatest effect.

The boss tomcat's feet moved so fast that for the first half second of running he didn't move at all. Finally, his claws found purchase on the tarmac, and he shot off like a bullet from a gun.

Rex watched with amusement as all around him the alley cats went vertical.

'That was fun,' Wolf chuckled.

'Where did you go?' asked Rex, wondering how it was that the wolf had not been visible when the alley cats surrounded him.

'I know this area,' Wolf replied dismissively. 'It's not my first run-in with that bunch. Actually though, I remembered something and went to check on it.'

The something that Wolf remembered was the piece of material from Jimmy's trousers that got stuck between his teeth. It had taken him ages to work it out from where it was jammed in. It carried not only the scent of his human's killer from contact with his skin but also some of the man's blood.

He led Rex to it, the one inch by three-inch piece of trouser leg lying forgotten on the concrete where he left it more than a day ago.

'Is this any good?' Wolf inquired, thinking that it probably was.

Rex took a good sniff, drawing in every scent the scrap of material had to offer. It hit him like a slap to the face, setting off an alarm bell in his head.

Dancing back a pace in surprise, Rex blurted, 'I know this human.'

The wolf's eyes flared a little - it was not what he had expected the dog to say. It prompted an immediate question.

'How?'

Andy was tired and that was making him grumpy. Another thing making him grumpy was the rushed breakfast and the fact that he was now hungry. He knew if he made a point of it, Richard would just accuse him of being hangry, so he remained sullenly quiet.

Or, at least, he tried to. His decision to punish his partner by refusing to speak wasn't exactly working, and when the smell from a café serving fat breakfasts reached his nose, he could no longer hold his tongue.

'What is it we're doing out here again?' he grumbled the question grumpily at the back of Richard's head.

All he got in return was, 'Shhhhh.'

Richard was doing his Black Ops soldier thing again. With his back pressed against the wall, he had sidled up to a corner and now he was peering around it. Satisfied that the coast was clear, but not taking his eyes off the loading yard into which he was peering, he gesticulated urgently for Andy to come to his shoulder.

'Dispatch just messaged,' Andy reported grumpily. 'They want to know if we found that snake yet.'

They were supposed to be all the way across town where a resident had reported the loss of his king cobra. Apparently, it had been missing for two days and the owner had been searching his house fruitlessly for it since he first discovered it was not in its tank. The report from the owner coincided, somewhat suspiciously, with the house two doors along reporting that their child's rabbit had gone missing mysteriously from the cage in its bedroom.

Frustrated that his partner couldn't get onside with what he considered to be their mission, Richard hissed, 'We'll get to it, all right? This has to take priority.'

'Why?' Andy wanted to know.

Content that they could move forward, Richard stepped out into the loading yard.

'Because the wolf is dangerous. You saw it,' Richard pointed out. 'And now it's recruited a dog to help it. What if it recruits more? What if, two weeks from now, we're facing some kind of wolf army?'

Andy gave himself a moment to consider what that might be like. Richard had already displayed some superhuman skills in not only finding the wolf last night but in then capturing it. Putting his hunger aside for a moment, Andy had to admit the idea of a wolf army was quite scary. Perhaps Richard was right, history was filled with stories of foot soldiers who turned the tide of the war with their heroic actions.

'What makes you think he'll be here?'

Richard tapped his nose, indicating that he held some insider knowledge.

'The killer always returns to the scene of his crime.'

Andy frowned. 'But I thought the man was stabbed?'

Richard had been about to say something clever about setting a trap for the wolf, but his mouth stopped halfway through opening and closed again. Flustered, because Andy made a valid point, Richard scrambled to think of a response.

'Maybe that's just what he wants us to think,' Richard tried. 'Would that not be a clever way to divert everyone's suspicions?'

Andy's frown deepened, his forehead almost vanishing as the skin concertinaed in on itself.

'But it was the wolf's owner who was killed,' Andy made another pertinent observation.

Having his partner constantly trump his statements with accurate yet inconvenient facts was beginning to annoy Richard.

'Exactly. Everyone knows that almost all murders are committed by the person closest to the victim. In this case it's not a person but a wolf. Well known killers, wolves. Everyone knows that.' Richard did his best to make it sound like that should be the end of the conversation.

Andy hadn't exactly run out of questions, but he was bored with asking them. What he wanted to do was satisfy Richard's need to explore the loading yard where the wolf's owner was murdered two nights ago. Maybe then they could stop in the café he could smell. Andy was beginning to fixate on the concept of a large plate of bacon, eggs, and toast.

To his great surprise, thirty yards ahead of them, the wolf and the German Shepherd dog walked into sight. Yet again, Richard had demonstrated an uncanny sense for where their quarry would be. Just when he was beginning to think that last night might have been a fluke, Andy was proven wrong.

Richard was equally startled. He had absolutely no idea that the wolf was going to return to this area, nor did he expect the dog to still be in tow. However, attempting to capitalise on his lucky guess last night, and how he almost captured the wolf when he fell over – he'd heard Andy telling the chaps back at the animal control centre about his amazing moves - Richard had decided to try his luck again. The bragging rights for bringing in the wolf would be unparalleled.

Now faced with the wolf, all he could think of to say was, 'Charge!'

It was precisely the wrong thing to do, for neither Rex nor the wolf had noticed the two humans. Richard and Andy were upwind so the likelihood of the animals detecting their scents was next to nil. Of course, there was a big difference between spotting the animals and being able to capture them. Even with the element of surprise on their side, had Richard kept quiet, the two animals would have proven impossible to sneak up on while they were awake and alert.

Reacting to the shout, Wolf sprang around to face the danger, saw who it was, and immediately started running away.

'Scarper!' he shouted to Rex as his powerful legs drove him from near stationary to full speed in just a couple of strides.

Rex had no trouble catching up, which surprised him a little. He didn't think he needed to comment, not yet anyway. Instead, he filed the detail away for later consideration.

Spotting a gap between businesses coming up, and a path that would lead them back to the road, Rex angled his body so that he would nudge wolf in that direction.

'Down here,' he panted. Rex had the scrap of material clenched between his teeth. It now had a very specific purpose: Rex planned to use it to track and catch the killer. For the time being, however, it was making it hard to breathe. He dared not open his mouth for fear he would lose the one piece of evidence he had.

'Where are we going?' the wolf wanted to know. 'And why are you slowing down?'

Rex gave no answer, he was too busy making sure that the two men from animal control saw where they went. At the end of the narrow passage, he was forced to wait until the first of the men, the tall skinny one, came into sight. Only once he was sure the idiot human was still chasing him, did he follow Wolf.

'Come on, Wolf,' Rex barked. 'They came from this direction.'

Wolf planted his feet. 'Yes, they did. Surely, that means we should be going in the opposite direction.' He believed he was making a valid point.

Still gripping the piece of material between his teeth, Rex tried to explain his thinking as swiftly as he could.

Five seconds later, and now imbued with righteous purpose, Wolf did his best to ignore the aches and pains he felt as he ran alongside Rex. They were about to even things up.

Carefully Extracting the Truth

Less than a minute after Rex and Wolf fled the area, George and Albert arrived. They were on foot since the hotel was spitting distance from the sweet shop.

'This is the place, eh?' George posed the question rhetorically, pushing the door to the sweet shop open to make the little bell tinkle once more.

Much like Rex, Albert had gone back to a place where he knew there was something to investigate. It had nothing to do with the wolfman's murder or the whereabouts of the wolf, which was the thing that he was really interested in, but because of what he found out over breakfast. In the final years of George's time in the police, he was involved in local organised crime, specifically the investigation and conviction of those behind it.

According to George, protection rackets were all run by a single man – a gentleman known as Fat Bernhard. George explained about Fat Bernhard's past and about Raymond 'Razor' Rutheridge.

It was well known that Fat Bernhard was behind the protection rackets, but several investigations had failed to produce any evidence that could lead to a conviction. The people he extorted money from all unanimously refused to speak out against him, and had they done so, they would not be able to identify Fat Bernhard anyway, because he was not the one making the collections.

What then did that have to do with the whereabouts of Albert's dog? The answer, potentially, was nothing whatsoever. However, upon loosely connecting a couple of dots, Albert had already formed a vague theory.

Essentially, the presence of hoodlums right next to the scene of a murder was too much coincidence for him to ignore. It was probably nothing, but nothing was exactly what he had to go on so far, which made the sweetshop a perfect place to start.

When he was last in the shop the previous evening, the displays near the counter were in disarray. The two men Rex cornered had taken to throwing items off the shelf to discourage the dog. It hadn't worked but it had made quite a mess. Everything was back to normal now, the shop looking neat, if a little cluttered from all the wares on display.

Albert and George wasted no time on pretence, making their way directly to the counter at the rear of the small shop.

Only the man was visible behind the counter, the lady was currently nowhere in sight.

Albert lifted a hand in greeting. 'Hello again. Please do not be alarmed. I'm not here to cause any trouble, but I do need to talk to you about the events of yesterday evening.'

The man started shaking his head before Albert had even finished delivering his sentence.

'No, no, no. Unless you're in here to make a purchase, I must ask that you leave.' He then added, 'Please,' when Albert did not immediately start moving. His tone was begging, imploring the two old men to go away.

It would have been very easy for Albert to about face and exit the shop. Indeed, there was a part of him that very much wanted to. Yet through his experience as a police officer, he knew the kindest thing he could do for this man was force him to overcome his fear.

Re-entering the shop from a storeroom in the back, the lady, who Albert assumed to be the man's wife, was talking and not paying much attention to her surroundings.

'That's all the new stock on the shelves, Lionel ... oh.' She caught sight of Albert and stopped talking midway through whatever she was saying.

'These men were just leaving, Doris,' said Lionel, keeping his eyes locked on Albert's as he reinforced his desire that they leave his shop.

Albert stepped closer to the counter.

'No, we were not,' he stated coolly. 'Look, I was a police officer for more than three decades. So was my partner here,' he indicated George standing to his left. 'So I ask that you will believe me when we say we understand the dilemma you currently face.'

'You can't possibly,' argued Doris.

George countered. 'On the contrary. You are forced to pay protection to men who arrive without warning and with the absolute knowledge that reporting them to police is more likely to result in injury or worse when the police fail to secure a conviction. You are utterly trapped and feel completely helpless. To you, the local police are completely inept and as much a part of the problem as the men behind the protection racket itself.'

Neither Lionel nor Doris spoke for a second, which gave Albert the chance he was looking for.

Dropping his voice to speak to them in soothing tones, he said, 'We are not the police. You could probably have guessed that for yourself,' he chuckled in a self-deprecating way as he made fun of his age and decrepitude. 'But that gives us power. We are not asking you to point the finger and identify anyone. You will not have to go to court and face your tormentors.' Albert could tell by their expressions, and by the fact the man was yet to reiterate his demand that they leave that he had at least managed to capture their interest. 'What I wish to confirm is whether the two men my dog cornered in here last night were men you have seen before.'

The seed was sown. It was an easy question that gave nothing away. The couple undoubtedly knew, either from experience, or through the grapevine, of others who had either refused to pay, or attempted to stand up to the organised criminals. Arms and legs break easily and some scars – the mental and emotional ones – never fade.

They would not willingly make themselves into targets, but they could answer Albert's question without doing so.

Both George and Albert were watching the man, but it was his wife who spoke.

'It wasn't the first time we saw them, actually. They were in here the previous evening too,' she revealed.

Her husband's eyes widened with astonishment.

'Shhh, love. You'll get us into trouble.'

The lady narrowed her eyes at Albert, then shifted her gaze slightly to look at George.

'Will I?' she asked. 'Is that what is going to happen?'

Albert's voice was solemn when he replied.

'I can assure you, Madam, that nothing you tell us will get back to anybody that could cause you any bother. But rather than have you say anything, I intend to tell you what I think is happening and you need only nod or shake your head to steer me. Is that acceptable?'

As if making a point, all Doris did in response was nod.

That put Albert on the spot. He chewed his upper lip with a lower incisor for a half heartbeat before taking a breath and getting started.

'I believe, from overhearing certain things that were said, the two gentlemen I met in here last night are relatively new to the area or new to the concept of running a protection racket. They are attempting to move in on the territory of an already established organised gang. I believe it is run by a gentleman called Fat Bernhard.'

He got a small nod from Doris's head.

Pressing on, Albert said, 'If they were here two nights ago to collect from you, they would not have returned last night. Thus, I must assume that they were not able to collect two nights ago.' Albert looked across at George. He was attempting to piece bits together as he went, using confirmation or denial that he was right or wrong as a guide to lead him. George indicated that he should keep going - an old double act manoeuvre that the two of them had employed many times in their professional lives together.

'The fact that they did not collect their protection money from you two nights ago would indicate that something happened to prevent it from taking place.' Two dots aligned in Albert's head. 'They were here to intercept Fat Bernhard's collector!' He blurted triumphantly. 'Yes,' he agreed with his own thoughts. 'They came here to get rid of the man they intended to replace. Terror tactics. Yes, that's it.'

George caught up with what Albert was suggesting.

'They took him through the shop, didn't they?' George's question was aimed at the pair of shopkeepers, but he didn't need an answer from them, he could already see what had happened in his head. So too could Albert.

Albert delivered the next part of the story. 'They wouldn't have wanted to kill him here, that would be too messy, so they were going to take him somewhere else. I think the man they murdered in the side road next to your shop disturbed them.'

Truthfully, the shopkeepers did not know what had happened. They knew the two old men were right about most of what they were saying because the two men Albert's dog had attacked had come in just moments after their usual collection agent arrived. The big one had struck him over the head using his fist, though it might as well have been a sledgehammer. They then bundled him out the back, with threats to keep quiet and that they would be back shortly.

They heard nothing else, and the two new men never returned that night. Terrified, they had stayed up half the night unable to sleep. In the morning, they awoke to find the police outside. Lionel had ventured as far as the police cordon to get a look at the body and was relieved to see that it was not Fat Bernhard's usual collection agent, a man they knew only as Brooksy.

Doris and Lionel were marvelling at the two old men. They had told them nothing, yet somehow the retired cops had pieced things together. They seemed to know more than the police. Admittedly, the police only came into the shop the previous morning to ask if they had seen or heard anything. The young detective posing the questions had been easily dissuaded from delving any further by the claim that they went to bed early and slept all night.

Albert tapped his chin twice as he ran the scenario through his head again and glanced across at his partner. George nodded his head, crediting Albert for a job well done.

‘You know, old boy, this probably means that you've just identified the murderers.’

‘Yes,’ Albert acknowledged. And they gave their names to one of the two constables who were here last night. That's assuming they were carrying genuine identity.’ Albert felt it was a fair chance that they had provided false identification. Either way, he and George needed to talk to the police.

The bell tinkled at the front of the shop, all heads turning to see who was there as their heart rates increased drastically. Pulses returned to normal again when they saw it was a young mother with her three children.

It effectively ended the conversation, but that was okay because George and Albert now had other fish to fry.

Rex was feeling buoyant. It would not have been possible for him to understand the scent he was looking for simply by listening to Wolf's description. However, finding the piece of material Wolf tore from the killer came as a big boost to the likelihood of him successfully catching the killer and the fact that he already knew the man increased his confidence tenfold.

They would get back on with the task of trying to find him shortly. First, Rex wanted to put a spanner in the works of the two animal control men who seemed hellbent on catching Wolf.

Rex chose the route they were currently taking because he believed the two animal control men must have a vehicle. He would be able to tell which one it was simply by smell, as could Wolf, or any dog for that matter.

The men were behind him, he made sure of that by pausing to be sure they had followed him. Now it was all down to a matter of luck. Would they find the truck? Or were they heading in the wrong direction?

'It will be something big but not really big,' Rex told wolf.

Wolf gave him a sideward glance. 'Big but not big? That's not exactly helpful,' he remarked.

Rex was about to concede that the wolf had a point and then try to give a more accurate description of what he thought they were looking for, when his nose picked up the scent anyway.

Just ahead was a large white van with double back doors and writing down the side. Details like the writing were invisible to Rex, but he knew a vehicle for transporting animals when he smelled one. Mostly it smelled like worry.

'Well, you found it.' Wolf circled around to the front of the vehicle. 'Now what?'

Rex walked to the edge of the pavement and carefully placed the piece of material he held against a wall. Trusting that it would not blow away, he turned to face the white van.

'Now we trash it.'

When Richard and Andy got back to where they parked their van, ten minutes had passed. Andy had wanted to give up at least nine minutes ago. This was all to do with his desire to eat something and to avoid conflict with their boss who still wanted to know how it was going with the search for the snake. If they didn't get on with what they should be doing soon, they were going to find themselves in hot water.

They lost the wolf and the dog in the labyrinth of alleyways running between the businesses, but Richard then insisted on searching for them. While Andy huffed and sighed and checked his watch, Richard examined the ground for paw prints and looked for tufts of fur on hedges or the edge of buildings because he said it would show which direction the animals had gone.

Surprisingly, Richard was still in a great mood despite not having come anywhere near to catching the wolf.

'I bet we get them next time,' he expressed his confidence.

'Why?' Andy wanted to know. 'Why are we trying to catch this wolf so desperately anyway? Why can't we leave it to one of the other teams?'

'Do you know who's been assigned to catch the wolf?' Richard asked, pausing in the street to make a point of it.

Andy stopped too, turning inward to face his partner. 'Yes. Claire and Ann are on it. So what?'

Richard made a face that suggested he shouldn't need to make the point he was about to make.

'Exactly, Andy. Those two hot pieces of fluff are after the wolf. If we can get it, we've got negotiation space.'

Now Andy was truly confused. 'Negotiation space for what?'

'Well, to ask them out, obviously,' Richard revealed his master plan. 'If they don't want to go out with us then they don't get the wolf. So we either get a hot date with two hot girls, or we get to look like proper heroes because we've taken the wolf in. But even if we give it to the girls, word will get out that it was you and me who caught it anyway.' He put a comradely arm around the shorter man. 'You stick with me, Andy, and good things will happen.'

Andy shrugged his shoulder to get rid of Richard's arm.

'Why would I want a hot date with either one of those girls?'

The question jolted Richard. He'd never really put much thought to his partners preferences.

'Oh, I'm, sorry. I hadn't realised you were gay.'

Andy's eyes popped out on stalks. 'I'm not gay! I'm married.'

This was news to Richard. 'You are?'

Andy started walking. He was going back to the van, and then he was going to get some food, and once his stomach had stopped rumbling at him, he was going to go and catch that stupid snake.

Over his shoulder, he shouted, 'I've got four kids, you idiot.'

It was at precisely that point that he spotted the van. More specifically, since he'd already been heading towards the van and knew where it was, what he spotted was that it didn't look like it had when they had left it.

The front grill was lying on the road in front of the van. That it had been chewed by a large animal could not be questioned. Both men could see the teeth marks. Both the driver's and passenger's door handles had been thoroughly gnawed. The door mirrors were both missing. Completely missing that is, as if someone had stolen them and made off down the street.

The tyres had survived the attack but there were many teeth marks visible in the rubber and both wheels at the kerbside were covered in suspicious yellow liquid. The rear bumper was hanging off on one side, one rear light cluster was smashed, and both front windscreen wipers were forlornly hanging off and would never be the same again.

Half a mile away, as they approached a park, Rex and Wolf were still laughing about it. A horn sounded as they crossed the road, the driver having to brake hard as both animals ran through the traffic lanes without looking.

They were on a mission. They needed to talk to as many dogs as possible and the park was the right place to do it.

'This is the place?' asked Albert, looking up at what appeared to be a workingmen's club.

Getting out of the front passenger seat of the taxi they'd hailed, George nodded his head.

'It makes for a rather good cover, don't you think?'

Albert had seen similar in his time. Criminals, especially organised ones, often chose to mask their activities behind a legitimate business. Public houses were a favourite.

The bar inside was open and serving drinks. A lone barmaid stacking glasses onto a shelf above her head paused to observe the two men as they entered.

Closing the door behind him, George went around Albert, heading directly towards the bar. He'd visited this workingmen's club before, but not since he retired. Approaching the sole member of staff visible, he calculated how long it might have been since he was last in this establishment. Unable to figure it out with any degree of accuracy, George decided it had to be the best part of twenty years. The only worrying factor in that calculation was that the décor did not appear to have changed at any point in the intervening years.

Albert looked around, taking in his surroundings. Most of the wall opposite them was dominated by the bar. It looked to have escaped from the sixties, the wood panelling inset with faded yellow frosted-glass panels, something Albert hadn't seen in many decades. Around the inside of the large room, the walls were also wood panelled to a height of about four feet. Above that they were painted in a deep magenta colour.

To his left were the obligatory dart board, pool table, and dance floor. There was a raised stage against the far wall where a band might play.

The lady behind the bar, a woman in her forties wearing clothes a size too small and a decade too young, as if she had raided her teenage daughter's wardrobe rather than her own, placed the last glass above her head.

'What can I get you, gents?' she asked, her tone neutral.

George took the lead. 'We're here to speak to Mr Grimshaw,' he announced. 'Please tell him George Benjamin-Mackie is here to see him. We're old ... acquaintances,' he selected the best word for their relationship.

The lady's right eyebrow had twitched in surprise at the mention of the crime boss's name. Perhaps she didn't get many people coming in asking for him. Or perhaps it was that those who knew they could find him here came in through a different door. Either way, without a word, she moved across the bar to a phone mounted on the wall.

It wasn't possible to hear what she said; she spoke quietly and had turned away, although she was glancing over her shoulder at the two men, perhaps so she could describe them more accurately to whoever was at the other end.

Whatever the case, when she put the phone down, she said, 'Someone will be down for you shortly, gentlemen.'

The shortly turned out to be less than two minutes. From a door to their left, adjacent to the bar, a tall, thin man appeared.

'Follow me, if you will, gentlemen,' said Kenny the Snake, making sure to avoid any words that would expose his lisp.

'That's Kenny the Snake,' whispered George as he fell into step next to Albert. 'He's got a terrible lisp and it's almost impossible to get him to say anything with an 'S' in it.'

Kenny led them from the bar area and through the door into a dimly lit corridor. There was natural light coming from a window set high above on the landing of a set of stairs.

They got no further than just inside that door before they were instructed to stop. Kenny the Snake had turned about to face them. From a door to their right, a younger man appeared. In his right hand he held an electronic device with a long, thin wand.

'Still checking people for wires?' George asked Kenny.

All he got in response was an impassive expression.

Albert had known what was happening, of course, but had not expected it. Back in his day, they used to pat you down because the technology was far more primitive and thus clunkier. He had not seen modern listening devices, except on the television, but knew from his children that they were now so small they were almost impossible to detect without a machine.

'Lift your left arm, lift your right arm,' Kenny the Snake instructed, his somewhat odd sentence avoiding the use of a plural.

Albert and George complied, having no reason not to, and the younger man got busy with the wand. It made a buzzing noise as it passed over Albert's jacket pocket, the sound reminding him of the noise a lightsabre makes in the *Star Wars* films.

'Phone?' Kenny the Snake guessed. 'Take it out,' he commanded.

Again, Albert complied, George proactively doing the same.

The process took no more than a few seconds, the young man with the wand nodding his satisfaction at Kenny the Snake before retreating back to the room he had come from.

The security check complete, Kenny the Snake led them to the foot of the stairs and up, not stopping to question if either man was fit enough to ascend them.

The stairs led to a landing at the top and another door. Once through that they were in a corridor decorated with the same wood panelling and paint as they saw in the bar. Here though the floor was covered in carpet instead of floorboards.

At the far end of the corridor, Kenny the Snake stopped outside a door, grasped the handle, then knocked and waited to be told to enter.

The voice that echoed out from within was a deep, booming bass.

'That's Fat Bernhard,' commented George.

Before he got a look at the man inside the office, Albert idly wondered if perhaps the name Fat Bernhard would prove to be one of those ironic nicknames because he was in fact as skinny as Kenny the Snake.

Once the door swung wide enough, Albert saw that was not the case.

Kenny the Snake held the door open for them, standing back so they could enter. Fat Bernhard was behind his desk, sprawled in a wingback seat that groaned and protested each time he moved. Once they were inside, the door was closed behind them and Kenny the Snake moved around them to take up position adjacent to his boss's desk.

George didn't hold back in approaching the mob boss, marching across the carpet, and extending his hand for it to be shaken.

'You're looking well,' George remarked, lying through his teeth. Fat Bernhard looked like a heart attack waiting to happen. 'Have you lost a little weight?'

The mob boss frowned slightly, shifting his weight to lean forward in his chair.

Albert questioned whether the chair was about to collapse. The man had to weigh in excess of four hundred pounds. He also heard an odd squeaking sound and heard the man in the chair suck in a sharp breath as if he'd just hurt himself.

'Never mind all that,' Fat Bernhard dismissed George's question. 'To what do I owe the displeasure of this visit? You can't tell me that you're working undercover,' he laughed a little at his own joke.

The giant mob boss's attention was on George, but he glanced at Albert continually as if sizing him up and wondering when he was going to speak. Albert chose to stay quiet, content to let George do the talking for now.

George advanced another pace, grasping a chair positioned to the side of the desk and swinging it around so he faced the mob boss when he sat in it.

'I'm sure you'll not mind me taking a load off these old legs,' he commented, a trace of humour in his voice. 'How about if we dispense with the bit where you claim to know nothing about anything and complain that you are just a hardworking businessman trying to make ends meet? I have a question to ask that will not implicate you in anything if you answer it.'

Fat Bernhard leaned a little closer, his stomach threatening to shunt the desk across the floor as it pressed against it.

‘Now why would I want to tell such awful lies, Mr Benjamin-Mackie? I am, and have always been, a legitimate businessman. Yet for decades, the police, which includes you,’ he poked a porky digit at George, ‘have conducted a campaign of slander and hate, trying to tear me down because you believe me to be associated with persons who might be up to no good.’

Albert noted that both Fat Bernhard and Kenny the Snake were wearing versions of the same outfit. Fat Bernhard’s jacket would go around Kenny about four times, but it was a pinstripe suit with a grey silk cravat over a white cotton shirt. Albert could not see Fat Bernhard’s feet, hidden behind the desk as they were, yet he was willing to guess the man wore white spats over black Oxford shoes.

That was exactly what Kenny the Snake was wearing, and so too the young man with the wand. It was like a uniform of sorts. Albert made a mental note to ask George about it.

Despite the barriers thrown up by Fat Bernhard, George pressed on.

‘I think you've got a new gang operating in the area, Bernhard,’ he stated. ‘I think they've been moving in on you for a short while, and they are creating problems. There was a murder two nights ago, and another death last night that while not suspicious, appears to be related.’

Fat Bernhard relaxed, sinking back into his chair, and pushing away from the desk with a satisfied smile on his face.

‘Now how would I have any idea what you're talking about, George?’

George glanced across at Albert before returning his gaze to the mob boss.

'Why so coy, Bernhard?' George wanted to know. 'You had us checked for wires, so why not help me to catch those behind the recent killing. I think they snatched one of your men.'

Albert and George both saw it when Fat Bernhard stiffened. His reaction was only fleeting, but it was automatic and sufficient to tell them they were right about his man.

Now on the defensive, Fat Bernhard turned his attention to the man he did not know.

Raising a pudgy arm to point towards Albert, he said, 'I want to know who this one is.'

It was time to introduce himself.

'Albert Smith,' Albert offered Fat Bernhard a tight smile but did not approach the desk or offer his hand to be shaken. He understood that there was often a necessity to cooperate with organised criminals, especially when removing them could destabilise the balance of power and cause greater harm. Nevertheless, he wasn't about to be friendly.

George added, 'Albert lost his dog, I'm helping him to find it.'

The confusing comment threw Fat Bernhard, his forehead rippling as he tried to work out what possible connection a missing dog could have to anything.

Albert saved him by bringing the subject back on track.

'I met the man I believe to be responsible for taking your ... employee,' Albert chose the word carefully and spoke at a volume above normal conversation to ensure his words penetrated Fat Bernhard's thoughts. 'He was with another man, a giant who is over seven feet tall. It is those two men that we are trying to find. They are affecting your business and,'

Albert had to bite down how much he wanted to cripple Fat Bernhard's rotten enterprise, 'killing people. They must be stopped so any information you might be able to give us will be helping yourself as much as it helps us.'

His line delivered, Albert waited to see how the mob boss would respond.

Annoyingly, Fat Bernhard stuck with the lines he was used to.

'I'm just an innocent businessman, gentlemen. I know nothing about any of these matters. I don't have a gang, I have a firm, a business if you like. The gentleman to my left is one of my employees, isn't that right, Kenny?

Kenny nodded dutifully. 'That would be correct, Chief.'

George sighed. 'This helps no one, Bernhard.'

Fat Bernhard nodded to Kenny the Snake, a clear indication that he expected his guests to now leave.

'If you have any further questions, on this matter, or any other, please feel free to keep them to yourself, gentlemen,' Fat Bernhard offered as a parting shot.

Walking ahead of Kenny, George and Albert arrived back in the corridor. There were voices ahead of them, yet there was no one visible.

'I think it's time we started removing some fingers,' said a man's voice.

The sound of a spoon tapping against the side of a coffee mug let Albert know the two men were somewhere out of sight making hot beverages.

A second voice answered the first.

'Collections are down by twenty-five percent and that's five of us have gone missing now. I can tell you I'm not going to be next,' the second voice remarked forcefully. 'I have no intention of becoming a permanent feature at the landfill.'

Panicked, Kenny the Snake shouted to get their attention.

'Gentshhh!' he rasped, forgetting or accepting that he had too little time to come up with a response that would not expose his lisp. 'Gentshhh, sssshhut up!'

From wherever they were, the two men stopped talking and burst into a fit of giggles.

'Hey, up, it's Hissing Sid!' cackled the first voice. He soon shut up though when he popped his head into the corridor and saw the two strangers looking at him.

Fat Bernhard had come to his door, a dour expression on his face.

George shot him a smile, pushing the door to the stairs open once more with one hand as he said, 'Totally legitimate, Bernhard, totally.'

Once they were back on the street outside, Albert remarked, 'I can see why he's been so hard to catch. He doesn't give anything away for free.'

'I'm told he has the building, his car, and his home swept for bugs twice a day. Hence the man with the wand. He's paranoid, but I guess being so has kept him out of jail.'

Across the street, a car door opened and the person inside started to get out.

Albert and George spotted the movement at the same time.

'Uh-oh,' muttered George. 'I think we might be in trouble.'

At the park, Rex and Wolf had calmed down from their excitement after destroying the animal handler's van. The time for mirth was put behind them as they got down to the serious business of pursuing their investigation.

'What is it that you think that we will find here?' asked Wolf.

Rex had a simple theory about the strip of material between his teeth. There was a distinct scent to it, one carrying cinnamon and liquorice among the other undernotes.

'The scent on the killer's clothing is very specific,' Rex explained. 'If we ignore his scent, and focus on what we can smell beneath it, that will lead us to find where those particular smells came from. You said yourself that you've been chasing other men who smell the same.'

'That's right,' the wolf agreed. 'But I haven't been able to locate its source. How is it that you think you're going to achieve that at the park?'

Rex was glad his companion had asked because now he got to show off his brilliance.

'Watch this,' he invited, heading towards a trio of dogs a few yards away. Their humans were all chatting, leaving the dogs to roam untethered for the time being.

One was a Schnauzer, another a Whippet, and the third was a fine-looking German Shepherd, but they had one thing in common despite their variation in breed. They were all lady dogs.

'Hey, ladies,' Rex sashayed over to where they were standing. He instantly had their attention. 'I'm rather hoping you gorgeous girls can help me out.' He was laying the charm on a little thick, but the occasion called for it.

The German Shepherd said, 'My you're a big one. I haven't seen you here before.'

Rex dropped his piece of material at their feet, giving the German Shepherd his best smouldering gaze. He was hot on the trail of a killer right now, but remembering a certain Afghan hound he met in Arbroath, he couldn't help but wonder if there might be time to return here later.

'My name is Rex,' he introduced himself. 'I used to be a police dog, but now I'm more of a freelance detective. I'm actually competing with my human to see who can solve this particular case first. You see, he thinks eyesight is better than smell.' Rex added a snigger because it was called for.

The ladies all sniggered too, the suggestion of sight over smell quite laughable in their opinion.

'I'm Gabrielle,' announced the German Shepherd. 'This is Minnie and Candice,' she introduced the Whippet and the Schnauzer in turn.

The Whippet was already sniffing at the piece of material.

'Where is this from?' she asked.

The German Shepherd nudged the Whippet's flank. 'Never mind that, Minnie, take a look at this hunk of meat.'

Rex had been about to ask the Whippet if she recognised the scent, and intended to prompt her to focus on the underlying smells behind the stench of human and blood. However, the German Shepherd's comment gave him cause to look at her.

'Huh?' Rex questioned, turning his head to follow her gaze.

By the time he did, all three lady dogs had lost interest in Rex and his piece of stinky cloth. They were going around him to explore a far more interesting target.

Namely the wolf.

In a husky voice filled with gravel, the wolf made all three lady dogs swoon.

'Hello, ladies. What are three lovely girls like you doing in such a dangerous environment?'

'Dangerous?' questioned the schnauzer. 'The park's not dangerous.'

'It is now I'm here,' the wolf rumbled in his gravelly bass voice.

The three girls who Rex had hoped to quiz about the piece of material, were now all enraptured by the canis lupus. He rolled his eyes, or might have done if that gesture meant anything to a dog.

'Wolf,' he called to get his new companion's attention. 'Wolf, remember the killer?'

'Killer?' questioned the Whippet.

'Yeah,' growled the Wolf in his ridiculously forced deep voice. 'Me and my sidekick ...'

'Sidekick?' Rex repeated the word, an unhappy expression ruling his features.

Wolf carried on as if he hadn't spoken.

'... are on the trail of a man who killed a human I knew. I've been tracking him for two days and I'm getting closer. Can you ladies help me?'

The German Shepherd was having trouble getting her mouth to work; it seemed to have gone dry and she hadn't blinked for almost a minute.

The Schnauzer answered for the group.

'Sure thing, gorgeous, whatever you need. Is it to do with this piece of cloth?'

Rex tried to get a word in.

'Yes. As I was saying ...'

The Whippet whipped her head around to glare at him.

'Shhh!' she hissed in his face. 'Your boss is talking, sidekick. Show some respect.'

Rex might have responded, but the Whippet was already focused on the wolf again. Her eyes, like those of the other two lady dogs were wide and full of wonder as they stared, unabashed, up at the wolf's rugged features.

'Don't speak harshly to him ladies,' Wolf chided. 'He's just doing his best. Without him to support me ...'

'Support you?' Rex questioned, thinking that he might 'accidentally' mark the wolf's head next time he went to sleep.

'... I couldn't be the hero that I am,' the wolf finished.

Minnie the Schnauzer almost fainted.

'Just get them to sniff the stupid piece of cloth, will you?' grumbled Rex, dropping it at their feet and backing off as he muttered under his breath about heroes and where they could stick their investigations.

When Wolf asked, all three willingly put their noses to the strip of material. Each got the pungent scent of blood and the distinct odour of the man the cloth had been in contact with.

'There's lots of cinnamon,' remarked Gabrielle.

'Liquorice too,' added Candice. 'It's almost buried under the stench of blood. What happened to the man who was wearing it?'

Wolf showed his teeth.

'He had a run in with my top jaw and my bottom jaw,' he growled. 'Otherwise known as thunder and lightning.'

The three lady dogs gasped.

'You bit a human?' Candice voiced her startled shock.

Rex couldn't believe what he was hearing. 'I bite humans all the time,' he injected though he got no response. 'Can anyone hear me?' he questioned. 'I recently organised a raid on a boat shed with an army of dogs, jumped off a cliff with a regiment of alley cats to divebomb a flock of angry seagulls, and smashed through a window to save my human from certain death.'

He thought the ladies were ignoring him or had perhaps just tuned him out, but Minnie glanced his way, frowning her disapproval.

'Yeah, but you're not a wolf, are you?' she pointed out, immediately dismissing him again.

Rex went back to muttering under his breath as the lady dogs discussed the source of the scents on the piece of cloth.

'I think we need to recruit some more noses,' said Gabrielle.

While Rex took his frustrations out on a small patch of heather which was doing its best to establish a toehold at the edge of the mowed area of grass, the lady dogs began to bark.

In seconds, more dogs began to arrive, many being chased by their humans, some dragging their humans behind them as was the case with a Bull Mastiff and a duo of St Bernards.

With Rex looking on in a bemused manner, the dogs explored the scent profile of the small piece of cloth while Candice, Gabrielle, and Minnie regaled the new dogs with tales of the wolf's incredible bravery and his mission to avenge the murder of a human he knew.

As strategies go, Wolf had to admit coming to the park was a winner. Especially so when a voice declared a result.

'This is from the factory on Keswick Road. Near to it, anyway.'

A circle appeared around the speaker, an old West Highland Terrier, as all faces looked inward to hear more.

Around them, a circle of confused humans were discussing what had gotten into their dogs. Some were trying, and failing, to pull their pet away from the ever-growing pack, other were attempting to untangle their leads. Still more, the less physically fit or able were still arriving having been left behind when their dog ran away.

'It's unmistakable,' the West Highland Terrier insisted.

Gabrielle tutted, 'He's right. I knew I recognised it. I haven't been along that way in a while, but now he's said it, I can smell the sugar hiding under the cinnamon.'

'Nowhere else in this town will you find cinnamon and liquorice in the same place,' the Westy insisted, getting a ripple of agreement from the assembled pack. 'The human who wore this must have spent a significant amount of time on Keswick Road to have picked up the smell on his clothing.'

Wolf barked to Rex. 'We've got our target. Let's go!'

'Oh?' Rex tilted his head to one side. 'Got a use for me again now, have you, hero?'

Wolf made an apologetic face.

'I wouldn't have thought to come here, Rex. I can't do this without you.'

Rex had a dozen smart replies lined up on his tongue, but with a sea of dogs looking at him expectantly, and the wolf acting so benevolent all of a sudden, he knew employing any of them would make him seem petty.

'Righto,' Rex snarled his response in a determined manner. 'Let's go find ourselves a killer.'

When Wolf howled his agreement, it was followed by a chorus of ear-splitting wails as the pack around him attempted to emulate his sound. Only a Bloodhound got close, but the overall effect was terrifying to the people in the park.

Children in the playpark began crying, a young couple having a snog behind a tree stopped abruptly when the squirrel above them dropped his acorns on their heads in fright, and the dogs' owners responded in a mixed manner.

Some shouted for their dog to hush, some backed away, worried the pack of snarling, howling hounds was on the brink of going berserk, and yet others simply froze to the spot, a cold chill spreading through their bones at the unearthly sound.

Before anyone could react, Rex and Wolf started running and the pack went with them, more than forty dogs belting hell for leather toward the edge of the park and the road beyond.

The humans, shocked, bewildered, and confused, bellowed for their dogs to return, swore and spluttered their outrage, blamed each other, but ultimately watched their dogs vanish into the distance.

Only one dog remained where the pack had been, a small, red Dachshund still tethered to her human and not possessing the required mass to break free.

'Good girl, Marjory,' cooed her human, a lady in her twenties called Maisy.

Marjory stared at the dust trail left behind by the pack of dogs she dearly wanted to follow and barked a reply that would make a dockworker blush.

Richard and Andy were watching the recovery truck reverse up to their van. A call to dispatch to report the current condition of their official transport required them to admit where they were. Andy blamed Richard and forced him to make the call to their boss.

It resulted in a stern lecture on doing what they were assigned to do and not swanning off on missions of their own. Someone else had been sent to deal with the snake in their stead and word of their predicament had swiftly spread through the rest of the animal control crews when their call to base was overheard by Claire and Ann.

The objects of Richard's desire were back there to drop off after successfully rounding up a stray Beagle. It was chipped so the owner would get a call shortly.

Their presence at the base, as they prepared to go out again, also meant they were listening when the switchboard went nuts.

'Did you hear that?' asked Richard.

'I'm still not talking to you,' grumped Andy, making the recovery man chuckle.

He shook his head and got on with the job of hitching up the battered van. It was a simple task, but when he grabbed the controls to tilt his load bed, he discovered one of the two idiots was in the cab of the van.

'Hey! Hey, dummy! Get out of there! I'm about to load that!'

'Listen,' Richard insisted, gesturing urgently for Andy to come closer. 'There's a pack of dogs racing along Rigby Road. And get this, Andy. They say it's being led by a wolf.'

‘I don’t care!’ snapped Andy. ‘They said they are going to dock us a day’s pay,’ he reminded his partner. ‘How would you like to be the one to explain that to my wife?’

‘But ... the wolf,’ Richard repeated, thinking that ought to be all the explanation he needed. ‘We can be heroes!’

‘Hey!’ the recovery man raised his voice. He was getting impatient.

‘Stuff this.’ Richard jumped onto the driver’s seat and slammed the door shut. ‘I’m going, Andy. You can stay here and be Mr Mediocre, or you can earn back that day’s pay and prove we were the right men for the job all along.’

‘Hey!’ the recovery man shouted the word this time, unable to fathom why neither of the two men were paying him any attention.

Sufficiently motivated by the desire to avoid his wife’s wrath, Andy ran for the passenger door as Richard fired the van into life.

A wad of chewing gum rolled out of the recovery guy’s mouth. ‘Hey, you can’t drive that!’

With the rear bumper dragging along the street, Richard stuffed the stick into first gear and cranked the steering wheel hard to the left. The van barrelled into moving traffic, horns blaring and cars swerving as they braked and skidded to avoid a collision.

‘Yeah!’ Richard pumped a fist into the air, punching the ceiling of the van and then having to pretend his fist didn’t hurt. ‘Let’s get the wolf!’

‘Yeah!’ echoed Andy, getting into the spirit, ‘Let’s avoid my wife kicking me in the pants!’

Albert and George were in the street outside the workingmen's club giving Eliza a jolly good listening to.

'Why would it not occur to you, Dad, that I might have people actively involved in trying to bring down the local crime gangs? Did you not think that perhaps it might have been a good idea to speak to me before you started your own investigation?'

George attempted to get a word in but got no further than his top lip twitching before his daughter continued her rant.

'Not to mention the fact that these are well known dangerous individuals. What would you have done if they decided to take offence to you just turning up at their place of business? We all know it's a front, but until any of us get the evidence we need to put them away, it will remain just that.'

Albert raised his hand. 'If I may,' he tentatively attempted to get involved in the thoroughly one-sided conversation.

'No, you may not,' snapped Eliza. 'I've got a good mind to blame you for this, Mr Smith. My father wasn't out attempting to solve crimes and interrogate local gangsters until you showed up.'

Now that his friend was being attacked, George could stay silent no longer.

'That's enough now, love. Poking our noses in was all my idea. Albert just wants to find his dog.'

'That's as maybe, Dad. The net result, however, is that the two of you arriving here has probably made Fat Bernhard nervous. One of my officers alerted me to your arrival the moment you went into the bar. Yes, we are watching the place, Dad,' she added with an aggressive snap because she felt her father ought to have expected it. 'Something is happening in Blackpool, a change in the dynamics. It seems likely there is a new player in town, and that alone might be sufficient to make some of these wily criminals act out of character. If they slip up, we will be there to swoop on them. We, the police, not you, two retired grumpy old codgers.' She accentuated her last comment by poking a finger at their chests.

Albert thought being called an old codger was a little harsh, but could see no advantage to be gained from arguing the point. Inadvertently, they had stumbled across a police operation already in play.

Eliza had fallen silent, waiting for either of the two old men to start arguing or attempt to raise a valid point to defend their actions. It was at exactly that point that her radio squawked into life.

'DCI Benjamin-Mackie, you wanted to be informed if there were any sightings of the wolf.'

Without taking her eyes from her father or Albert, the senior detective lifted her radio.

'DCI Benjamin-Mackie receiving, do you have a location? Are animal control responding?'

Whoever was at the other end of the radio in the police dispatch centre was doing a poor job of keeping their emotion in check.

'Everyone is responding!' he replied in a tone bordering on flustered. 'There's a whole pack of dogs racing inland along Rigby Road. I don't know where they're going, but reports are that they are moving fast and causing multiple problems.'

Albert sucked some air through his teeth and closed his eyes. He was willing to bet there was a large German Shepherd right at the head of that pack of dogs. He'd seen it happen before though he was at a loss to explain quite how it came about each time.

Frowning a little as she tried to picture what the officer in dispatch was telling her, Eliza sought some clarity.

'Confirm you said a pack of dogs,'

'That's right, current estimate is somewhere close to fifty. All different breeds, most of them wearing collars, and all being led by a wolf.'

Eliza shot her eyes at Albert, a question hanging in the air for him to answer.

Wearily, Albert nodded his head. 'This will be Rex's doing.'

In her head, Eliza was attempting to work out where the dogs could be heading. Rigby Road did not lead anywhere in particular, it ran inland from the coast. She had too many things to be doing to be worrying about some dogs. However, if she could find Mr. Smith's dog and send him on his merry way, perhaps her own father would stop getting himself into trouble.

Grumbling at the distraction, she nevertheless backed towards her car, inclining her head so the two men would know to follow her.

Into her radio she said, 'Keep me informed on the pack's whereabouts. I'm en route to intercept.'

Injured?

Rex leaned into the corner. The pack was moving at a fair pace as it came into Keswick Road, and that meant the taller dogs, who cornered less easily than those with a low centre of gravity, struggled to make the turn.

Rather than lose dogs along the way, Rex got the impression that the pack had grown in numbers during their run through Blackpool. They'd definitely picked up two outside a supermarket as they shot by.

Now, according to Gabrielle and a few of the other dogs, they were nearing their destination. This was good news, but all it did was put them in the general vicinity of an area where the killer they were looking for had been. The wolfman's killer had spent enough time here to pick up the scents hanging in the air, but that didn't mean he was still here.

Thinking they ought to slow down now so a carefully controlled sweep of the area could be conducted - they all had the scent of the man now from the piece of cloth - Rex glanced across at the wolf.

He looked to be in discomfort.

Rex remembered that he had been able to smell blood on the wolf when he first met him. Wolf dismissed it when Rex quizzed if he was injured, and since there was an obvious tear to the wolf's ear, Rex had let it go.

Now he suspected the wolf might be carrying a more serious injury.

'Everybody hold up,' Rex barked to be heard, and put the brakes on himself. As he did so, he glanced at the wolf once more and saw the relief pass across his face. He was hurt, for sure. However, it was something Rex would have to ask about later. The sound of sirens heading in their direction let them know they had a limited window in which to find their quarry.

'Everyone split up,' wolf wheezed. 'Search for the human. You've all got his scent. If you think you've found him, bark to bring us all to you.'

There's Somebody at the Door

Inside a house directly opposite the Rock factory on Keswick Road, Jimmy squinted at the window.

'Can anybody else hear dogs?' he asked.

Muldoon cracked a smile. 'I like dogs. Specially those long ones that look like sausages.'

From the street outside a cacophony of barking and yelping was filtering through to drown out the television show Jimmy was watching. It being the middle of the day, they had very little business to conduct, and Jimmy felt content that staying out of sight was the right thing to do.

He knew his plan was proceeding exactly as he intended. They had successfully created a problem for Fat Bernhard. Snatching five of his men would make him nervous, but Fat Bernhard and his protection racket was not the goal. Jimmy's sights were set far higher.

Losing one of their team last night was a blow, but ultimately little more than a bump in the road. They could manage with seven.

Fat Bernhard would have his men out looking for them, but Jimmy believed the old mob boss's motivation to eliminate the threat Jimmy posed would be less to do with money and rather more about the fear that news of the problem would reach Raymond's ears.

The thought brought a smile to Jimmy's lips. Fat Bernhard's men were out looking for them, but they had no idea who they were. Jimmy's team would not be found, not by Fat Bernhard, the police, or anyone else.

Fat Bernhard would deploy his men in pairs now Jimmy felt certain, but he didn't need to take any more of them. Not yet at least. The old mob boss would be watching the businesses where he knew Jimmy's team had struck and expecting to catch them when they returned to make the next collection.

Only Jimmy wasn't going to be so foolish. He had no intention of returning to any of the places they had already been. No, if they had to, they would continue targeting other firms under Fat Bernhard's thumb. All he had to do was keep the pressure on and wait for the inevitable effect that would cause.

Anticipating his opponent's strategies, always thinking two or three steps ahead was why he came with a team of eight. You might think more would be better, but not if you want to move surreptitiously and stay below the radar. A small team, as demonstrated by special forces teams such as the SAS, are far better able to operate undetected.

'What is going on outside?' Jimmy demanded to know. It was getting hard to think with all the yapping and barking.

What he didn't know, was that the dogs had identified the house Jimmy and his team were staying in. Outside his front door they were beginning to converge.

Assuming the question was directed at him, Muldoon levered himself out of the two-seater sofa - the only chair in the house that could accommodate his frame – to head for the door.

Jimmy meantime, limped through to the back of the house where he assumed it would be quieter. He needed a little peace to be able to think. Things were going according to plan, but they were far from done yet.

Unavoidably curious about the noise he could hear, Drew went to the window. His eyes were widening in disbelief before he got a proper look at the seething mass of canines stuffed into the front garden of the little terraced house. Somehow, despite the din coming from outside, he heard Muldoon unlatch the safety chain on the front door.

Drew had enough time to begin to scream, 'Nooooooooooo!' before the sound of barking trebled in volume. The noise from outside was now inside, as dogs flooded the building.

Home Invasion

Both Rex and Wolf had been trying to get to the front of the pack. When they heard the shout that someone had found a scent trail for the human in question, they raced to see if the report was accurate.

The sirens were coming closer, the noise instilling an even greater sense of urgency. They believed they were close to finding the human who killed the wolf's human, and for Wolf it returned the taste of the killer's blood to his mouth.

He wanted to taste it again.

They could not, however, get anywhere near the house. Their noses assured them this was the right place. The street outside stank of the wolfman's killer, and they found a car which stank of blood and the scent of the man Wolf bit.

They had found his lair, yet their overexcited, over enthusiastic pack of willing canine accomplices were now in their way.

The first dog through the door went straight between Muldoon's feet. It was a Pomeranian called Pixie. He wasn't entirely sure what was going on and had been following the other dogs because it seemed like the right thing to do. When the pack started forming in front of the door, Pixie was able to weave between their legs and bodies to arrive at the front. When it opened, he ran inside.

The Pomeranian wasn't much to worry about as home invasions go, but right behind him were the two Saint Bernhards. Their lumbering mass, which could only just squeeze through the door side by side, met with Muldoon's sturdy legs, and flipped him into the air like a broken garage door.

After that, dogs of all breeds and denominations flooded through the lower level of the house.

'Let us through!' barked Rex.

'Yes, let us through!' agreed Wolf.

It was no use. Though they could be heard by the dogs nearest to them, farther ahead, where the bottleneck of hounds were all trying to get into the house, there was too much noise for most to hear, and too much excitement for those who could hear to respond or obey.

Deeper inside the house, Jimmy heard the explosion of dogs coming his way. Blind serendipity had placed him near the rear door of the house, the only escape route at this point.

Still trying to force their way through the mass of dogs in their way, Rex and Wolf were stuck in the street outside the front garden. Their desperate efforts stopped when they heard a strange grating, abrasive dragging sound swing into the end of the road.

Racing towards them was the abused looking white van they trashed earlier. Framed in the front windscreen were the two idiots from animal control. That the men inside had spotted them could not be questioned. Rex and Wolf saw the men shouting and pointing at them.

When two police cars drift-steered into the street behind the van at breakneck speed, Rex knew they were out of time. His concern that they might be captured doubled the moment he looked for an escape route and found another police car hurtling towards them from the opposite direction.

'Wolf, come on! We're gonna have to scarper!' Rex barked at his companion.

Through clenched teeth, Wolf growled, 'I can smell him. He's right in there. All I've got to do is get to him.'

Wolf attempted to climb the Labrador in front of him. Such was his determination to catch his human's killer that he was about to attempt to run across the backs of the dogs blocking his path.

Rex lunged, knocking the wolf back down to the pavement.

'There's no time!' Rex urged, nudging the wolf along the street with his shoulder. 'There'll be another chance. He can't come out this way anyhow. But he might have gone out the back. Let's find an alleyway, escape the two idiots from animal control, and see if we can catch the killer running away.'

There was no way for Wolf to argue with Rex's logic. He knew the dog was on the money, and the chance of getting caught if they didn't move soon was high.

As the animal control van screeched to a stop mere yards from their location, the dog and the wolf made a break for it, scrambling to the right to get away and vanishing through the press of dogs still gathered in the street outside the house.

Cornered and Outnumbered

'Stay here,' Eliza ordered. Her eyes were locked on her father's where he sat on the back seat of her car. After a second, she shifted her gaze to stare directly at Albert, making sure that he understood her instruction too.

Before either man could respond, she was out of the car and running across the street, barking into her radio as she went.

They were one street over in Ashton Road, Eliza opting to park there because she didn't want to get caught up and trapped if the officers in uniform blockaded the street to round up the pack of dogs.

'Tenacious woman, that daughter of yours,' Albert observed.

'Yeah, she's a real firecracker,' George agreed though it was obvious he wasn't truly appreciating his daughter's brilliance at this time.

Albert stared out of the window for a few moments, drumming the fingers of his right hand on his thigh while he questioned his options.

'Do you think we should...'

'... Ignore what she said and go look for ourselves?' George completed Albert's sentence. 'You're damn skippy we should.'

Albert and George were out of the car and on the street four seconds later. Just in time, as it happened, for Jimmy to burst into the street twenty-five yards away.

Escaping the house, with his laptop under one arm, several weapons tucked inside his jacket, and a wad of money stuffed into his trousers, Jimmy had leapt the fence at the end of the garden and limped away as fast as he could. Landing in an alleyway that ran between the two rows of houses that backed onto one another, he soon found a turning to lead him to Ashton Road.

Muldoon was hot on his heels, though he had run through the fence at the back of the garden rather than attempt to jump over it. Jimmy could hear his henchman's enormous feet thumping on the concrete as the lumbering ox came after him.

There were others too, a quick check over his shoulder showed Jimmy that there were three more of his team behind Muldoon. Since two of the others were still out somewhere, that was six of the seven accounted for. He could work out who was missing and whether that was a problem later. If any of them were taken by the police, he doubted it would be a problem - the police had nothing on them.

It would be a bigger problem if Fat Bernhard managed to identify who they were and grabbed one of his team. The police would interrogate in such a way that any of them could happily withhold what they knew. Fat Bernhard and his men would ask the same questions, but in a very different way.

However, all those thoughts slipped from his mind as he skidded to a halt in Ashton Road, his disbelieving eyes staring straight at a man he did not expect to ever see again.

Now frozen to the spot, Albert swallowed hard.

'George,' Albert called to get his partner's attention. 'Do you remember I told you about the two men in the sweet shop?'

George frowned. 'Yes? That's who we are after, isn't it?'

'Well,' Albert said, 'We found them.'

Jimmy paused, just for a moment so he could listen. The house they had been using was no longer an option - they could not return there. Indeed, the entire area was one which they now needed to vacate. He had no idea what was going on with the dogs or why so many of them had converged on the house. For a moment he had worried it might be the wolf coming after him again. Drew was adamant it had been a wolf that chased him and Ryan last night.

However, he hadn't seen the wolf, it appeared to just be a pack of dogs. Nevertheless, the police were swarming Keswick Road, their sirens off now, but they had been good enough to alert him that they were coming.

Seeing the two old men getting out of a car gave Jimmy an idea. It was a gloriously criminal idea that involved committing several crimes simultaneously and therefore it met with Jimmy's instant approval.

'Who are you?' he demanded, approaching Albert and George. His strides were purposeful and determined even with the limp. Muldoon, giant that he is, appeared behind him on the street just a moment later.

The sight of Jimmy's henchman was enough to make George gulp and take a small step back.

'I know, right?' Albert remarked. Addressing Jimmy, who was getting dangerously close and looking unlikely to change course, he said, 'I'm one of the good guys. I guess that's probably a problem for you, isn't it? Because you're one of the bad guys.'

Whatever Jimmy had been expecting the old man to say, that wasn't it. A laugh burst from his lips.

'Okay, well, I guess I can get a proper answer later when we have a little more time and some privacy.' Over his shoulder he shouted to his team. 'Lads, we have a new mode of transport. It'll be a bit of a squeeze,' Muldoon took up a lot of space, 'but I'm sure these nice gentlemen will be happy enough to ride in the boot.'

Jimmy dropped the jovial expression, his face hardening as he glared at Albert and George. It was no casual threat. He fully intended to find out who the old man was. That Albert interrupted his business once could be ignored as an inconvenience. Appearing a second time just a day or so later could not be written off as a coincidence. Jimmy did not believe in such things.

Albert and George were faced with a tough choice. Even as young men, two against five was a fight very few would win. When one included a man the size of Muldoon on the opposition, any positive outcome seemed highly unlikely.

Neither Albert nor George considered themselves to be young men.

So did they fight, and hope that someone would come? Did they sacrifice their dignity and cry for help? Running away did not seem to be an option - they were not fast enough to get very far. If they chose none of those options, all they were left with was to accept their fate and clamber willingly into the boot of Eliza's car. And that did not appeal one bit.

'What do you reckon, Albert?' George asked, the nervousness he felt evident in the timbre of his voice.

Exhaling a deep breath before drawing in a fresh one, Albert reluctantly raised his fists. Getting taken by men he knew to be willing to kill was no option at all.

There was steel in Albert's voice when he replied, 'I guess if I'm going to go out, I'd like to know I did so fighting.'

Seeing the two geriatric old men shuffle into fighting poses drew a fresh snort of laughter from Jimmy.

Muldoon, seeing that there was a fight to be had, and knowing it was his job to lay down the beatings when they were necessary, jogged to get around Jimmy.

Jimmy thrust out an arm, blocking Muldoon's path.

'Whoa there! I rather think somebody else should do this. I want to be able to ask some questions later.' He didn't think this was going to take much. The pensioners had to be well into their seventies, possibly older. Jimmy didn't know and did not care.

He was going to give them each a sharp tap on the chin. Just enough to convince them to desist with their silly nonsense. Then they could get stuffed in the boot and dealt with later.

Albert and George stepped closer to each other, positioning themselves so they were almost back to back. With the car behind them, they only had to defend one hemisphere, yet in an instant, they were surrounded by six men.

Intending to deal with it himself, Jimmy tensed his muscles. The blow to his jaw as George's uppercut connected with it shocked him. He'd failed to give the pensioners sufficient credit, though as his head rocked back to its normal position, he wasn't going to make the same mistake twice.

Four of his team were laughing, but all were weighing in, grabbing the two old men before either had the chance to land another punch.

Albert struggled against the hands clamping his arms against his body. In no more than a few seconds, he was going to get stuffed into the boot of the car. Once in there alongside George, they could holler and hammer as much as they wanted but the likelihood of being rescued was slim.

So it was with great relief that when he caught a glimpse of the street behind his attackers' heads, he saw his dog bounding towards him.

Dogs Everywhere

Back in Keswick Road, the police were doing their absolute best to bring some form of calm to the utter bedlam around them. There were dogs inside a house that was quickly identified by the first officers on the scene as being a potential base for criminal activity. They didn't know who had been living there yet, but they found wads of money, weapons, and blood-soaked bandages all within a few seconds.

Gathering and cataloguing any evidence required emptying the house of the three or four dozen dogs currently inside it. That might not seem like too tough of a task. All a person with any sense would need is a bone, or a biscuit, or a tasty treat of any kind. Unfortunately, what the first police officers in the house were greeted with as they attempted to start ejecting the dogs, were two idiots from animal control.

Just outside the front door, as the dogs exited, they spotted two men with control poles in their hands and immediately performed a rapid U-turn.

'Where is he?' demanded a tall thin man wearing the uniform of the town's animal control unit. 'Where's the wolf? I saw him right outside the house.'

Right on his shoulder was a short, fat man wearing the same uniform. He too was looking around as if desperately trying to spot something.

Standing in the doorway to the house as dogs streamed back around her legs, and feeling like someone lost in an overflowing stream, Constable Matilda Greg wondered if she could get away with employing her baton. She didn't wish to hit the dogs with it, just the two idiots who were defeating her best efforts to get the pack of hounds out of the house.

'What are you two doing?' she demanded to know. 'There are dogs running freely in every direction and you two appear to be from the animal control unit. Why are you not rounding up the dogs?' Her questions were delivered in a gruff voice that was little more than a growl emitted between clenched teeth. Constable Greg had already been having a bad day before this particular incident.

Her partner for the day, another constable going by the name of Sean Flynn, was complaining of gastric troubles as a feeble excuse for his constant flatulence. That she had to be stuck in a car and constantly breathing in his stench was something she considered to be cruel and unusual punishment. Now several hours into her shift with him, she was just about ready to kill. Kill her partner, kill the idiots from animal control, kill anyone who looked at her sideways ... she really wasn't fussy about her target so long as she could find an outlet for her rage.

The grimace on the face looking at him, and the unspoken threat of violence it contained was sufficient to cause Richard's feet to stop moving. This happened so suddenly that Andy bumped into him.

They both heard the police constable's questions, and unable to think of a suitable answer, they decided that perhaps what they ought to do is begin rounding up the dogs.

'Rex! Sic 'em!' Albert knew his shout was unnecessary, but it filled him with great joy to be able to give Rex his favourite command.

'That's him!' Wolf barked. The man he first saw two nights ago was right there in front of him. Rex had delivered in a way that Wolf found surprising. Without the dog at his side, he would have been captured already, but even if he had managed to evade the idiots from animal control, he doubted his method of sniff and hope would have brought him back to the man he sought.

The pain in his chest was getting worse. It was enough to make Wolf question whether it would get so bad that he would have been forced to abandon his hunt for his human's killer. Starting when the giant hit him with an old piece of wood, there was something sharp digging into his skin. It wasn't big, but he couldn't manoeuvre his head to get to it. Worse yet, he was starting to wonder if the slight nausea, chills, and dizziness he felt were associated with it.

Of course, none of that mattered now because his quarry was right there, mere yards away, and all the wolf could think of was biting and tearing and the satisfaction that would bring.

Rex's thoughts were not much different, but his were laced with a hefty portion of guilt. His human was in trouble and that was down to Rex. Not that his human managed to stay out of trouble when Rex was at his side, but had he been there, where he knew he ought to be, Rex might have prevented the drama unfolding before his eyes.

He put his head down and charged.

Jimmy heard the old man shout something though the words failed to make sense. Until he heard the barking, that is.

When his head whipped around to gawp open-mouthed at what he believed to be two dogs charging toward him, his heart caught in his chest. He remembered the pain of being bitten only too well.

Albert was right in front of Jimmy when the man turned his head and got to see his eyes widen in horror. He also got an arm free as all six of his attackers found themselves momentarily distracted.

Drew, another man to have been terrorised by the wolf, though he managed to escape unscathed when he scaled a wall and ran across the roofs of some garages to get away, slackened his grip on Albert's arms.

It was all Albert needed. Still held around the chest by another man, he put all he had into throwing his head backwards. It connected with something, a clonk resounding through Albert's skull as the man let go with a grunt of pain.

Drew turned his head to see what was happening, which meant the punch Albert aimed at his jaw landed firmly on his nose and lips. It was followed up by a knee to the groin as Drew recoiled from the blow to his face.

The six men still had the upper hand, and they were all armed, but panic needed less than the space of a single heartbeat to create disarray. One second, they were about to stuff the old men into the car's boot, steal it, and drive nonchalantly away. The next, they were scrambling to be anywhere else.

Jimmy was the first to abandon the task of grabbing the pensioners. He could regret letting Albert go later. Right now, the only thought in his head was escape.

With a lunge, he shunted George out of his way, screamed for everyone to get in the car and dived in through the passenger's door. From there he clambered into the driver's seat.

Already off balance, George received a second shove as the man holding his shoulders pushed him away. By the time he fell to sprawl across the road, the man was halfway into the car.

Two more were diving into the back, and Muldoon was around the other side on the pavement, trying to get in from that side.

The engine fired into life, roaring with power as Jimmy snatched at the gear lever and floored the accelerator.

Albert grabbed the backdoor nearest to him, hoping he could grasp a foot or something to stop the men from getting away, but his grip, far weaker than it had been as a younger man, had never been sufficient to overcome the physics involved.

The car took off in a shower of fine road grit and dirt, the tyres burning rubber as it fishtailed down the road. It sideswiped a parked Volvo as Jimmy fought to get control, three of the doors still open as his team struggled to get the last of their limbs inside.

Wolf's rage at seeing his prey evade him again was incandescent. He and Rex had been less than five yards from the car when it began to move and got within two yards before the car's greater ability to accelerate tore it from his reach.

Albert was half watching the car go, partially keeping an eye on George to make sure he hadn't hurt himself when he hit the ground, but mostly focused on the one member of Jimmy's team who hadn't been fast enough to get into the car.

Having reeled backward from the punch to his mouth, Drew was lucky the knee to his groin had missed the mark. The upshot though, was that he was a yard too far away to get to the car before it took off.

Left in the street, he got to stare with disbelief as his colleagues made good their escape in a cloud of smoke and dust. He didn't get to stare for long though, just enough time to swivel his head back around to lock eyes with Albert. Then his world went sideways.

Rex had been alongside Wolf when they both saw the men scramble for the car and he knew they were going to get away. He heard Wolf's disbelieving bark of horror and wished they could have moved faster. Though the wolf denied it each time he broached the subject, Rex could tell the animal was injured.

The wolf winced when he ran and when he thought Rex wasn't looking, he worried at a patch of fur on his chest. Worse yet, Wolf was beginning to develop a new and worrying scent. It wasn't one Rex was familiar with, but his brain assured him it was the smell of infection. So he'd slowed down to keep pace with the wolf rather than run as fast as he could to leave him behind as they followed the killer's scent through the alleyways behind the houses.

That was until they burst into the open and he could see and smell his human. Then he ran as fast as he could, but somehow Wolf had found the strength to match his speed, his new effort powered, no doubt, by the sight of his target.

Had he not gone slower so the wolf could keep up, he would have caught all the men in the open and they would not have been able to escape in the car. As it was, he wanted to obey his human's command but there was only one man left.

As wolf tore senselessly after a car he could never catch, Rex put down his head and ran straight through the man standing opposite his human.

For Albert it was one of those moments when he wished his eyeballs were fitted with a slow-motion camera and instant replay function.

Drew was there, facing him, holding his mouth, and looking both panicked at being left behind and ready to retaliate to Albert's punch. Then he wasn't.

For a second, it was as if Drew had ceased to exist. Had Albert blinked it would have seemed as if the man had vanished in the time his eyes were closed.

When Drew came back to earth almost two seconds later, it was to land painfully in a crumpled heap more than a yard from where he started.

Rex skidded to a stop and reversed course.

Albert watched the downed man for a few seconds. He was writhing and moaning, trying to work out which bit of him hurt the most. Content that he wasn't about to get up, Albert closed the distance to help George back onto his feet.

Accepting the hand up, George got his feet back under his bottom and pushed himself upright.

'Thanks, old boy,' George gave Albert a comradely pat on the back. 'I rather think we had a lucky escape there, wouldn't you say?'

Albert's attention was on his dog. The moment George was back on his feet and Albert could be sure his friend was okay, he abandoned him to check on Rex.

'Where have you been, Rex?' Albert knelt so his dog could come to him.

Rex felt torn. All the excitement had given him something of a head rush, and now that the one remaining human who'd been attacking Albert was on the floor, all his senses were telling him to follow up his initial strike. Rex believed a quick bite and yank on a juicy piece of leg or arm would deter the human from any thoughts of getting up.

However, an even greater draw was the desire to make sure Albert was okay, so it was with little hesitation that he bounded across to lick the old man's face.

Only by hooking a hand around Rex's shoulders did Albert managed to stop the dog's enthusiasm from knocking him over. Albert was hugging the dog and Rex was licking Albert's face and chomping at his wrists in an excited manner while whining how pleased he was to be reunited with him.

'It's good to see you too, boy,' Albert felt a tear coming to his eye, and found a spare moment to swipe at it.

In turn, Rex was checking over his human. The old man seemed no worse for wear, certainly no different from the last time Rex had seen him. He appeared to have found a human companion, not that Rex believed he was being replaced. That his human was not alone came as some relief, and Rex was overwhelmed with joy to have the old man back at his side.

Yes, it had been enormous fun to tackle this mystery by himself, and he knew that given a little more time he would be able to see it to its conclusion. However, worry for what might be happening to the old man had been plaguing his mind ever since he ran away to help the wolf. It was far more important to make sure his human was safe than it was to prove his point that the nose was better than eyeballs every day of the week.

Albert finally broke off the hug. Mostly this was because his legs were protesting, and he needed to stand upright again.

Rex turned around expecting to see the wolf. It was time to introduce his new companion to his human. But when he looked, the wolf was nowhere in sight.

'Oh, no.' Rex knew exactly what had happened. Too focused on bringing down his own human's killer, Wolf had chased after the car until it disappeared from sight and then just kept going anyway. Rex had done the same himself on more than one occasion albeit that he wasn't attempting to avenge a death at the time.

A gasp of frustration escaped Rex's chest. He glanced back at Albert, and then down the road again. The wolf's scent was on the air, so too the exhaust note left behind by the car the killer had escaped in. Both would soon dissipate, blown away by the breeze or simply absorbed by the other smells around them.

Now he was faced with a difficult choice. Reunited with his human, he wanted nothing more than to stay with him. However, if he wasn't swift to go after the wolf, finding him again might prove to be impossible. He did not owe the wolf anything. It might be more accurate, in fact, to say the inverse was true. But Rex believed the wolf was injured.

No, that wasn't right, Rex corrected himself. Rex was utterly certain that the wolf was carrying an injury that might prove to be life threatening, but even if it were not, it was reducing the wolf's physical abilities. In the moment when he needed them most, that loss of strength might mean that if Wolf cornered his quarry, rather than emerge victorious, he might lose.

In the end, the decision was an easy one. Moreover, he knew that his human would act much the same if the roles were reversed. Rex had seen the old man put his life on the line for people who were almost complete strangers on more than one occasion in just the last few weeks.

Against a ticking clock, Rex closed the distance to place his head against his human's thigh and lean into him a little. He could not tell what was going to happen next and wanted to feel the warmth of his human companion again before he set off.

With a heart rending last look up into the old man's eyes, Rex turned and started running.

'Rex!' Albert bellowed as loudly as he could. 'Rex!'

Rex heard but he did not look back. The scent trail he needed to follow was already fading. Had he left it any longer to pursue the wolf ... let's just say he was glad to know his pace was faster.

'Where's he going?' asked George.

Albert knew the answer, at least he thought he did. A small lump had formed in his throat, the presence of worry filling his life again as he watched his favourite friend round the corner at the end of the road and vanish from his life once more.

Mercifully, he did not have to provide an answer to George's question, for a distraction arrived in the shape of George's daughter, Eliza, and several uniformed police officers.

Just down the street, two of Fat Bernhard's men decided they had enough footage and turned off the phone they were using to record what had happened.

'Not the Cypriots then,' commented Crab O'Halloran.

His colleague, Big Dave, nodded his agreement. 'They sure didn't look Cypriot to me. That's got to be the guys though, hasn't it?'

Crab, so called because he was missing three fingers which left him with a thumb and pinky on one hand, shrugged.

'We'll ask the boss what he thinks, but the old men led us right here and there can't be all that many seven-foot giants in the town.'

Much like the police, Fat Bernhard had an investigation underway. He needed to know who was behind the disappearance of his men and was becoming desperate to put a stop to it. Until just a few hours ago his efforts had been yet to produce any fruit. But putting the squeeze on a couple who owned a sweet shop on the seafront, the same premises where Brooksy disappeared from two nights ago, they had been able to get descriptions of two men who had been attempting to extract protection money.

According to the couple, who cracked quite quickly when Big Dave broke the first bone, an old man with a dog had interrupted the two men making their collection. They also confirmed that the two men had grabbed Brooksy the previous night and that the murder of a street act known only as 'the Wolfman', was likely to be at their hands too.

They almost got to follow Jimmy, Muldoon, and the others when they drove away, and were planning to grab the two old men for questioning when the police appeared. They waited for a few seconds, to see if the police would move on, then driving as casually as he could, Big Dave performed a three-point turn, and drove away from the police officers now crowding around the two old men in the middle of the road.

Half an hour later, Albert and George were nursing their bruised knuckles over pints of stout in a public house called The Three Feathers. It was past lunchtime, and they were waiting for some food to be delivered when Albert's phone rang.

To fish it from his pocket required Albert to shuffle around on the chair. He'd removed his coat when he came into the public house, and it was folded on the chair next to him with the phone tucked securely in an inside pocket. When he finally got his hands on the infernal device, the name displayed on the screen was that of his eldest son, Gary.

'Hello, Son.'

'Dad, where are you? I thought you said you would be heading back first thing in the morning.'

Albert scratched his head and sighed a tired breath. 'Yes, about that. I've, um, I've misplaced Rex.'

Not certain he had heard correctly, Gary repeated his father's words.

'You've misplaced Rex? He's not a pair of reading glasses, Dad. I would have thought your dog, given his size, was rather hard to misplace.'

'Okay, I'll put it another way. Rex met a wolf who is the only witness to a murder and appears to have taken it upon himself to solve the crime. I last saw him a short while ago when he interrupted me getting beaten and kidnapped by a gang of protection racket hoodlums. After saving me, he then ran off after the wolf again.'

George picked up his pint, sniggering quietly to himself.

Sitting at his desk in London, Gary squinted into the middle distance, running his father's statement through his head a couple of times before he was ready to respond.

'Had that story come from anyone else, I would have dismissed it instantly. Since it's you, Dad, I shall take it as gospel. Are you all right?'

Albert picked up his own pint, the half-drained glass hovering in the air as he considered what he wanted to say.

With a wry smile, he replied, 'So far, son, yes.' Then he drank half of the remaining liquid in three swift gulps.

Spotting his partner's nearly empty glass, and knowing it was his round anyway, George downed the rest of his drink and went to the bar.

Gary had his eyes closed and his forehead nestled in his right hand. He always imagined that it would be his teenage children who turned his hair grey or forced his hairline to recede. He had never once anticipated that it might be his father who caused him the greatest stress and worry.

'Do you need me to come to you, Dad?' he asked, praying that the answer would be a negative.

Albert nodded his head towards George in answer to an unspoken question. George had just raised his glass and his eyebrows in Albert's direction to confirm a second drink would be welcome.

It wasn't rare for Albert to have a drink at lunchtime, but it was rare for him to have more than one. He always felt that it made his head a little floaty and impaired his decision making.

Nevertheless, given the day he'd been having, he chose to excuse himself.

To answer Gary's question he said, 'No, son, there's no need for that. My greatest concern was that Rex might get lost or hurt. Seeing him just less than an hour ago, it's clear he has a better handle on things than I do currently. I'll catch up to him shortly and we'll both be home as soon as we can.'

Gary breathed a sigh of relief.

'Okay, Dad. Well, I'm here if you need me. One of us can come to you if you need us. It's only a few hours' drive.'

Normally, with one of his children on the phone, Albert would find some small talk with which he could engage them, asking about his grandchildren perhaps. Today, he had other things on his mind and just as George was turning away from the bar, a fresh pint of stout in each hand, the door to the pub opened and Eliza walked in.

Eliza nodded to the landlord on her way past the bar, asking for a diet cola. She did not stop to wait for it to be poured, continuing directly onwards to take up one of the chairs opposite Albert and George. They were both sat with their backs against the wall on a bench seat with a small round table in front of them.

Shucking her jacket, and placing her handbag on the floor, Eliza started talking even before her bottom found the chair.

'Now, this is an activity I can approve of, gentlemen. A pint or two and some lunch for two retired gentlemen seems about the right pace.'

George blew a loud raspberry.

'That's what I think of that, love,' he remarked. 'Neither one of us is quite over the hill yet, my dear. I think perhaps you ought to give us a little more credit.'

Undeterred by her father's words, Eliza put both elbows on the table and leaned forward. She was making eye contact with both men, waiting for either one to speak again so that she could cut over them. There was only one voice of authority here, and it was hers.

Her problem, in this situation, was that both of her opponents had played this game many more times than she had. They simply waited for her to speak.

When the silence stretched out for long enough, the pressure to fill it became too much for Eliza.

'I did not say over the hill,' she argued.

'So you would concede that we still have something worthwhile to give in this investigation?' Albert fired in quickly before she could say anything else.

Eliza made a scoffing noise. 'Absolutely not,' she replied without needing to think of her answer. Focusing on her father, she attempted to make her position very clear. 'Dad, I love you very much, but you are no longer a police officer and you have not been for a long time.' She shifted her gaze to meet Albert's. 'And the same can be said of you, Mr. Smith. Neither one of you have assisted the police in our efforts to apprehend any of these criminals so far today and I must insist that you play no further part. Do I make myself clear?'

'Absolutely crystal, love,' George replied while refusing to make eye contact with his daughter.

Albert raised his glass in salute. 'You'll have no further trouble from us, Detective Chief Inspector.'

Satisfied with their answers, Eliza gathered her things once more, folding her coat over her left arm.

When she was standing again, she said, 'Then I shall bid you both a good day and pray that you manage to stay out of trouble.' She swivelled on her heels, turning halfway towards the bar, before she thought of something and turned back. 'I was able to confirm with animal control that they are yet to capture your dog, Mr. Smith. I will, however, keep you informed of any developments.'

Albert dipped his head to acknowledge and thank her.

'Just one question,' Albert stopped Eliza before she could escape. 'The ... gentlemen,' Albert selected his word carefully, 'who made off in your car. Have they been found? I assume that your car is fitted with a tracker.'

Seeing her father lean forward to hear her answer, Eliza was overcome with an almost overwhelming urge to throw something at the two old men.

'Now why would you need to know anything about that if the two of you are going to be in the pub minding your own business for the rest of the afternoon?' she asked, her tone innocently teasing them to give her an honest answer.

'It doesn't have to be a secret, love,' George pointed out. 'We were jolly near kidnapped by those men. It's only natural that we might be curious to hear whether they were caught. Otherwise, we might spend the rest of the day looking over our shoulders.'

From the side of his mouth, but in plain sight of the Detective Chief Inspector looking down on them, Albert whispered, 'Nice one, George.'

Eliza rolled her eyes. 'If you must know,' her words came out clipped and tense. 'The car was abandoned in a carpark near the seafront. I have a team going over the car now to look for fingerprints and DNA. I have another team going over the house, though I'm not sure they're going to find anything other than dog saliva and fur.' she nodded her head at Albert. 'You confirmed two of the men were those your dog cornered last night, yes?'

It was a rhetorical question, but Albert nodded his head in confirmation anyway.

'The identification they supplied to the officers at the scene were fake.' The revelation came as no surprise to Albert who had predicted it at the time. 'The address was the same for both men – something that should have been spotted at the time. I had someone there twenty minutes ago; it's a real house, but no one is living there. They've given us the slip, but everyone is looking for them now. Nevertheless, gentlemen, I doubt there will be any need for you to be concerned about seeing them again. They will not be foolish enough to remain in Blackpool.'

Albert frowned. 'What makes you so sure?' he wanted to know.

To Eliza's way of thinking, the answer was obvious.

'They just lost their base of operations, and they are on the run. Only a complete moron would stay in Blackpool when half the police in the town are looking for them. Now, gentlemen, if there's nothing else you need, you'll have to excuse me. I have police investigations to which I must attend.'

This time, when Eliza turned away, she did not turn back. At the bar she paid for and took a sip of her cola before placing it back on a beer mat and leaving through the same door she had come in through just minutes before.

Neither man said anything for several seconds, each silently contemplating what had happened so far today, what they had seen and heard, and what they wanted to do now.

George was first to interrupt the quiet.

'What's with your dog, Albert?' he wanted to know. 'To me, it seemed as if he had a specific purpose in mind when he ran off. Also, he appears to be running around with the wolf who is, I guess, potentially the only eyewitness to the murder the other night – that's what you said to your son, too. Then there's the small matter of him turning up at the house of the man we suspect to be the killer. I'm not really one for coincidence,' George remarked, 'and I remember what you always used to say about coincidences in police business. So tell me, Albert, what's with your dog?'

Albert took a sip of his drink. It seemed like the right thing to do because he did not have an immediate answer to give to George. There was something ... different about Rex. Albert was aware of it, but could not articulate his own thoughts on the subject to say what it was that made him stand apart from other dogs.

Because George was waiting for an answer, and looking at Albert in anticipation, Albert felt he needed to say something.

'I don't really have an answer for you, old boy. However, I agree that Rex does not act as one might expect. Sometimes it seems as if he's trying to solve the case alongside me. In fact, I have caught myself wondering if he was trying to tell me something once or twice.' Seeing George frown deeply, Albert accepted that he needed to explain a little more clearly. 'Look, I'm not saying he thinks he's some kind of canine detective ...' Albert ran out of words and chuckled to himself. 'Honestly, I don't really know what it is I am trying to say. There is something different about Rex'.

George nodded his head and picked up his point once more.

‘Yes, there is,’ he agreed.

The food arrived before the conversation could continue any further. Hearty steak and kidney pies with mashed potatoes, fat garden peas, and a jug of onion gravy for each of them.

While they ate, Albert allowed his mind to weave through the confusing maze of visible and audible clues he had heard and seen since he arrived in Blackpool less than twenty-four hours ago. There was something troubling him about the man from the sweetshop, the one with the limp.

He knew his name was Jimmy because his colleagues had used that name. It was probably the same first name on his fake identification – Albert didn’t credit criminals with much imagination. Knowing a first name - it was probably James on his birth certificate - didn’t give Albert much to work with. He had no address for the man, no knowledge of his associates, and no ability to anticipate where he might go next.

Focussing harder on what his brain was trying to tell hm, Albert decided it was Jimmy’s face. There was something familiar about it, but he couldn’t yet work out what.

There was a second thought going around in his head - a small voice that refused to be ignored. Eliza sounded convinced when she said Jimmy would have left the area, but the voice disagreed.

Jimmy came across as someone with a plan. It boiled down to Albert questioning why a man would come to a place like Blackpool and attempt to overthrow the ruling mobs who were already well-established. There were so many other places a criminal could set up shop. Why not pick a softer target?

Albert found it confusing, but also informative. The man with the limp, the one he knew as Jimmy, had to have chosen Blackpool specifically. It could not be an accident and it could not be coincidence. Therefore, if Jimmy had come to the town with a plan, Albert doubted he was going anywhere just yet.

He finished off the last piece of pie crust with a glistening morsel of kidney balanced on the end of his fork and a final swipe of mash. With his lunch complete and his belly now full, Albert explained his thoughts to George.

When Albert was done, George asked, 'What do you reckon then? Ready to misbehave a little more?'

Master Plan

'What are we still doing here, Jimmy?' Chappers Chapman wanted to know. 'Surely, we need to get out of here. The police are all over the place we've been staying in, and I for one would like to move on before the net closes.'

They were in a café on the seafront, the only punters in the place on a dreary day in late autumn. The old woman serving tea, cakes, and sandwiches had no interest in what they were saying, so they were talking about what had just happened and how it was that the police managed to find them.

What they were not talking about was the fact that they left Drew behind. By the time they realised he wasn't in the car, it was too late to go back for him. Jimmy called his phone, but a woman answered. When she introduced herself as Detective Chief Inspector Benjamin-Mackie, Jimmy ended the call without speaking. The team then ditched their phones, considering them to all be compromised. They all had backups, still in boxes and waiting to be activated.

Jimmy had been planning this for a long time.

In many ways, Drew being taken by the police was vastly superior to a rival gang getting him. He was far less likely to crack and give away key facts under police interrogation since they would not resort to cutting bits of him off in their quest to extract answers. Nevertheless, it was yet another thing to worry about and their number was now down to six.

There were only five of them sitting at the table. Number six wasn't at the house when the canine-led raid on their hideout had occurred. He had been at a newsagent on the corner buying cigarettes and was on his way to their location now.

Muldoon could be relied upon to not have an opinion, and Jimmy was the one with the master plan. However, the other three men at the table were of a singular voice and they were all voting to call the conquest of Blackpool quits.

Jimmy smiled at them.

'It's all going to turnout just the way I said it would, chaps. All you need is a little faith and a little patience. There was nothing at the house that we needed, it was just a place for us to be. The police cannot tie it to us, because we were squatting there not paying anyone rent. So let's not bother to talk about the house again, shall we? What we should be focusing on is advancing the plan.'

'You keep talking about *the plan*,' Francis felt like it was time to voice his concerns, 'but the rest of us don't really understand how it is that you expect to topple Raymond Rutheridge.'

Vic joined in, 'Yeah, you were all about this old, fat man running a protection racket in Blackpool and how easy it was going to be to take it all away from him.'

The team were acting in an agitated manner; a temporary result of the sort-of police raid. They were more commonly calm, and difficult to fluster. Recruiting them had been easy enough, but finding highly specialised, hard men with no former criminal record had been tough. Jimmy believed they would soon be entering the next stage of his plan where they created the power vacuum he intended to fill.

For that, he needed them to regain their composure. It was time for him to steady the boat.

‘I did indeed state that taking over the protection racket in Blackpool would be easy. Would any of you say that it has been difficult so far?’ he encouraged his colleagues to speak up.

‘We’ve lost two already,’ Vic pointed out.

Jimmy nodded. ‘Ryan suffered a heart attack, Vic. You broke into the morgue to read his notes. I accept the blame, since I recruited him, but I put his loss down to bad luck. Drew is with the police, but he isn’t going to give them anything, just as none of you would.’ Jimmy paused to make eye contact with each of the team. ‘I doubt we will get him back anytime soon, but we can manage with six and we all knew running into the authorities was an occupational hazard we each needed to accept.’

‘What about the wolf?’ asked Francis. ‘He attacked and bit you, he chased Drew, and then today the house got raided by a pack of dogs.’

Jimmy let a smile creep onto his face.

‘What are you suggesting? That we are being tracked by a wolf and he has recruited dogs to help him?’

Francis’ cheeks coloured. ‘Well, no.’

Jimmy moved the conversation along.

‘What opposition have we come across so far? We've taken out five of Fat Bernhard’s men with barely any effort at all. And we are well on our way to taking over his entire operation. If you're referring to the minor hiccups such as having to kill a man because he saw Muldoon grabbing one of Fat Bernhard’s men or the fact that I got bitten by some rabid wolf, then those events, just like the police taking Drew, are just bad luck. Can I explain the pack of dogs showing up at the house followed closely by the police? No, I can't. I'm not going to let it worry me though. You shouldn't either. This is just stage one.'

'Stage one?' echoed Francis. 'What comes after stage one?'

Jimmy had not planned on revealing the full extent of his ambitions for the town, nor his reason for selecting Blackpool until they had full control of the protection racket. Today's events were accelerating things and that in turn forced his hand. It was a good thing though - an opportunity, not a problem.

If he was right about what would happen next – and his entire strategy was based on the belief that he could predict not only Fat Bernhard's moves, but those of the bigger fish up the food chain from the overweight mobster – an opportunity was about to present itself.

Jimmy checked around, lifting his head in an unnecessarily exaggerated gesture of making sure no one was listening so that his team would know he was about to talk about something top secret.

Leaning inwards to the centre of the table while making a small gesture with one hand that everyone else should do the same, Jimmy began to whisper.

'This was never about the protection racket, fellas. No one can ever get rich running a protection racket. We are here to take over the whole town. And here is how we're going to do it.'

Over the course of the next few minutes, Jimmy laid out exactly what he believed was going to happen next and how the six of them were going to take advantage. Yes, it would be violent, but they were violent men.

When he was done, they were all on board. Muldoon was always going to go along with whatever Jimmy said and the other three were agreeing, even though what Jimmy was proposing terrified them, because to not do so would make them look cowardly.

Now all they had to do was wait and see if Jimmy was right.

Betraying a Friend

Not so very far away, Rex was trying to convince the wolf that he needed to see a vet. Rex was surprised at himself for making such a suggestion, for he loathed trips to the vet. It seemed to him that on almost all occasions when he went to the vet he felt perfectly fine going in and felt much worse coming out. The vet, whoever it was, always wanted to poke, prod, and generally fiddle with him.

His human would hold him and stroke his ears which was all very nice, but then the vet would jab him with something sharp, or worse yet get out the thermometer.

However, Rex also recognised there were times when he truly needed the help of a vet. He had been cut and required stitches, he had been sick and required medicine, and now he was certain that the wolf needed treatment too.

'I'm just tired,' argued Wolf. 'All I need is some rest. I haven't had a lot in the last two days.'

'What's that smell then?' asked Rex. 'And don't ask me what smell I might be referring to. It smells like infection to me.'

They had returned to the area the wolf was most familiar with – close to the shore and not far from where his human was killed. Behind a shop selling alcohol, they found shelter inside some boxes. It was tight inside which meant their body heat soon warmed the place. Wolf would be asleep soon and Rex could not deny the attraction of a good nap.

He couldn't lie down to sleep though, not until he talked some sense into the wolf.

‘Hey, I’m talking to you. You’re sick,’ Rex nudged the wolf’s shoulder with a paw, drawing an irritated growl.

‘I'm sick all right. Sick of this conversation. I just need some rest, and you're stopping me from getting it. Even if I was sick, which I'm not, nothing is going to stop me from catching the man who killed my human. Now if you don't mind, I'd like to rejuvenate my energy levels a little. If you want to make yourself useful, keep your nose attuned and wake me if you smell anyone coming.’

As a gesture that the conversation was over, the wolf burrowed his head a little deeper into his front paws and went still.

Rex drew in a slow breath, held it for a second, and then let it go. It was decision time for him, and he knew it was going to be a tough one. To do what he believed to be right, he was going to have to betray the wolf's trust. Wolf could lie all he wanted, but he could not fool Rex. The lethargy was one thing, but the smell of infection was another entirely.

In the back of his canine mind, Rex was certain that his new friend needed help. He waited until he was certain Wolf was asleep, then he left their temporary shelter and ventured back out onto the streets of Blackpool.

If he found his human, he could lead him back to the wolf and would trust the old man to know what it was that he needed to do. The old man could be quite intuitive for a human. Rex couldn't calculate what the chances were of finding his human though, so he was searching for another smell at the same time, that of the idiots from animal control.

Getting taken by them was hardly a favourable outcome, and while he was certain Wolf would not thank him for it, he also believed it might save his friend’s life.

With that in mind, he headed for the seafront.

'Nice place,' Albert made his obligatory remark as he got out of the taxi. They were at George's house where he said they needed to collect something. He'd been cryptic about it, refusing to divulge what he had at his house that would help them, but Albert played along.

He still believed the fastest way to get himself reunited with Rex was to track down the same man who Rex seemed to be after. It was a wild guess, or possibly you could call it a hunch, but since Jimmy seemed to be at the centre of what was happening, and Albert could place him close to the scene of the murder on the night that it happened, he was content to put him in the frame for the crime.

Right or wrong, Albert intended to track down Jimmy with the belief that when he did so he would find his dog.

George handed the cabdriver a crisp twenty pound note before leading Albert to the front door. He had to fish in his pocket to find his keys, then made them both wait on the doorstep as he squinted at the bunch to find the right one.

'I really should remember to pack my reading glasses more often,' he grumbled to himself. With the door finally open, he led Albert inside.

A small white cat appeared a moment later, rushing out from a room to their right to see who was there.

Guiltily, George admitted, 'I forgot to feed him this morning, actually. It's one of the reasons I needed to come home.' He led Albert through to the kitchen, talking as he went. 'I awoke to a message from Eliza to say that she had bumped into you in the middle of the night.'

'I thought you lived with your sister?' Albert questioned.

'She's away with some friends on a coach tour in Belgium,' George replied over his shoulder. 'She's due back tomorrow evening. Eliza clearly hasn't gotten around to letting her know what I have been up to, or I would be getting messages from her to tell me off as well.'

The white cat followed George and began winding around his legs, rubbing against them as George reached into a cupboard to extract a box of generic supermarket kitty crunch.

Once the cat was happily face down in its bowl, George inquired whether Albert wanted a cup of tea.

Albert shook his head. 'No, thank you,' Albert replied without needing to think. 'I really ought to not hang around. Finding Rex again is something of a priority. I need to get on my way back to Kent.'

Accepting Albert's first answer and not seeing any need to press him on the subject, George dismissed the idea of a cup of tea in favour of looking for the item he came home for. He began rummaging in kitchen drawers, commenting that it had to be in here somewhere.

'What is it you're looking for?' Albert asked.

George's hands stopped moving for a second and though he didn't turn around, he did turn his head to look over one shoulder.

With a sly grin, he said, 'You'll see.'

Albert rolled his eyes, accepting that was all the answer he was going to get until George found what it was he was looking for.

George moved to another drawer, yanking it open and pulling items out to dump them on the countertop.

As if an idle thought had just occurred to him, he asked, 'What is it you need to rush back to Kent for, anyway? That was your son on the phone earlier in the pub, wasn't it? What's going on in Kent?'

Albert had no reason to keep a secret, so leaning against the refrigerator while George continued to delve into the nooks and crannies of his kitchen drawers and cupboards, he explained a little more about the Gastrothief.

'Aha!' George took a box from the back of a drawer. It was made of brown cardboard and could have contained anything for there were no markings or symbols on the outside that Albert could see. His curiosity to learn what was inside was forced to wait though when George asked another question.

'You really think there's some master criminal somewhere kidnapping chefs and stealing equipment? What for?'

Albert let a tired laugh shake his shoulders as he shrugged.

'I wish I had the faintest idea. I can make no sense of it, but I cannot deny the evidence trail that I have found. What I really need is one key piece of information to tie it all together. If I just knew what it was all about, I might be able to trace it back to someone.'

George had the box in his hands, but was making no attempt to open it or look inside. Albert was finding it a little infuriating. However, from the look on George's face, what he held had been all but forgotten in favour of hearing more about Albert's Gastrothief.

'You said you ran across two men in Biggleswade who were attempting to kidnap a chef. But you don't think they were behind it?'

Albert bit his lip, considering for a second what he believed, and why he believed it.

'They were career criminals,' Albert replied after a second. 'At least, that was the impression I got. They were operating on somebody else's instructions. The same two men were in Keswick, and my son, Gary, found information suggesting that they were heading for Arbroath. Obviously, they never got there because they both died in Biggleswade.'

'But didn't you say you got involved in something in Arbroath?' George finally moved to the table and put the box down, though the lid, annoyingly, remained in place.

Albert nodded. 'Yes, that's right, but it was nothing to do with the Gastrothief.'

'What about that chap who you said went missing at the end?' George asked with a frown.

'Argyll?' Albert confirmed. He opened his mouth to speak, but then wasn't sure what he wanted to say, and it took him a moment to form a sentence. 'I don't know what to think about what happened to Argyll. He just vanished.'

'Don't you think that maybe if your theory about this Gastrothief is correct,' George made air quote symbols with his fingers around the term Gastrothief when he said it, 'then maybe they took him. Not the two who died in Biggleswade, obviously, but another pair.'

The thought had occurred to Albert in the past, most especially at the time when he was in Arbroath. However, there was nothing to indicate that his suspicions had any foundation. Not then, and not now. Choosing to dismiss the conversation and move on with the current investigation, he nodded his head towards the little box.

'Are you ever going to open that?'

George flipped his eyebrows, a gesture that said he'd all but forgotten the device when he found himself drawn into Albert's tale of a master criminal.

The lid came off with a flourishing hand gesture as George said, 'Ta-dah!'

Albert peered inside, his forehead wrinkling.

'I haven't seen one of those in decades. Goodness, it must be forty years or more. Where on earth did you find it?'

George took the device out of the box, placing separate pieces on the countertop. He popped the back off the main component, checking the batteries were in place before pressing a button on the side.

'They were throwing them out. As I'm sure you can imagine, this is considered to be ancient technology now. If I showed this to half the chaps joining the police now, I should think very few of them would even know what it was.'

Albert agreed but had to ask, 'It's all very interesting, but why are you showing it to me? Why did you want to come here to collect it?'

George gave Albert a sly grin. Then without a word, he pressed another button on the side of the component, fiddled with it for a second and then pressed yet another button.

Half a second later, the device replayed Albert's voice, crisply repeating his previous sentence.

The device, since I'm certain you are wondering, was what passed for a secret recording device in the seventies. A tiny microphone would be attached inside a person's clothing which led to a small tape recorder that could be hidden inside a pocket. At the time it was considered to be high tech. Both George and Albert remembered when such devices started to be made available to them. It happened years after such things had been readily available to organisations with better budgets.

In a flash, Albert understood what it was for.

'There're no electronic components in it, are there? Fat Bernhard's clever chap with the wand thingy won't be able to detect it, will he?'

George's smile was that of a lion who had just made it inside a zebra-only nightclub and was now taking off his stripey pyjamas to the horrified stares of all the other patrons.

'No, Albert, it doesn't, and it won't. All we need is to get him to talk - to get any of them to talk - And we'll have them.'

Summoned

In his office at the end of the corridor on the top floor of the workingmen's club, Fat Bernhard was sweating. To be fair, he sweated a lot, the layer of insulation between his muscles and his skin ensured his body ran a few degrees warmer than it should at all times. That, however, was not the primary reason for his perspiration at this point.

He was on the phone with Raymond 'Razor' Rutheridge, the big boss in Blackpool. When Raymond called, which he did not do very often, one answered the phone and prayed. Primarily, one prayed that the reason he had dialled your number was because he wanted you to kill someone, not because he was giving you fair warning that he was about to have you killed.

Raymond was one of the men who had made a true fortune out of organised crime. He ran all the big-ticket enterprises, and it was with his blessings that Fat Bernhard was permitted to run the protection racket for him.

What Fat Bernhard's men did not know was that their boss had to pay Raymond a monthly dividend for the pleasure of conducting his business. Essentially Raymond ran a protection racket to collect money from the man running his protection racket. If Fat Bernhard ever failed to pay on time and in full ... well, let's just say that Fat Bernhard was sweating and not without good reason.

Fat Bernhard was not the only minor player in town, but he was the smallest fish in the pond, no pun intended. All the other bosses, if they were to band together, could theoretically challenge Raymond for the dominant spot, but none were brave enough to even whisper such things in the privacy of their own homes. The nickname 'razor' had been well earned in his early years, and Raymond took great pride in dispatching anyone who displeased him in person to make sure no one questioned the legend.

'Yes, Raymond, that is correct, there have been a few minor issues this week.' Fat Bernhard could only guess how Raymond knew he had men missing and had failed to make several collections over the course of the last week or so. He'd always thought it highly likely Raymond had a mole positioned somewhere in his firm. It could be any one of his men, Fat Bernhard knew. Raymond probably had moles positioned in everyone's organisation, as well as the police force, and probably the local council.

He held his breath as he waited to see what Raymond was going to say next. He did not sound angry or displeased, but Fat Bernhard was not going to draw another breath until he knew one way or another.

'Far be it for me to dictate how you run your business, Bernhard. So long as you are content to continue giving me my cut, and don't find any silly excuses, it can remain none of my business, wouldn't you say?'

Fat Bernhard breathed a sigh of relief - he was off the hook.

'Yes, absolutely, Raymond. I'm already putting maximum effort into resolving this minor and relatively insignificant invasion of my turf. I can assure you there will be no perceptible change in service.'

Bernhard had not realised that he was talking himself into a verbal trap.

'That was quite absolutely the wrong answer, dear fellow. A problem for you is a problem for us all, wouldn't you say? Your business is my business,' Raymond growled into the phone. 'The very fact that the news has reached my ears, means that you are not resolving this issue. I am led to believe that you have lost five men. Five men in a week.'

Fat Bernhard doubted that pointing out it was nine days and not a week would do him any favours and chose to stay quiet.

Attempting to be cooperative, he said, 'We shall redouble our efforts, Raymond. We have already identified the group we believe to be at the centre of this trouble and will be dealing with them very soon.'

'Yes, yes, very good. However, I rather think that we should all have a meeting. A problem for one of us can soon become a problem for all of us. I have already spoken with the other bosses. My men will collect you from the yacht club in one hour.'

Fat Bernhard swallowed hard. He was being summoned, and there was no room for him to negotiate. Failing to appear when summoned was tantamount to spitting in Raymond's face and would be treated in much the same manner as if he had.

He hated the sea, positively loathed setting foot on a boat, and knew he would be seasick long before he got to Raymond's yacht. He also knew he had no choice.

'I shall leave straight away,' he promised.

With no better plan in place and no starting point, Albert and George returned to where it all began - the sideroad where the wolfman was killed, and the sweet shop where Albert first came across Jimmy and his giant accomplice.

Albert had no idea what he hoped to achieve by visiting the beleaguered couple for a third time, but their business was the one that he knew to be targeted by those involved in the protection racket and, to the best of his knowledge, they were yet to make this week's payment.

Since he doubted there was any mileage in attempting to convince Lionel and Doris to give evidence against those who were preying upon them, he hoped instead to take the onus away from them.

The loose plan was to have George inside the shop, nosing around, and waiting for Jimmy to come for the money he was yet to collect. Albert would be outside watching for Rex and the wolf.

Neither truly expected Jimmy to appear at the sweet shop – it was the longest of long shots. The police knew who he was and even though they had no evidence of any wrongdoing, he was wanted for questioning in connection with the items found in the house on Keswick Road.

On top of that, what Albert and George had been able to tell Eliza proved sufficient for her to want to question Jimmy and his friends about their whereabouts at the time of the wolfman's murder.

Albert didn't care whether Jimmy was caught or not because his focus was on getting Rex back. This time, if he was able to grab his dog, he was going to get the lead attached and no matter what Rex wanted to do, Albert wasn't going to let go again.

The two former police officers discussed all this in the cab on their way to the seafront, laying out a couple of contingency plans, and trying to formulate responses in advance should things not go their way.

All of it was discarded the moment they arrived outside the sweet shop. The steel mesh shutter was down, the business very clearly closed for the day.

It left them wondering what their next move might be until they spotted Doris getting out of another taxi, just a few yards ahead.

Lionel followed her, exiting onto the pavement after his wife. The man had his right forearm in a cast which was held across his body by a sling. His wife was sporting an awful black eye.

Someone had given them a brutal beating.

Racing to escape the confines of the taxi to find out what had happened, Albert inadvertently slipped the cab driver a fifty-pound note. It was more than three times the value of the fare, but as the cabbie watched the two old men hurry along the pavement, he shrugged and pocketed it anyway.

Albert and George did not notice, but the cab they had just exited took off down the street far faster than was necessary as the driver did his best to get away before his most recent customer realised his error.

Albert almost made the mistake of asking, 'Are you all right?' but stopped himself before the words left his mouth, for clearly such a question invited a barrage of abuse.

Instead, he asked, 'Which of the gangs was it? The old, or the new?'

'The old ones,' Lionel confirmed. Doris wouldn't make eye contact, hiding her wounds by casting her eyes to the ground.

George moved forward to help Doris with her keys. Her hands were visibly shaking, the need to return to the scene where they had been attacked, and the memories that evoked, enough to cause a fresh wave of nervousness and nausea.

'Here, let me help you with those. Albert and I can at least assist you to get inside and settled.'

They didn't fight him, the lady handing over a bunch of keys so that George could unlock and raise the shutter, then unlock and open the door. It took more than a minute, and five keys, the lady doing her best to confirm when George had the right one in his hands.

Inside, George locked the world outside once more, certain that was what they would want.

'Thank you,' said Lionel, a world-weary sigh escaping his lips. He looked utterly beaten. 'I don't know what you two gentlemen are here for, but unless you wish to buy a sweet shop, I'm afraid there's very little that we can do for you.'

'You intend to sell?' Albert confirmed.

Husband and wife were clinging to each other, much as Albert had seen them do more than once already. The comfort they took from each other was a blessing that he believed would ensure they got through this together.

It was the husband this time who answered Albert's questions.

'This was the last straw,' he stated with an air of finality. 'It's one thing to reduce our profit by extorting money from us each week, but another thing entirely when they hurt my wife. They'll get no further money from us. We're leaving tonight. We'll close the business and deal with the financial fallout in due course.'

'I'm sorry to have to ask you,' Albert started, 'Can you tell me why they hurt you?'

This time it was Doris who replied.

'They wanted to know who the new people are. That man who was in here last night and the giant who was with him - the ones your dog cornered. We could tell it was members of the original gang because they all wear this ridiculous outfit with spats on their feet, but it was two men we had never seen before. One was missing three fingers from his right hand and the man he was with kept calling him Crab.'

Her husband interrupted, 'The other one was called Kenny and he had the strangest way of talking.'

Doris agreed. 'Yes, he spoke slowly as if he had to consider every sentence he was going to say.'

Albert and George exchanged a glance; they both knew the second man was Kenny the Snake.

'They didn't believe us when we said we had no idea who they were. And the guy with the missing fingers got really mad when we said we had given them this weeks' money and had nothing for them.'

Albert thought perhaps they had missed their chance and needed to confirm if Jimmy had returned already.

'Have you given the man with the limp the money? Has he been back already today?'

Lionel sighed, glancing at his wife who gave him a tight lipped smile it.

'No, we were lying,' he admitted. 'I don't know if he could tell I was lying or if he didn't care. But that was when he broke my arm.'

Albert decided it was time to go for broke. This was either going to work or it was not, either way it was a risky strategy he was attempting to employ. His only goal was to get Rex back, and maybe this was the way to do it, maybe it was not. But doing something felt better than doing nothing.

'You need some time to pack, yes?' he asked the couple.

'Here he is. Right on time. What did I tell you?' Jimmy looked about at his colleagues, a smug smile of satisfaction on his face.

'How on earth did you know that Fat Bernhard was going to come to the yacht club?' Chappers Chapman wanted to know.

'What can I tell you?' Jimmy voiced a rhetorical question. 'I have a sixth sense for how these things work.' He gave a cryptic response, then relented to reveal the truth. 'Everything we have done in the last week and a half has been about getting to this point. I told you about Raymond Rutheridge earlier, yes?'

'Yes,' Francis answered for the group. 'You told us he is on a yacht somewhere and never comes into British waters. Anyone approaching his superyacht is likely to get blasted unless they are the coastguard or Royal Navy.'

Jimmy nodded, pleased that the chaps had been paying attention.

'Exactly. We have created sufficient disruption to Fat Bernhard's business, that the big fish in these parts, Raymond Rutheridge, has summoned him to his yacht. Raymond probably heard the first rumblings of a problem a few days ago and would have sailed here from the Canary Islands, or wherever he was, planning to head off this issue before it could become a problem.'

Vic interrupted. 'How does any of this help us? You said you want us to take over the whole operation in Blackpool.' Vic took a second to make sure Chappers and Francis were backing him up. 'That means we need to take on and beat Raymond. He can see people coming for miles around, Jimmy. How is it that you propose to sneak up on him? It's not like we are heavily armed.'

They had guns, but only a few small calibre handguns, hardly what they needed to mount an assault.

Jimmy continued to smile at his team.

'You worry too much, chaps. This is how it is going to go down …' Jimmy laid out the precise order of events and how they would now unfold.

Giving them the plan a piece at a time as he had avoided swamping them with too much information or scaring them into believing they were taking on the impossible. By the time he finished, the black limousine in which Fat Bernhard arrived had departed, and they had watched him waddle into the yacht club and down onto one of the jetties.

Vic, Chappers, Francis, and Marvin, the man who missed all the fun with the dogs because he went for cigarettes, were quiet, each idly fantasising about all the money they were going to make. Jimmy had it all figured out and he even revealed how it was that he knew so much.

That one piece of information, the revelation about his heritage, gave them the final boost in confidence they needed. Jimmy was right, this was going to be easy.

According to Jimmy, a motor cruiser would shortly be arriving to collect Fat Bernhard. It would take him out to Raymond's yacht and that was how they were going to strike.

Soon it would be time for them to move.

'Is that it there?' Francis pointed a finger out to sea where an indistinct blob, that was less grey than all the grey around it, was slowly changing into the shape of a boat.

Jimmy sucked in a deep breath.

'Are we ready then, chaps?' he asked. 'I rather think it's showtime.'

The grey-haired old lady running the cafeteria had been counting down the minutes until her shift ended and was looking forward to stopping for a small sherry at the Duke of Cumberland public house on her way home. Had there been any other customers this afternoon, she might be trying to move the six gentlemen along - they had finished their beverages more than an hour ago.

However, when they suddenly pulled out guns and started donning balaclavas, she gasped so hard her top set of dentures fell out.

Cyril, Fat Bernhard's right hand man, had an umbrella in his left hand which he held above the mob boss's head. It wasn't raining, but there was a fine mist in the air, the kind that stuck to your clothes and soaked straight through them.

Fat Bernhard could see Raymond's motor launch coming to collect them and knew it was time to make their way to the end of the pontoon.

Just as they arrived where they expected to be picked up, they heard a thundering of footsteps coming their way.

Rex could barely believe his eyes. His nose wasn't picking up anything due to the stiff breeze blowing inshore, but he knew what he was seeing. Being a dog, Rex wasn't sure if the right term to employ was irony or coincidence, but the fact that it was his eyes and not his nose that found his target caused a snort of surprise to escape his mouth.

Whichever the right term was, he had no time to lose. The wolf was utterly determined that nothing was going to stop him from catching his human's killer and Rex believed he would not be able to get Wolf the medical attention he needed until Wolf had tracked and tackled his quarry.

With that in mind, Rex turned tail and began running as hard as he could, returning back to where he left his poorly friend.

Inside the sweet shop, Albert and George were playing shopkeepers. The couple, Lionel and Doris, were upstairs packing suitcases and gathering those items they felt they needed to take with them as they abandoned their shop.

It had taken some convincing, but through a process of wearing them down, the two old men convinced the shopkeepers to let them remain in the shop until the couple were ready to leave.

That Jimmy, or any of his friends might choose this short period of time to return to the sweet shop was an absolute longshot, and both George and Albert knew it. However, Albert maintained that staying in this area and hoping he might spot Rex was his best bet.

Despite believing that this was his best strategy, Albert was nevertheless utterly startled when a Rex shaped blur sprinted past the front of the shop. At the time, Albert was watching out the front window to see if anyone was around.

'Rex!' Albert yelled as he got the door open.

George joined him in the street.

'Did you see your dog?' he asked.

Now Albert was faced with a dilemma that he had not anticipated. He'd seen Rex and wanted to follow, but that meant leaving the shop unattended.

'He went that way,' Albert pointed. 'I'm going to follow,' he remarked, starting to walk while twisting his torso to let George know his plan. 'Stay here. Hopefully I'll not be long.'

George gave his old friend a thumbs up and stayed in the doorway, watching Albert as he hustled to where the side road cut up between the parade of shops.

Rex had heard his human's voice, and under any other circumstances would have turned around and gone back. However, he was too excited at the prospect of ending the wolf's hunt for his human's killer. If he could do that, this would all be over, and Rex knew that his human would be able to help him get the wolf the medical attention he needed. Hating himself, even though he knew it was the right thing to do, Rex kept his head down and his legs pounding, skidding to a stop when he arrived back at the wolf's lair.

'Get up!' Rex barked loudly. 'I've just seen him! But we've got to go now! I think he was about to get on a boat.'

Rex believed this was a test for his friend. Wolf was either going to get up and get going, thus demonstrating that he did just need a rest, or he was not going to be able to, and in so doing would prove Rex's point that Wolf needed help.

Wolf sucked in a deep breath, focusing his mind and ignoring the reports coming in from all over his body. He felt weak, and a little shaky. His hearing seemed to be affected, as if there were something blocking his ears and his heart was pounding far faster than it ought to be in a resting state. Nevertheless, he got to his paws with a determined growl.

Turning to face the dog, he drew back his lips to growl, 'Show me.'

Albert headed up the side street and back past the scene of the murder. There was no longer any sign of the crime scene tape. That had been removed, either by the police or by somebody who thought it would make a nice souvenir of their visit to Blackpool. He was heading for the loading yard and parking area behind the businesses, imagining in his head what might have occurred here in the last few nights.

'Rex!' he called his dog's name over and over. 'Rex!'

Looking around, and pausing to listen, he heard the sound of approaching claws on the street and swivelled to face it. He did so just in time to see Rex and the wolf burst from an alleyway and into the loading yard.

'Rex!' Albert called his dog's name again, but this time with the joy of knowing that he had found him.

Rex was terribly torn, his duty to his human and his responsibility to help the wolf conflicting and twisting his conscience as he wrestled with what to do.

To the wolf, he barked, 'Keep going, I'll catch up in a moment.' Albert had his arms out to greet Rex and was attempting to block the dog's path.

It would take almost no effort at all to evade his human, but that would be bad dog behaviour and above all else Rex loved the old man.

So he stopped, skidding to a halt a couple of yards before he reached him. Wolf kept going, zipping past the old man on his right side, Albert paying him almost no attention as he focused on Rex.

'Come on, boy. It's time to stop this now. I need you to come with me.' Rex's lead was in the shop, of course, left in the pocket of Albert's coat. He had taken it off because he was inside and too warm with it on.

Meeting his human's eyes with his own, Rex tried hard to make the old man understand.

'It's almost done. We just need to catch the killer. Then I promise I'll come back to you, and I'll be a good dog. Actually,' an idea bloomed in Rex's head, 'you should come with us. Some human help might be really useful once we've caught him.'

Then a nagging worry that the wolf might intend to kill his quarry drove Rex to get his paws moving once more.

'Come on!' Rex barked at Albert. 'Come on, I need your help!'

Rex nimbly sidestepped Albert who swung an arm in a vain attempt to snag his dog's collar. Already moving at speed, Rex pounded out of the loading area, back onto the pavement, and was flying along at full speed by the time he whipped past George standing in the door of the sweet shop. He continued to bark over his shoulder, encouraging his human to follow him.

Albert had no idea what the dog's incessant noises were about, but he was going to follow anyway.

George met him in the street. He had his own coat on and was carrying Albert's in his left hand.

'I thought you might want this,' George remarked as he chucked the garment to his companion.

Albert caught it one handed and slid it over his shoulders in one smooth movement.

'What about the shopkeepers?' Albert asked.

'I let them know we had to leave,' George replied, the two old men hurrying along the street at something close to a jog. 'They said they were about to leave anyway. They are going to lock up, and told me not to worry.'

Seventy yards ahead of the two old men, Rex was back at Wolf's side, and both animals performed a hard left turn to enter the yacht club.

'Where are they?' the wolf barked his frustration. His nose wasn't giving him what he needed. The inshore breeze was carrying the scents away too fast, stealing away all traces of the smell he wanted to follow.

Humans working at the yacht club shouted at them as they sped past. Both animals ignored them, the sound of human speech of no concern to either dog or wolf in their quest to find the killer. There were yachts to their left and right and straight ahead, and the pontoons split off to give them multiple routes they could take.

Wolf's breathing was laboured, giving Rex fresh cause for concern. However, just when he was about to suggest they pause so he could get his breath back, Rex saw movement.

Using his eyes once again, Rex saw one of the men from the killer's team. He was fiddling with a rope, kneeling on the pontoon as he unwound it.

Rex had just enough time to nudge his companion in that direction, so they both saw the man clamber on board a motor cruiser. They were already running hard, but had to break into an all-out sprint as their brains calculated the distance between them and the boat which was already beginning to move.

Hurrying along the seafront, Albert and George were watching when the animals ran into the yacht club. They had no idea, nor could they guess what might be motivating their movements, but they now believed they stood a great chance of catching Rex.

'All we've got to do is have the chaps at the yacht club close the gates,' panted George between breaths. 'There's no way out unless they go for a swim.'

Albert was allowing himself to feel hopeful. George was right; having gone into the yacht club, his dog could climb on board a boat, but unless he found a boat that was going somewhere, Rex was effectively trapped, and Albert could finally catch up to him.

So it was with great dismay, that he saw a large, sleek cruiser beginning to pull away from the far end of a pontoon. The movement drew his eyes. The cruiser was leaving, heading out to sea no doubt. He was about to dismiss it, when his incredulous eyes caught two streaks of fur pursuing the boat.

'Well, I'll be,' George muttered, unable to come up with anything else to say.

The cruiser was picking up speed and pulling away from the pontoon, but it wasn’t accelerating fast enough to escape Rex and Wolf.

A bark echoed across the water, Rex’s excited encouragement for the wolf to jump. Both animals leapt into free space, hanging in the air for a second before they crashed onto the sea-level deck at the back.

Albert’s feet faltered, his brain and his heart arguing for a second as he tried to work out what he could possibly do now. His beloved dog, Rex, was heading out to sea. Whatever it was that Rex was trying to achieve was putting him in great danger. If Albert didn't go after him, would Rex ever find his way back to shore?

At the entrance to the yacht club there ought to have been a man in the security booth. He wasn't there because he was currently arguing with the club’s undersecretary about all the people and then animals he failed to keep out of the exclusive club’s premises.

The security guard argued that his barrier failed in acting as a deterrent when it came to stopping large dogs. As for the humans, the security guard felt it quite pertinent to point out that the six men escorting two other men against their will, were doing so at gunpoint.

The focus of their somewhat heated discussion was largely due to the undersecretary, a civil servant by trade, refusing to believe any of the nonsense the security guard was telling him. Obviously, the tale of armed gunmen was a complete fabrication, and he could see through the petty functionary’s lies.

For the paltry wage the yacht club paid him, Carl the security guard was happy to hand over his uniform and walk away. The option to punch the undersecretary on the nose, something he’d considered more than once in the past, was going to be part of his severance.

The upshot of his absence from the front entrance was that Albert and George also waltzed through unopposed.

'You're seriously planning to go after him?' George wanted to know.

What Albert could not adequately express to his old friend was that after losing his wife, he poured all his affection into the one live being left in his house. Rex was his companion, and in many ways his protector. But he was also more than that. Rex, and meeting Rex's needs, gave Albert purpose and he could not consider what his life might be like without the dog around. It had been enough in recent weeks to place himself in peril to ensure the dog survived, and Albert could not remember a time when he was more worried about his canine companion.

To answer George's question, Albert nodded his head. 'Yup. Look, there's no reason for you to come with me. I don't know who or what is on that cruiser, but I'm willing to bet it's Jimmy.'

George grabbed Albert's arm to stop him moving and swung him around so they were face to face.

'Are you serious? Do you hear yourself? You're suggesting that your dog is attempting to solve a murder.'

Albert tore his arm free, but did so as gently as he could, gripping George's hand so he could place it back at his friend's side.

'I don't know what to think,' he admitted. 'But I am going after him.'

'How?'

Albert sucked in a deep breath. He'd already spotted his means of giving chase. He couldn't say he was happy about it, or even if he was going to survive trying to retrieve his dog. Regardless of the danger inherent in attempting what his brain proposed, Albert knew he was going to do it anyway.

In fact, the only question left in his head, was whether he could talk George out of attempting to follow him.

The Big Reveal

When Raymond's cruiser arrived at the yacht club, the men on board expected to find Fat Bernhard waiting for them. So it came as no surprise when he was on the pontoon surrounded by several of his men.

Their instructions were to collect the overweight mob boss and his right hand man, so the rest of the men were going to be left on the pontoon. There would be no discussion regarding the subject - failing to carry out Raymond's instructions to the letter always met with severe reprimands.

It was Raymond's total control of the Blackpool underworld that cost the men on the cruiser their lives. It had been so long since anyone opposed them that it did not even occur to them to be wary of the additional men waiting with Fat Bernhard.

Coming alongside the pontoon, men front and aft had thrown ropes to temporarily secure the cruiser, but the moment they stepped down onto the pontoon, Jimmy's men shot them with silenced handguns.

Inside the cab of the cruiser, the two remaining men of the four-man crew, questioned what it was that they had just heard. The pop pop of silenced handguns was not a sound they were unfamiliar with, but inside the insulated cabin, and over the sound of the cruiser's twin engines, they were unable to work out what they might have heard until it was too late.

Jimmy's team stormed the cruiser, taking no more than a few seconds to get up to the cabin where the final two men of the four-man crew were hastily dispatched.

The only people at the yacht club who could have seen what happened were the security guard from the front gate and the undersecretary. Neither man was looking the right way though. The undersecretary could only see clouds as the damp soaked into his clothing where he laid in a puddle and held his nose. Carl the security guard, now wearing nothing but his boxer shorts, a vest, and his shoes, had his back to the events on the pontoons as he headed for the exit. Though mildly concerned that he needed a new job, he was happily massaging his knuckles.

Muldoon picked up the bodies from the pontoon, dumping them out of sight on the back deck of the cruiser before collecting the other bodies from the cabin to do likewise with them.

Fat Bernhard, advancing with Jimmy's gun digging into his back, made his way inside the boat's lounge area.

'Muldoon,' Jimmy called, his voice raised to attract his henchman's attention.

The lumbering giant appeared a moment later.

'Yes, boss?'

'Can you drive this thing?'

Muldoon nodded his head. Pleased, Jimmy twitched his head in the direction of the cruiser's control room.

'Go ahead then. Send the rest back here, please.'

Muldoon departed, leaving Jimmy alone with Fat Bernhard and Cyril.

Nervous, and angry because he was nervous, Fat Bernhard could keep silent no longer.

'Who are you? Do you really think that you can take over my operation?'

Before Fat Bernhard could say another word, and in answer to his second question, Jimmy swivelled his gun around so it was pointing at Cyril and shot him twice in the chest.

To say that Fat Bernhard was shocked would be an enormous understatement. He liked to think that he was used to violence, but in truth it had been several decades since he was personally witness to anything worse than a paper cut.

Cyril crumpled to his knees and then keeled over to his left to form a ragged heap on the carpet.

Jimmy was smiling. More specifically, he was smiling at Fat Bernhard, and it was a warm smile.

'You don't recognise me, do you?' Jimmy asked.

Fat Bernhard blinked twice slowly, staring at the younger man. His expression was a mixture of disbelief and curiosity now that the crazy man before him was suggesting they'd somehow crossed paths in the past.

'I guess I should not be surprised,' Jimmy remarked. 'It has been quite a few years,' he chuckled, 'and I was just a boy when you last bounced me upon your knee.'

Fat Bernhard's brow furrowed as his confusion deepened.

Jimmy's smile faltered, as just the first tendrils of irritation crept in. Surely, he hadn't changed that much as he'd grown; the old man ought to at least recognise Jimmy's father in his face.

'James?' Fat Bernhard hazarded a tentative guess. 'James is that you?'

Thrilled that he wasn't going to have to explain, Jimmy threw out his arms.

'Grandad!'

Fat Bernhard could feel the ground moving beneath his feet, and it wasn't just the fact that they were at sea and the deck was heaving with the waves.

'I need to sit down,' he murmured, glancing around to spot a couch onto which he could collapse.

Jimmy tucked his gun away and grabbed a chair as he crossed the room to sit close to his grandfather.

'It's so good to see you again after all these years, Grandad. I wondered if you would figure out that it was me before I came to find you,' Jimmy commented.

It jolted Fat Bernhard out of his reverie.

'What on earth have you been up to, James? Have you been killing my men?' He realised what he just said and looked across at Cyril. 'Why am I asking you that?' he asked himself. 'I've just seen you kill my best lieutenant.'

Jimmy chuckled as if it was funny.

'Yes, Grandad. Him and five more. I needed to demonstrate how weak your men had become. Your entire organisation has been letting you down, Grandad. It was easy for me to come in and take over. Imagine if it hadn't been your grandson. Imagine what might have happened to you then?'

Fat Bernhard could not believe what he was hearing, but it seemed as if his grandson, who he had not seen since his age could be measured in single figures, was suggesting that he was here to help him.

'What are you saying? That you've been trying to take over my protection racket so that somebody else wouldn't? Do you have any idea how bonkers that sounds?'

Jimmy chuckled again. 'Grandad the time has come for you to have a successor.' Jimmy added quickly, 'I'm not suggesting that I want to push you out. I believe I probably have a lot to learn from you. However, it is clear to me that your organisation has lost its touch. You used to run all the organised crime in this town. I am here to get you back on track and return our family name to the top of the tree.'

Suddenly Fat Bernhard realised the enormity of what his grandson was suggesting.

'You plan to challenge Raymond?' he gasped, his belly filling with fear at what might happen to him if his grandson were to go through with such a crazy plan. Would Raymond count Fat Bernhard as equally responsible? Fat Bernhard knew that was exactly what Raymond would think.

The smile dropped from Jimmy's face.

'Challenge? Goodness no, Grandad. I'm just going to kill him. He has no idea that we are on his boat, or that his own men are dead. When we come alongside his yacht, we're just going to kill everyone. Then, with the vacuum we have created, you and I are going to ascend to the top.'

'Does your mum know you are here?' Fat Bernhard questioned. His daughter had disowned him a long time ago, moving out as soon as she was old enough. The friction started long before that, his little girl discovering what her father did for a living and shunning him while still living under the same roof. There had been a brief period of reconciliation, and for a time, he had been allowed back into her life. Young James became the apple of Fat Bernhard's eye until his daughter discovered that her father had stepped down as the head of crime in Blackpool, but hadn't exactly gone straight.

He had not seen Jimmy in almost twenty years.

Reunited with the boy he knew, his heart ought to be filled with joy, but the man before him had such dangerous intentions that all Fat Bernhard could feel was fear.

Any further conversation was cut off by the arrival of four of Jimmy's colleagues. They were all now armed to the teeth, having liberated the stash of weapons kept on board Raymond's cruiser. Again, it was exactly as Jimmy said it would be, and now they had the weapons they needed to assault the crime boss's stronghold.

They were a mile out to sea and a speck on the horizon was slowly transforming into the shape of a superyacht.

Huddled on the transom at the back of the cruiser, Rex attempted to get Wolf moving again. The run and the leap to get on board had taken more out of the wolf than he dared to admit to his companion.

'I just need a minute,' Wolf lied, attempting to cover up how bad he now felt. What started as a small wound on his chest, had spread throughout his body. He could feel it, the first touches of eternal blackness attempting to grip him. He was close to catching his human's killer though, as close as he had been since that first night, and he intended to see the job through. His human would be avenged, and so far as Wolf was concerned, if it was the last thing he ever did, he would accept death's bitter embrace with content.

'We really need to keep moving,' Rex nudged the wolf's shoulder with his muzzle. 'We are getting too wet here, and the cold and the extra weight of the water in our coats will just make everything harder. At least let me help you get into the dry.'

Reluctantly, and having to fight to not grunt against the pain and discomfort he felt, the wolf got back onto his paws. They had to clamber up from the platform they were on at the very rear of the boat, exposing themselves as they went over the transom and onto the rear sundeck.

Rex was beginning to doubt that Wolf still had the energy or capability to take down his human's killer and was beginning to suspect that it would have to be he who did it in Wolf's stead. For the first time since meeting the wolf, Rex was beginning to question his own decisions. He believed they had identified the killer, and they had tracked him, soon perhaps they could corner him, but what then?

With no human to back him up, Rex could chase and bite, but he had no ability to arrest. Worse yet, they were on a boat with no way of getting back to shore. He was choosing to focus on one problem at a time, hoping that he could end Wolf's quest to catch his human's killer. After that, Rex really wasn't sure what he would do next.

Glancing back at the grey sky hanging forlornly above a dark sea, Rex knew for certain that he was on his own. There was no way his human would be able to follow him this time.

Focusing on what he could do, he kept Wolf moving until they were tucked away from the spray kicking over the sides of the boat.

A quarter of a mile behind and keeping the cruiser in sight as they skipped across the waves, Albert and George were in high-speed pursuit.

Shouting to be heard above the noise of their engines and of the wind whipping past their faces, George shouted, 'Albert, of all the ideas you've ever had, this is by far the worst! How do we even know how much fuel is in these things?'

Albert gave a shrug, but then realised that George probably wouldn't be able to see it. His friend raised a good question. They had not the faintest idea how much fuel was in the two jet skis they were riding.

'What if we run out of fuel?' George wanted to know. Accentuating his point by looking over his shoulder, he then added, 'I can barely see the shore.'

'Don't worry,' Albert shouted in response. 'The chaps we stole these from are bound to report them missing. I expect the coast guard will be after us before too long.' To be extra contrary, Albert shot George a broad grin and gave him a thumbs up.

Neither man was used to stealing things. Back in the day, they might have commandeered a vehicle or a bicycle or something in the pursuit of a criminal, but his was hardly the same. Abandoned on the side of the jetty, the two jet skis still had their keys in the ignition. Albert and George could hear the owners, who were in a shower block just a few yards away, undoubtedly warming up and getting dressed. They were chatting, discussing their plans for dinner, when Albert snuck in and relieved them of their wetsuits.

George had expected Albert to appeal to the two men for help, thinking that they could ride pillion behind the jet skis owners. Albert, however, had other ideas. They were based, quite nobly, on the belief that they might be riding into danger and ought not to be endangering anyone else in the process. In many ways, it could be argued that stealing the jet skis was doing the owners a favour.

A few minutes later, and with Blackpool disappearing into the distance behind them, both men were feeling the effects of the cold air and water upon their skin. On the side of the pontoon, they had stripped down to their undies before wincing and whining their way into the cold, clammy wetsuits.

They were both still wearing their socks and shoes, electing to put them back on once they were wearing the wetsuits rather than go barefoot. Their wallets, phones, and keys went into one of the plastic baggies Albert carried everywhere in case Rex did his business.

Back at the yacht club, the two young men came out of the changing room to find neatly piled clothing next to where their jet skis had been. The look of confusion they shared was less to do with the theft than it was to do with how obvious it was the clothing they found belonged to two old men.

They were going to be a laughingstock when their friends found out they'd been jacked by pensioners.

Out of sight of their owners, the jet skis, with Albert and George astride them, were nearing the cruiser. They were not, however, closing on it fast enough to arrive before it reached what Albert perceived to be its destination.

In the distance, he could just about make out a single blob ahead of them. This close to the waves, it had taken him a while to work out what he was looking at. Now that he could, and since there wasn't anything on the horizon to which they could be heading, he had to question who owned the superyacht.

Ahead of them, the cruiser was beginning to slow, the engine noise reducing as they neared Raymond's superyacht. The change did not go unnoticed by Rex, who lifted his head and sniffed deeply, testing the air to see what it contained.

This far out to sea, and on the deck of a moving boat, he wasn't getting any scents that were of use to him.

Nudging the wolf with his muzzle once more, Rex said, 'Something is happening.'

At the controls of the cruiser, Muldoon eased back on the throttle, approaching the superyacht on its starboard side. Jimmy was at his shoulder, giving commands. He wanted to see if there was anybody waiting for them.

Raymond was notoriously paranoid, and the last thing Jimmy wanted, in what he perceived to be his moment of victory, was for there to be an ambush.

The superyacht was devoid of life. The lights were on, illuminating the inside of several portions of the yacht, which was arranged over several decks. As they watched, shadows moved about, passing to and fro inside as people moved around. After a few seconds of observation, Jimmy was content that their arrival was going to come as a complete surprise.

Fat Bernhard squinted out through the window at the superyacht beyond. There was something unnerving about not seeing anybody waiting for them. He was used to there being armed guards on the deck whenever he'd arrived in the past.

Jimmy tightened the grip on the assault rifle he held. The other members of his team were all on deck already, hidden from sight but ready to storm the superyacht.

'Time to go,' he said. 'Are you ready, Grandad?' he asked, adding, 'Don't worry. This will play out exactly as I have planned. They have no idea we are coming and will be caught totally off guard. Before they know what is happening, we will have control of their ship. When the coast guard find Raymond's yacht adrift tomorrow, they will discover a bloodbath on board and almost all of Blackpool's organised criminals lying dead. The police won't look at you because I will provide you with an alibi and they have no idea who I am.'

'You make it sound so very neat,' Fat Bernhard mumbled, terrified almost to the point of hysteria.

Jimmy slapped his grandfather on the shoulder. 'It will be. Come on, let's go. If there is anyone coming to meet us, they will expect to see you.'

'He's not coming?' Fat Bernhard tilted his head at Muldoon, thinking the giant would make a nice barrier if there were any bullets flying around. Hiding behind Muldoon would provide some cover – it wasn't as if any of the other skinny wretches had the required girth.

'Muldoon?' Jimmy asked. 'No. Muldoon hates bullets and guns. He'll be staying here on the cruiser. We'll need this to get back to shore.

Without another word, Jimmy led his grandfather out onto the deck of the cruiser as Muldoon guided it around to a platform at the rear of the superyacht. Had any of them looked in the opposite direction, they would have seen the tiny white trails of foam left by two jet skis as they approached.

Fat Bernhard required the help of two of Jimmy's team to get him safely onto the deck of the superyacht. The moment he felt steady, he shook off their arms as if they were making a fuss and made his way up the short flight of steps onto the open rear deck.

Once there, his eyes widened in mute horror, and he sucked in a gasp of horrified air.

On the bridge of the cruiser, Muldoon watched with equal horror as two dozen of Raymond's heavily armed troops surged out from their hiding places. It was a classic sting ambush, Jimmy and his men all caught in the open. If any of them so much as twitched, they would be cut to ribbons.

Muldoon gave brief thought to throwing the engine into reverse and escaping, but a single shot through the window to the left of his head deterred him from touching the controls again.

Raymond's men were coming for him, advancing on the cruiser with their weapons ready. They were well-trained and slick - too good for Jimmy to have ever hoped to beat.

As Jimmy, his grandfather, and the five members of Jimmy's team were led inside the structure of the superyacht, nobody noticed the one set of eyes watching them.

Rex sniffed the air again, got nothing of use, and wished he'd stayed on land with his human.

'What do you think?' asked Albert.

When he replied, George had to fight against teeth that wanted to chatter.

'I think it's brass monkeys out here, Albert. I'm so cold I can't even feel my bollo ...'

'I mean about the ship,' Albert interrupted George, cutting off what he was going to say. 'I've got to say I am a little apprehensive about getting any closer. That thing has drug lord written all over it.'

'Then it's Raymond Rutheridge's,' George replied, 'Which would make perfect sense. He's probably come here because he's heard what has been happening.' He twisted around to look back toward Blackpool. There was no sign of it.

'I guess that makes sense,' Albert conceded. 'We've thought all along that the new player was messing with the protection racket. Maybe he was working for the top man all along.'

George inclined his head, acknowledging Albert's theory.

'Could be. Maybe Raymond decided to take it over, but didn't want to get his own hands dirty, so he outsourced to a contractor. I can see how that might happen.'

Both men knew that whatever the case might be, the whole thing was far too big for them. The only sensible play was to back off. They had chased the cruiser out to sea, but now it was docked up against the back of a superyacht owned by a man who would not hesitate to kill them.

‘I just want my dog,’ Albert complained to himself, his words too quiet for even George to hear. It was decision time, but really there was no choice to make. Albert couldn’t bring himself to head back to shore without Rex and that left him with only one option. ‘I’m going to sneak up from behind the cruiser,’ he announced.

‘That’s risky, Albert,’ George understated his opinion. ‘If you get caught, they will kill you.’

Albert refused to take his eyes off the cruiser. Rex was on it somewhere.

‘You should head back,’ he murmured loud enough for his friend to hear. ‘I have to get Rex.’

Before George had time to answer, Albert twisted the throttle again, easing his jet ski forward without creating much noise.

Two seconds later, George appeared alongside.

‘I’m too cold to ride this thing all the way back. I think we should take the cruiser.’

Albert wanted to argue, but he too worried about the cold creeping deeper into his body. He’d survived a recent dance with hypothermia and didn’t fancy giving it a second chance. If they could sneak up on the cruiser and find Rex, it wasn’t as if he could carry the dog back as a pillion passenger on the jet ski. And what about the wolf Rex was with? Albert was willing to bet his stubborn, headstrong hound wouldn’t leave him behind, so it had to be the cruiser or nothing.

Wondering how he managed to get himself into these situations, Albert coaxed his machine quietly up the back of the cruiser where both men tied them to a handy cleat.

'Rex?' Albert called, keeping his voice quiet.

They were on the low platform at the back of the cruiser, where Rex and Wolf had landed earlier. Three small steps led them up to the lower sun deck, but that was as far as they got.

'Lost are we, gents?' The question was posed in a jovial manner by a man holding a stubby machine gun. It was pointed loosely at both Albert and George, the gunman undecided about which he was going to shoot first. He was looking down at them from the upper deck roughly fifteen feet above their heads.

'Here, Spence,' he called over his shoulder without taking his eyes off his latest captives. 'Come and have a look at these two James Bond wannabes.'

Albert and George were frozen to the spot, or would have been if they could stop shivering.

A second man appeared alongside the first, his eyes doing a double take when he saw the silver-haired pensioners quivering on the aft of the boat. The two gunmen had been sent to check damage to the cruiser and return the weapons Jimmy's team took. They had been about to return to the superyacht when one spotted the jet skis approaching.

'Crikey, Tom! Is MI5 having recruitment problems?' Spence laughed at his own joke, Tom spluttering as he joined in.

Rex and Wolf hit them like a pair of furry wrecking balls.

Both men pitched forward, their arms pinwheeling in free air as they flipped over the top rail of the safety barrier.

Albert and George had to jump out of the way so the gunmen wouldn't land on them, barely getting clear before Raymond's troops clattered to the deck in a jumble of limbs.

Rex woofed his delight, his front paws on the top rail and his tail wagging as he looked down at his human.

The job wasn't done though. The men might have fallen a few feet but that wasn't enough to put them down. The oar George hit them with was.

Albert got to watch as his former sergeant whacked it down onto the crown of first one head and then the other as both gunmen scrambled to get up.

'That ought to do it,' George cackled.

'Where did you find that?' Albert wanted to know.

George inclined his head. 'It was over there.' Discarding the oar, he knelt beside Spence. 'Yup, still breathing,' he declared after checking each for a pulse.

Albert stared up, scanning the edge of the top deck. Rex wasn't there any longer and he couldn't hear his dog's claws heading his way either.

'Rex!' Albert hissed as loudly as he dared. 'Rex! Where are you, dog?'

Rex couldn't hear Albert because he wasn't within earshot. He wasn't even on the cruiser. Wolf had barely moved on the ride out to the superyacht, and he only started moving when he caught a whiff of his human's killer. Jimmy had stepped out onto the cruiser's deck, but before he and Rex could attack, Raymond's men had swarmed the ship.

They hid, accepting that they were going to have to bide their time and wait for the right opportunity, but now Wolf was arguing. They both had to watch as the man Wolf wanted was taken away. He wanted the satisfaction of getting revenge himself, it wasn't enough that the killer might die by someone else's hand.

'I'm going to find him,' Wolf growled.

'You're too weak,' argued Rex. 'If I push you hard enough, you'll fall down.'

Wolf snarled his response, 'Don't try me, dog.'

Rex darted ahead, getting in front of the wolf.

'Look, you can die here on this boat, or you can come with me. That's my human back there and he will get us back to dry land. He can take you to humans who will make you well again. It doesn't matter if you aren't the one to hunt down your human's killer, Wolf. Let it go while you still can.'

'Are you going to try to stop me?' Wolf asked, his top lip quivering as he showed his teeth.

It was a threat display, but not one that scared Rex. He knew the wolf was on his last legs. He also believed he had done all he could to help. If the wolf wouldn't listen to reason now, Rex was going to get back to his own human and help him to escape. Rex wanted to find a dry spot on the carpet of a public house somewhere and sleep there by his human's feet.

Rex bowed his head.

'No. I'm not going to stop you,' he sighed. Walking back toward the cruiser, he offered the wolf a parting comment. 'Good luck.'

On the cruiser still, Albert's search for his dog had yielded no results.

'Where the heck did you go to this time, dog?' Albert demanded. No one heard his question, and no one answered. He was trying to move stealthily, staying out of sight in case there were any other gun-toting criminals around.

George appeared, walking in a half crouch which was clearly proving difficult to maintain and causing him some discomfort.

'I didn't see him,' he let Albert know he hadn't been able to find Rex either. 'We can't stay, Albert. If he doesn't come back, we are going to have to go.'

Albert knew his friend was right. If Rex wasn't on the cruiser, then he was on Raymond 'Razor' Rutheridge's superyacht. They had been lucky so far, but following his dog there was asking for a terrible death. George had already put his life at risk and gone far beyond the call of friendship in trying to find Albert's dog. But just as Albert was going to accept the terrible burden of defeat, he spotted the dog coming back his way.

He grabbed George's arm. 'Here he comes now,' he squealed, elation filling his voice. 'If this is really the superyacht of a major gang boss, we ought to be bringing the coastguard and everyone else down on their heads. We can scarper first, but maybe we should call your daughter, she can arrange direct action, especially when we tell her we think that Jimmy character is on the ship. What do you think?'

George dug the plastic baggie with their phones and other paraphernalia out of his wetsuit.

'What's that doing in there?' Albert asked, pointing at the ancient miniature tape recorder.

George shrugged, delving into the bag to retrieve his phone.

'I dunno. I just stuffed it in there when I emptied my pockets. Here.' He passed the plastic bag to Albert so he could get to his own phone. 'Grab your dog and let's get out of here.'

Albert agreed wholeheartedly with that suggestion, but as he twisted around to head for the edge of the cruiser, hoping Rex was about to arrive there, George grabbed his shoulder.

'No signal,' George announced, showing Albert the symbol in the corner of his phone's screen. 'I guess we are too far out to sea.'

'The radios?' Albert asked, nodding his head toward the bridge of the cruiser.

George snapped his fingers. 'Great thinking. I guess that's why they made you a superintendent.' He slapped Albert on his shoulder to get him moving. 'Get your dog, get the ropes untied, and let's get out of here before someone else finds us.'

There was no mistaking the urgency in George's voice. Every extra second they spent where they were, the likelihood of getting caught increased.

Albert went forward just as George snuck into the cruiser's structure.

Rex was right there, crossing the rear deck of the superyacht to get to the cruiser. His tailed wagged, and his eyes sparkled. His human was ten yards away, but why was he standing so still?

As he watched, the old man slowly raised both his hands, looking beyond Rex and upward to the deck above where two new men with guns had their muzzles trained on his chest.

'Don't move,' one ordered, his voice calm and certain it would be obeyed.

Rex rushed to Albert's side, spinning around to track where the old man was looking.

The gunmen's' faces showed surprise at the unexpected arrival of a dog, but it changed their intended strategy very little. Something unheard passed between them and the man who had not yet spoken disappeared from sight.

'What's that in your hand?' the remaining gunman asked, nodding with his head at the plastic bag hanging from Albert's right hand.

As if remembering that he was holding something, Albert looked across at it with a curious expression.

'It's my phone, and the lead for my dog. I don't know what's going on here,' he tried to bluff. 'My dog ran off and jumped on the back of that cruiser behind me. I'm just here to get him back. I don't want any trouble.'

The gunman's face was impassive as he stared down into Albert's eyes. Whatever emotion he was feeling, his face refused to betray it.

'It's too late for that,' he said. 'Take the phone out and toss it in the water. And put the lead on your dog if you value his life. If he barks at my partner, I'll shoot him.'

Albert felt like screaming at the sky for all his rotten bad luck. All he needed was a few more seconds, and he could have been back on the cruiser with Rex and charging across the waves towards Blackpool. Instead, now he was really trapped.

Doing as instructed, Albert cupped the plastic bag in his left hand and reached in with his right. His fingers found the phone, but also George's ancient recording device. He knew the sensible thing to do was toss it overboard with his phone.

Footsteps were approaching, the second gunman working his way around the superyacht to find the intruders.

Making a show of it, and fumbling because his fingers were numb, Albert lifted his phone so the man above him could see it and then launched it out to sea. The man's eyes tracked it, just for a second or two and when he looked back at Albert the old man was connecting the lead onto his dog's harness.

The plastic bag was now empty, discarded on the deck by Albert's left foot.

Rex twitched, his muscles bunching as the second gunman came into sight. He understood what the guns represented and that he needed to help his human escape.

Sensing that his dog might attempt something foolhardy, Albert tightened his grip on the lead, pulling Rex closer and crouching slightly so he could loop his free arm around Rex's neck.

Once his partner arrived next to Albert, the first gunman retreated from sight, appearing less than a minute later down on the rear deck of the superyacht. Neither spoke, the twitch of a muzzle in the direction they wanted Albert to travel was sufficient to get him moving.

Albert didn't look back, not even once. They hadn't spotted George, that much was clear, or they would have boarded the cruiser to fetch him too. Since they hadn't, Albert was fervently hoping that George had seen what had happened and had the good sense to take the cruiser and escape.

It was the only sensible play. George could radio for help and save himself. Attempting to do anything else would just get him killed.

Albert was directed inside the structure of the superyacht, where warm air greeted him like an affectionate hug. He knew it would be a while before the warmth penetrated him enough for the shivering to stop, but being out of the cool breeze was an enormous relief.

There were voices ahead, muffled conversation drifting out from somewhere deeper in the yacht. A double width set of stairs led upward to a large open plan room where more than twenty men were gathered. Albert's brain labelled it as a stateroom. It was the sort of room he could see the US President holding a meeting in.

The assembled men were formed into two distinct groups. Albert recognised Fat Bernhard instantly, but the expression on the old gangster's face was vastly different to the haughty superiority Albert witnessed at the workingmen's club.

Fat Bernhard had the look on his face of a man gripped by utter terror. He was on his knees on the carpet in the middle of the room, his hands raised to shoulder height as if begging for his life. A yard behind him were six more men, including Jimmy and the giant from the sweet shop. Albert recognised the other four, of course, from their altercation in Rigby Road.

That they were also on their knees told Albert that his assumption about Jimmy working for the top boss to bring down Fat Bernhard was incorrect. It meant Albert knew even less about what was going on than he had hoped.

The men on their knees were all in the middle of the room and facing to Albert's left, so when he arrived, they all had to look over their left shoulders to see him. The conversation stopped abruptly.

'We found another one, boss,' announced the gunman closest to Albert. It was the same one who had done all the talking so far. Then he chuckled. 'I'm not really sure what to make of him though. He says he lost his dog.'

A ripple of amusement went around the room, not that the seven men on their knees in the middle found anything to laugh about.

Trying to hold his bladder and wondering if his voice would betray him and come out as a squeak when he spoke, Albert scanned around the room. It was easy to pick out the man in charge.

A tiny man wearing Cuban heels and a dandy suit over a shirt left open to his navel was sitting alone on a three-seater couch directly in front of Fat Bernhard and the six members of Jimmy's team. His hair was jet black and slicked backward across his scalp with something that made it look wet and greasy. His face bore a three-day stubble and there was a small scar above his left eyebrow.

Raymond had men arranged around and behind him - clearly his protection detail. Elsewhere in the room, the men Albert could see, he assumed to be other gang bosses and loyal lieutenants.

It would do him no favours to reveal that he knew the big boss's name, certainly it would expose the ruse that he was only there to get his dog. However, Albert also knew that they were never going to let him off this boat alive.

Before Albert got a chance to speak, the man on the couch, Raymond 'Razor' Rutheridge, lasered his eyes at the two men who had brought Albert into the room.

'And you thought it was a good idea to bring him into my conversation, did you? You checked him for bugs, yes?'

It was the infamous paranoia that George had spoken about, the organised criminal's friend if they wanted to stay out of jail.

Albert could not see them, but he could feel the nervousness radiating off the men to his left and right.

'Um, no, boss,' replied the talkative one, gulping in worry over his error in judgement. 'He's just an old man, and he's all wet, boss.'

Raymond bounced onto his feet, his face instantly a mask of rage.

'What? You don't think they can make waterproof listening devices?' he raged.

The eyes around the room were glaring at the two gunmen standing just behind Albert. It was enough to make Albert feel uncomfortable too, and now he really started to worry they would find the recording device.

It had been hard fighting against the numbness in his fingers as he took advantage of a very brief period when the gunman was watching Albert's phone vanish beneath the waves. In that tiny window of opportunity, Albert activating the tiny tape recorder and tucked it away where he prayed they would not find it.

Now he got to test out whether George's claim that an electronic sweep for devices would not detect it.

Raymond clicked his fingers, getting an instant reaction. A man began moving around the room, coming from the far side and around the backs of those all now watching Albert. He carried a familiar electronic device with a flat paddle wand about eighteen inches in length. If Albert had to guess, he would say it was an upgraded, or updated version of the one Fat Bernhard's man had used on him.

The man with the wand covered the ground in fast strides and the gunmen to Albert's left and right each took a step back to give him space to work.

Rex growled, a low bass note of threat. He wasn't sure what was going on, but he didn't like it and could smell fear coming from his human.

Albert jerked his lead and shushed him, reaching out with a trembling hand to stroke Rex's ears. Then, he waited, nervously holding his breath, and waiting for the device to beep. When the man with the wand stepped back and gave a curt nod in Raymond's direction, Albert physically sagged with relief.

Trusting that George was even now racing for safety and had already alerted the police, the coast guard, the Royal Navy, and possibly the A-Team, he chose to go for broke.

'Well, I'm glad that's over,' Albert said, with as much forced confidence in his voice as he could muster. 'I must say that you have a beautiful yacht, Raymond.'

Using the mob boss's name had the exact effect that Albert hoped it would.

Raymond's eyes flared in surprise, and his were not the only ones. Murmurs and whispers passed between the assembly of organised criminals all staring in his direction. Even the men on their knees looked Albert's way with curious expressions.

Sensing that he might be able to deflect attention away from himself, Fat Bernhard started talking.

'He used to be a police officer, Raymond. He was at my club this morning, poking around and asking questions.'

Not to be left out, Jimmy joined in on the action.

'Yeah, that old man and his dog interrupted me making a collection two nights ago. Then he turned up when a pack of dogs and the police raided our house just a few hours ago. It's him you want to be pointing the gun at, Raymond. My grandad and me weren't coming to attack you,' he lied. 'It was just a show of force to let you know how effective we could be and how we should be trusted with far greater responsibilities.'

Fat Bernhard turned his head a little, looking at his grandson with incredulous eyes.

'You killed four of his men at the dock, you idiot.'

'Oh, yeah,' said Jimmy, falling quiet once more.

Ignoring the men assembled on his carpet, Raymond gave the old man in the wetsuit his full attention.

'Who are you?' he asked. 'Make with some fast answers or I'll have my men start cutting bits off you.'

As threats went, Albert thought that was a pretty good one. He was also convinced that it wasn't hyperbole. Thankfully, his plan, as it was, involved him talking.

‘My name is Albert Smith,’ he announced. ‘I really am in Blackpool on holiday with my dog. But, as Jimmy claimed, I walked into a situation two nights ago where he was shaking down a rather nice couple for some money.’

Raymond interrupted, ‘Oh, boohoo. Like I care about whether the people we extort money from are nice or not. I run protection rackets through this tub of lard here.’ The mob boss aimed a kick at Fat Bernhard's midriff, doubling the overweight man over as a whoosh of air left his lungs. ‘I also manage prostitution, smuggling, and drugs trafficking. I have several politicians in my pocket and extort money from dozens upon dozens of wealthy people.’ He lifted his arms and looked about as if drawing attention to his palatial surroundings. ‘This is how I afford such a lifestyle. Unfortunately, because sometimes I demonstrate a lack of judgement in leaving imbeciles in charge of some of my minor operations,’ Fat Bernhard got another kick at that point, ‘I am required to return to this awful coastline to make sure things are operating as they should.’

‘So, Jimmy isn't working for you then?’ Albert asked, the open question intended to make Raymond say a little more.

Almost everyone in the room reacted in some way. Some made a scoffing sound, others gave a little chuckle at the old man’s ridiculous suggestion, and some gasped.

‘Really?’ asked Raymond. ‘That's really the best you can do? You've made it all the way onto my personal yacht where shortly you will die, and you don't even know what's going on?’ Raymond seemed amused to be giving away all his secrets so freely.

Feigning ignorance, Albert ruffled his brow and did his best to lead Raymond just a little further down the rabbit hole.

‘I thought Jimmy reported directly to you. I've been listening to him for some time,’ Albert lied, making it up on the spot. ‘Isn't he in line to take over drugs and prostitution from you? I thought you were looking to retire?’

Raymond looked around the room in disbelief. Making eye contact with several of the other men present, who all looked equally dumbfounded by Albert's latest statement.

‘Are you looking to replace me, Raymond?’ asked a man with glittering gold teeth and a shaved head. ‘My girls bring in plentiful profit every month.’

‘Yeah, Raymond, we’ve been working hard for you,’ protested another man. ‘Just last month I extended our crystal meth distribution and have increased our bottom line by almost fifteen percent. If you want us to do better, you just have to say, there’s no need to light a fire under our butts.’

‘It's not true!’ Jimmy protested. ‘I've never said any of those things.’

Raymond growled, silencing everyone so he could speak.

‘That’s enough. If I want your opinion on how to run things, I will give it to you.’

Albert watched as dissent spread around the room. All around Raymond, the other bosses were swapping meaningful looks. They believed they were being undermined and that Raymond was considering terminating their services. It was making them nervous, and while that made Albert’s environment even more lethal than it had been a moment before, it was also stirring up a hornet’s nest that might provide an avenue for escape.

Across the room, a new man spoke up. His colleagues knew him as Garfield though he'd been Christened Hilary and did everything he could to forget the teasing he got at school. More than anything, he was ambitious.

'If you want someone new to run prostitution, I want to throw my hat in the ring,' he remarked, a hopeful tone in his voice. He was backed by the two men on his shoulders, clearly his sons if Albert was gauging the family resemblance correctly.

The comment sparked a new round of argument.

'Hey,' said the man with the gold teeth. 'No one is taking over my piece of the pie, all right? It's my empire and I built it.'

'Because I let you, Clive,' Raymond pointed out with another harsh growl. 'I decide who does what.'

'Oh, yeah?' Clive's response drew a few sharp intakes of breath from around the room. It was a direct challenge and the men in his immediate vicinity were edging away to leave him in a space by himself.

Albert was fighting to not look down at Rex. His dog was sitting by his side, placidly watching. Albert maintained a strong grip on his dog's harness, using his hand as an extra barrier in case anyone looked closely enough to spot the recording device nestled between Rex's assistant dog jacket and his fur.

He could not tell if it was recording, or what quality the recording might come out. More importantly one might think, Albert had no idea if either one of them was going to get out of this alive. If they did, he had a full confession on tape.

'Enough!' snapped Raymond. Glaring at Clive with hard eyes, he said, 'You and I will continue this conversation later.' He spun in place, making sure to look at everyone in the room. 'I have no plans to shift anyone from any of their current tasks. This is not a job swap opportunity. We gathered so we could speak with Bernhard about his loss of control and what he was proposing to do to regain the protection racket in Blackpool. It is now time to extract some answers from him and from the men he arrived with. First though,' he stopped spinning when he came to face Albert, 'take the old man and his dog below and dispose of them both.'

The instruction was aimed at the two men who caught Albert sneaking onto the yacht to retrieve Rex. They were glad to be able to obey after their earlier faux pas.

Grabbed roughly by his left elbow, Albert almost lost his balance as they pulled him away from the assembly of gangsters and their dreadful plans. He kept a tight hold of Rex's lead, terrified the dog would attack if Albert gave him the slightest chance.

Frantically, Albert looked around. Could he throw himself at the guards and create an opportunity for Rex to escape? Would Rex run if Albert commanded him to?

Back down the wide set of stairs, they reached the next deck where he was shoved and pulled to go around and across the floor to another set of stairs. These were more narrow and were leading down into the bowels of the yacht.

Albert knew that if he went down there, he wasn't coming back out.

'Where are you taking my friend?' snarled the wolf.

The sudden and unexpected guttural growl from their left created the distraction Albert needed. He dropped Rex's lead and reversed direction as he threw his weight at both guards.

Rex didn't need to be told, but it warmed his heart when he heard his human shout, 'Rex! Sic 'em!'

The deafening sound of gunfire robbed Albert of his hearing for a heartbeat as one of the men pulled his trigger less than a foot from his head.

The shots went wild, the weapon aiming nowhere as Albert's attempt to thwart them threw the shots off target.

Above them in the stateroom, everyone reacted instantly and differently. Raymond opened his mouth to send reinforcements after the men he sent away with Albert, but the words never left his mouth.

Unconvinced Raymond was not attempting to remove his empire from under him and concerned that challenging Raymond just a few minutes ago would ultimately result in his untimely demise, Clive chose to attack.

Raymond's guards were running for the stairs which left the tiny man exposed. All Clive needed was a weapon, something Raymond's security team had relieved him of before he was allowed to come on board.

Meanwhile, Jimmy recognised that if he wanted to survive, this was probably the only chance he was going to get. Leaping to his feet, he hooked a hand under his grandad's right arm.

'Come on, Grandad! We've got to go right now!'

Bewildered, and not able to react that fast, Fat Bernhard stayed where he was.

The rest of Jimmy's men were making a break for it.

Garfield saw the sudden disarray as a perfect chance to get rid of Clive. He'd always wanted to have a stab at the prostitution empire. All he needed to do was remove the man running it.

In the space of a heartbeat, while the echo from the burst of gunfire downstairs was still fading away, the entire stateroom descended into bedlam.

Two decks below, Rex lunged and sank in his teeth. He caught the flesh of a forearm, biting down hard and throwing his body violently to one side and then the next. The hand attached to the forearm released the gun it held as the man squealed in agony.

The second gunman was trying to get to his feet, fighting Albert all the way. Surprise combined with landing on top had provided Albert with a brief advantage. He pressed that home as best he could because the man he fought had almost five decades on him and was significantly stronger.

However, Albert wasn't trying to win. He knew he only needed to delay the man for a couple of seconds. Rex was fast and effective. If Albert could just hold on, his dog would do what needed to be done.

He didn't get a couple of seconds.

A cracking left hook caught Albert on the right side of his face. It stunned him and loosened his grip on the man's gun arm. Mercifully, Rex arrived in the very next moment, biting down hard on the gunman's bicep.

Albert dropped his weight, landing once more on the gunman's forearm to pin the weapon in place.

The screams of pain from both gunmen were drowned out by the fresh sound of gunfire coming from upstairs. Albert could only imagine what was happening, though it was clear the dissension and doubt he created had bubbled over into an all-out battle.

Remembering the first gunman with a gasp of panic, Albert twisted around to find the man using his uninjured arm to retrieve his gun. It would kill just as affectively if held in the man's left hand and there was no way for Albert to get to him fast enough to prevent the trigger being pulled.

The gunman was sitting on the carpet, blood pooling underneath his ruined right arm as he brought the gun to bear.

Knowing he was about to die, and wishing he had been able to get Rex to safety first, Albert closed his eyes.

An almighty clanging noise reverberated around the room when a large fire extinguisher whacked into the gunman's skull and bounced off across the floor. The gunman's eyes rolled up into his skull, and he folded into a heap on the floor, out cold.

Albert couldn't manage to convince his lungs to draw a breath, so shocked was he to not be dead.

'Can we go now?' asked George, appearing from around the corner. 'It sounds like World War Three upstairs.'

As if to accentuate his point, several bullets came through the ceiling above his head to thud into the deck no more than a couple of yards away

Albert accepted a grateful hand up, tugging Rex away from the man he was still attacking.

'Come on, boy! We've got to go now!' With a hand through his collar, Albert yanked Rex away from his victim and it was only at that point that he spotted the wolf. Throughout the entire fight the animal had not joined in at any point. All he had done was watch.

Albert figured there would be time to ponder what that was about later. Right now, it really was time to go.

'You have to come with us now,' Rex urged Wolf. 'You can hear the gunfire upstairs. Chances are your human's killer is already dead. Do the right thing now and survive.'

Wolf came out from his hiding place but was moving slowly; the lethargy and dizziness he felt was making it hard to concentrate on anything. It had taken all his effort to distract the two humans when he saw them with Rex. But he knew the dog was right. He desperately wanted revenge on his human's killer, but his only option now was to flee and fight another day.

The two men and the two animals began hustling towards the cruiser. It represented their one chance of survival.

They got five yards.

Just as they were nearing the room with the wide staircase descending from the stateroom, a man landed hard on the carpet at its base. He had jumped from top to bottom, striking the ground too fast to control his movement, but instead of sprawling and crashing to the floor, he tucked into a roll and came out of it running.

Running was not an accurate description though; limping was a far more fitting term.

A spray of bullets followed him, eating into the carpet like a voracious termite as the bullets followed his retreating feet.

It startled Rex when the man landed, and the bullets stopped him from giving pursuit, but there was no mistaking the man ahead of them – it was Jimmy, the wolf's human's killer. He was bleeding badly from a wound high on his left shoulder - a bullet wound, Albert instantly surmised.

Wolf saw him too, his top lip curling to reveal his canines. He was being helped along by both Albert and George, the men able to spot that the animal was ailing, but upon seeing his quarry, the wolf found a fresh reserve of energy.

He bounded away with Rex at his shoulder, both animals chasing Jimmy as he in turn fled to get back to the cruiser.

As the old men followed behind as fast as their legs could take them, two more men tumbled down the wide stairs from the stateroom. A glance revealed that there was nothing to fear from them - they were both dead. They looked to be members of Raymond's security team, now shot full of holes.

Jimmy heard the animals behind him and glanced over one shoulder. His only plan was to escape. He didn't know what had become of his grandfather, but had seen Chappers and Vic shot down before they could get off the carpet. It was a bloodbath in the stateroom, that anyone might escape unscathed was questionable.

Who might be left alive was not, however, Jimmy's primary concern at that time. All his effort was on surviving, and that included avoiding the dog and the wolf who were yet again chasing him. He was unarmed this time, but he did have opposable thumbs so as he ran through the doors to get onto the sundeck at the rear of the yacht, he reversed direction and slammed them shut.

Inside, Rex and Wolf had too little notice to slow down or change direction, both slamming into the glass as their quarry evaded them once more.

Albert and George arrived a handful of seconds later, flicking the latch to open the doors once more. By then, Jimmy had cast off the ropes and was running to get to the bridge of the cruiser. In seconds, they would be left stranded on the superyacht.

Fit and healthy, Rex streaked across the deck and directly onto the bow of the cruiser. Trailing him, and powered only by sheer grit and determination, Wolf made it onto the cruiser too just as the engines roared into life.

Albert felt like he was running on empty. His tired muscles were aching due to the cold that had seeped into them, and the fatigue was made worse by the effort of fighting the gunmen. His whole body argued when he demanded just that little bit more from it.

The cruiser leapt backwards a yard as the propellers bit into the water.

Rex was waiting on the bow of the cruiser, barking encouragement at his human and the other man who was with him as they both leapt into open space. Had the jet skis not been lashed to the rear of the cruiser they would have landed in the sea.

As it was, the harsh acceleration when the boat moved backwards caused it to run over the pair of jet skis. One snagged a propeller, making a God-awful noise and forcing Jimmy in the cruiser's bridge to back off the throttle.

Desperate to get away, Jimmy threw the drive selector into the opposite direction and yanked back on the throttle once more. This time the cruiser surged forward, smashing into the rear of the superyacht as he turned the steering wheel hard to port. The cruiser scraped along the back of the yacht for two seconds before bursting into free water.

Albert and George were lying on the deck, holding each other to make sure they were both safe and fighting against Rex who was doing his best to lick the skin from Albert's face.

They needed a moment to find their balance, making it slowly onto their knees as the cruiser picked up speed and began to bounce across the waves. Jimmy was driving it at a terrifying speed, heading back to Blackpool as if the devil himself was giving chase.

'What now?' asked George.

Clinging to the side of the cruiser as they made their way gingerly along it to get inside, Albert looked back at the superyacht. It was already growing small in the distance. What carnage had they left behind? Was anyone on board still alive?

'Did you manage to use the radios?' Albert shouted to be heard over the sound of the racing engine and the pounding waves.

‘Yes,’ George shouted in reply. ‘I was able to get through to Eliza. I could not give her my coordinates though; I couldn't work out how to make the ship tell me where I was. Hopefully the description of a superyacht somewhere off the coast from Blackpool will be enough. We need to get close enough to shore that I can use my phone because they're going to want to know what they're walking into when they find it.’

It was another understatement, but Albert agreed that they needed to make the call. First, they still had the small problem of Jimmy to deal with. Was he armed?

The answer to that particular question was no, and Jimmy was cursing himself for it. The weapons locker on the cruiser was right behind him, outside of the bridge, but he could not get to it. He saw the dog and the wolf and the two annoying old men get on board the cruiser before he escaped from the superyacht. The humans didn't trouble him too much, but he remembered the pain of the wolf's bite and that same wolf was looking at him through the glass of the door to the bridge right now.

Every time he glanced over his shoulder, the wolf showed his teeth. How was it that this creature continued to chase him? How did it find him? How did it track him to a ship in the ocean?

All these questions played through Jimmy's mind as he raced for the glowing lights of Blackpool in the distance. The sun was setting fast, making the coastline easy to pick out. As he squinted into the darkness, the lights of the Blackpool Tower emerged from the dimness ahead.

The yacht club was there somewhere, but he wasn't aiming for that. He didn't care where he came ashore just so long as he was able to get away from the wolf. He knew he would spend a long time trying to figure out where his plan had all gone wrong. He wanted to ascend to his grandfather's right hand side and lead the senior member of his family to become the primary force in Blackpool's organised crime network.

It had truly been years in the planning, the idea coming to him when he was still in his teens. He had studied, and watched, and learned, but though this attempt was a failure, it would not be for nothing. He needed to regroup and recruit a new team. He could not guess who might have survived the battle on board the yacht, yet he was willing to bet a power vacuum had just been created. Even if Raymond had somehow managed to survive, his position would be greatly weakened.

Jimmy's plan had not gone as he expected, but there was opportunity still.

The next time he glanced at the door behind him, the old man from the sweet shop was trying to get in.

Tentatively, Albert tried the door handle. As he expected it to be, it was locked on the inside. He looked around for a weapon, something he could use to smash the window so they could reach in and unlock the door.

Did they really want to do that?

If they got through the door, they would force Jimmy's hand and he would have to fight. Albert was willing to bet that Jimmy did not have a gun, for if he had, he would surely have fired at them by now. That did not, however, mean that he was not armed.

If they got the door open, Rex would attack on command, but if Jimmy was holding a knife...

Albert did not want to think about it. They could wait him out. Soon they would be close enough to shore for George's phone to pick up a signal. Help would come, they did not have to tackle Jimmy themselves.

'We are on!' George cheered when two bars lit up on his phone. He was already pressing Eliza's contact and holding the phone to his left ear when Albert turned around. 'Hello,' George shouted when the call connected.

'Dad. Where are you? Are you okay? What's happening?' Eliza snapped into his ear.

'Um ...' George took a moment to explain their current predicament, providing as much detail as he could. 'Our current trajectory will land us near to the Blackpool Tower. I think he's using it as a landmark to aim for,' George guessed. 'He might veer off before we get there, but if you've got any resources near the coast, alert them to look out for a cruiser moving at about a thousand knots.' his exaggeration encapsulated the situation perfectly.

Had Albert and George known there was a treasure trove of assault rifles and other weapons in the same room they were currently standing in, they could have ended their breakneck flight across the water now, and approached the coast at a more sensible speed with Jimmy in their custody.

Of course, they did not know, so as the lights came closer and closer, and they questioned whether the man at the helm was ever going to slow down, they chose to find somewhere they could shelter and brace for impact.

Albert had to pull the wolf away from the door. Wolf's eyes were locked on his target, and he did not want to let Jimmy out of his sight again. Had he not been so weak from the fever running through his body, he would have been strong enough to resist. As it was, he was barely able to stand, and when the old man dragged him by the scruff of his neck, he simply did not possess the strength to stop it from happening.

'This could get dicey,' George observed, a tremor in his voice because they both believed they were going to crash. Would the ship sink with them on it? Would they be in shallow enough water that it would not be a problem? Was the fool aiming for a jetty? There was a vast difference between beaching it at high tide and slamming into something solid.

Aft of the bridge, Albert and George found cabins from which they rescued mattresses. It was hard to move, the boat's deck was in constant motion, but they managed to create a crash zone for themselves and the animals where they hunkered down and waited for what they felt was going to be the inevitable impact.

When Jimmy glanced over his shoulder to discover there was no longer anyone looking in through the window, it did nothing to still his concern. Quite the opposite, in fact. His heart rate ratcheted up a few more beats per minute as he questioned where they might have gone. He knew there were weapons out there, but could he get to them?

Taking his eyes off his course for a moment, he went back to the door where he looked all around to see if there was anyone still there. He calculated that he would only need a few seconds, just enough time to open the door, run to the weapons locker, and run back.

He had time! He was certain of it, and he desperately wanted the security and confidence a weapon would give him.

With the flip of his fingers the door unlocked, and he limped as fast as he could across to the locker. Triumphantly he gripped the handle and twisted. Even if the dog or the wolf or the old men returned now, it was too late for them to stop him. He would shoot them dead before they could get to him.

Only the handle did not turn. Jimmy's heart skipped a beat as he tried again. It was locked! Raymond's men had put the weapons back inside and secured it. Jimmy needed the key! Or he needed something to smash his way in.

With a jump, Jimmy remembered his collision course with the shore, and ran back to look at how close the cruiser might now be to the lights illuminating the seafront.

The blood drained from his face.

In his haste to get back to shore, he aimed for the unmistakable lights of the tower, but in so doing had forgotten that right in front of it was the pier. Jutting out into the water, the steel structure rose from the waves like an iron giant, and he was aiming right for it.

The terrifying sound of the metal hull rending and ripping as the steel of the pier tore through it became an all-encompassing din that blocked out all possibility of hearing any other sound.

Albert and George had no idea what the ship had collided with, but as inertia caused their internal organs to compress, they were glad of the additional cushioning they'd created for themselves.

On the pier, squeals of fear came from the people working there and tourists alike, many of them rushing to the edge to see what might have created the sound. Others chose to just bolt back towards shore, parents grabbing children and running with them - fear that the pier was about to collapse into the sea driving them onwards.

The cruiser careened off the pier's superstructure without damaging the metalwork, though it scared the bejesus out of some mussels and other molluscs happily clinging below the waterline. It was taking on water, a huge gash in the port front quarter of the bow acting like a funnel to push sea water into the stricken vessel.

Jimmy got thrown forward upon initial impact, flying through the air and over the controls to smash into the front screen of the bridge. His left collar bone broke, and his right wrist, plus he received a gash to the top of his skull, the blood from which was running down over his face.

He clambered back to the floor, unable to decide which part of him needed nursing the most. He could feel the deck beginning to tilt, the cruiser listing to port as water filled the hold. He knew there was a button somewhere to engage some pumps that would eject the water, but he could also tell that he wouldn't need it.

The cruiser was still going at a rapid rate, heading for shore where it was going to beach on the sand. Jimmy needed medical treatment - he could not ignore that now, but he also couldn't just go to a hospital. The bullet wound to his right shoulder would draw the police, and they would have uncomfortable questions that would result in his incarceration, he felt entirely certain. At the very least, they would link him to one of the guns fired on board Raymond's superyacht, and there was no way he would be able to claim his presence as an innocent bystander.

With the cruiser hurtling towards the sand, Jimmy did his best to brace against the control console. The propellers continued to churn at maximum rpms because Jimmy had not the presence of mind to reduce their speed, so when the leading edge of the ship's bow dug into the seabed, the laws of physics tried their absolute best to flip the back end out of the water.

Twenty yards aft of Jimmy's position, Albert, George, Rex, and Wolf all got thrown into the air. Hanging for half a second a few inches off the deck, they fell back with a bump to gain just a few more bruises. Then all was still.

But it was not quiet.

They could all hear the engine racing and water rushing into the hull of the boat.

Clambering to get up, and getting in each other's way, Albert and George fought to get their feet beneath their bodies so they could get up and get moving.

'Time to go?' shouted George rhetorically.

Answering him, Albert agreed, 'Really very definitely time to go.'

Even with all the noise, they heard the uneven cadence of Jimmy's limping footfalls as he ran out of the bridge and onto the deck of the cruiser. It was listing heavily to port now, though it would go no further because the sand was supporting it where the hull had dug in.

Rex nudged Wolf.

'This is it, Wolf. Can you make it? I can chase him down if you want.' It wasn't necessary for Rex to say who he was talking about; that he was referring to the killer was not in question.

Looking up at Rex's face from his position on the floor, the wolf finally admitted, 'I don't feel so good. Can you help me?'

'Sure,' Rex replied. 'First, we have to get you off this boat.'

Albert had gone three yards before he realised Rex was not following and went back for him. When he arrived back at the hidey hole they'd been in, the wolf was getting unsteadily to his paws.

'You need a hand, don't you?' Albert observed, leaning his head back into the passageway to call for George.

Between them, they picked the wolf up and carried him to the edge of the deck where it was a drop of about three yards from the bow to the sand. Too far for them to attempt to jump.

The sound of sirens was already filling the air as emergency vehicles closed on their position. Ahead of them, weaving underneath the pier so he would emerge on the other side, the limping form of Jimmy could just about be made out by his shadow.

'We'll have to go into the water,' Albert stated what both men were thinking. Another dip when they'd just about warmed themselves up did not appeal in any way, but it was a more attractive proposition than breaking their legs by landing on the sand from such a great height.

Halfway back along the side of the cruiser, the drop to the water was less than a yard and a half. Rex jumped when Albert commanded him to, disappearing under the waves to bob back up a moment later. Instantly doggy paddling for shore, Rex heard the splash as the two humans holding his friend plunged into the frigid water behind him.

Rex shook himself once he was free of the sea, spinning about and bouncing excitedly on his paws. He was ready to give chase - it was chase and bite time, but if he was going to do it, going to corner the killer so Wolf could exact his revenge, then Rex needed his friend to be with him.

Wading through chest deep water, Albert and George neared the shore. They were holding the wolf, his paws and the lower half of his body in the water. The moment the wolf's paws found the sand beneath them, he began to struggle to be set free.

He hadn't intended to do so, but in his feverish state, the wolf shoved too hard against George, sending him toppling backward into the waves. Albert released the wolf, reaching back to grab his partner - they both needed to get out of the water.

'Are you sure you're up to this?' Rex asked. 'I don't think he's going to get very far. You can just let the humans deal with him.'

Shaking his head in a hopeless attempt to clear it of the fogginess he felt, Wolf growled in defiance of his own weaknesses.

'No, it's happening now.' He began loping forward, forcing his paws to move. With each yard he gained a little bit more pace until he was running. Turning his head, but without taking his eyes off the target one hundred yards ahead of him, he asked, 'Can you slow him down a bit for me?'

Rex felt no need to provide a verbal response. Instead, he put his head down and he ran as fast as his body would allow him to go. In a race against even the fastest man on the planet, Rex would run rings around them. Against an injured man, limping heavily and struggling to see from the blood running into his eyes, it took him no more than a few seconds to close the distance.

Coming up behind Jimmy, he made no attempt to slow down, running straight through the back of the killer's legs and flooring him in the process.

Jimmy could hardly believe it. Flipped into the air to crash back to the sand a second later, pain receptors fired in his legs like white hot coals had been placed under his skin. Lifting his head to put his chin on his chest, he got to see the German Shepherd slide to a stop and reverse direction.

Jimmy knew he was hurt, but the terrible bruising from the German Shepherd's blockish skull was just another injury on what was becoming a long list. He needed a vacation, but it was terror that gripped him more than any of the injuries he felt.

It was obvious to him that the wolf had been tracking him because he killed its owner. It had bitten him at the time and had been showing up everywhere he'd gone since. The wolf was responsible for Ryan's death so far as Jimmy could make out. Certainly, Drew claimed that the nightmarish creature had tracked and chased them that night. Now it was back to get revenge.

Rex turned around to head back the way he came. The human was lying sprawled on the sand and trying to get up. Rex did not know that he had broken three bones in Jimmy's right leg, but his only intention now was to make sure the killer did not escape.

Wolf had slowed again, his fatigue and dizziness demanding that he reduce his pace to a steady lope. He could see his quarry - the human was right in front of him. He needed no more than a few seconds, plus the will to do what he had promised he would when he witnessed his human die.

Watching the wolf approach, his body battered, bruised, and broken, Jimmy broke down and began sobbing.

'Pleeeease!' he begged. 'Please, I'm sorry,' Jimmy wept openly. It was a pathetic display for a man who had taken so many lives.

A yard behind him, Rex watched impassively. He did not want to be a part of what the wolf had planned, but he had given his bond to help the wolf track his human's killer and that came with the acceptance that the wolf was going to kill the man when he finally cornered him.

The humans would arrive, and when they saw what he had done, they would put the wolf to sleep. Rex knew that without question, but the wolf had been ignoring his injury for so long, Rex felt sure he was not going to recover anyway. If this last act would give him some peace, Rex would not stand in his way.

Wolf paused in front of his quarry, taking his time, and savouring the moment.

The human was still sobbing and screaming for anyone to come to his aid. On the seafront, thirty yards up the beach, the flashing lights of police and other emergency vehicles created confusing shadows. The humans were coming.

Wolf knew he had but a few moments left to do what needed to be done.

Taking his eyes away from Jimmy's pathetic form, he looked at Rex.

'I need your help again, friend,' he made the request in a simple manner.

Rex dipped his head, breaking eye contact.

'I cannot help you with this. I must draw the line.'

Wolf's sniggering noise caused Rex to lift his head again.

'Did you think I was going to kill him? I'll admit the thought crossed my mind, but I would never be able to get the taste out of my mouth if I did that. Humans taste awful.'

'Yeah, they do,' laughed Rex, amused but also confused about what the wolf wanted him to help with.

Wolf walked forward, closing the final yards between him and Jimmy.

'Remember the animal control van?'

Albert and George were making the best progress they could across the sand. It was a slight uphill slog to get to the seafront and they saw little reason to hurry.

Until they heard Jimmy's screaming, that is.

Fear stabbed through Albert's heart, terrified that Rex might be killing the man he had been chasing for two days, but as he came out from under the dark shadow cast by the pier, and squinted at the gaggle of forms fifty yards ahead, a laugh burst from his mouth.

'Are they …?' George couldn't believe his eyes.

Albert struggled to get the words out.

'Yes!' he spluttered, mirth stealing his breath. 'They are!'

Jimmy fought and cursed and flailed around with his broken limbs, but there was nothing he could do to stop the dog and the wolf as they emptied their bladders all over him.

The bright beam of a powerful flashlight illuminated them as the police invaded the beach. They had only a vague idea about what was going on and were operating entirely upon a garbled and confusing message from DCI Benjamin-Mackie.

She was somewhere else, coordinating something that was happening out to sea and involved the coast guard, the royal navy and no less than three police launches.

'It's a wonder she didn't call the A-Team,' a uniformed sergeant grumbled as he attempted to organise the officers at the beach.

By the time Albert and George reached Jimmy's location, the police were only a few yards away.

Rex and Wolf had backed off a pace, knowing the humans would want to get to the injured man. However, as everyone converged on their location, the wolf lost his battle against the fever ravaging his body. The eyesight became fuzzy, and with a quiet howl of despair, he collapsed onto the sand.

Rex was immediately on his feet, barking and prancing to draw attention to his friend.

He ran to Albert, grabbing the old man's right wrist in his mouth so he could drag him to where Wolf lay. 'He needs help!' Rex howled.

'Right, what on earth is going on here? Who was piloting that cruiser?' asked the uniformed sergeant as he attempted to get a grip on what was happening. Two of his officers were dealing with an injured man as that was a priority he could not ignore, but he wanted to know who the two old men in the wetsuits were.

'Dad!' A voice from the seafront drew everyone's attention.

It was Eliza, jumping down to run across the sand.

Murmuring quietly to Albert, George asked, 'Do you think she will kick me in the trousers before or after she hugs me?'

It turned out to be neither. Eliza was so relieved to find her father in one piece, she simply held him until the damp from his wetsuit soaked through her own clothes. Then she took control of the area, ensuring Jimmy was read his rights and that he was searched for weapons before the paramedics began administering first aid.

Albert was kneeling on the sand with Rex. They were next to the unconscious form of the wolf. Albert was no vet, but it didn't take a genius to tell that the wolf was seriously ill. His pulse was weak and thready, his gums pale and his nose dry. The wolf was circling the drain.

Blankets arrived, Albert and George taking one each to wrap around their bodies, and using two to insulate the wolf.

'Gotcha!' cheered a voice as it cast a shadow over Albert and Rex.

Rex looked up just as the animal control idiots looped the hoop from a pole over his head. He bucked and threw himself backward, but the loop snapped closed, trapping his head at the end of a three-yard pole.

'Ha! Try escaping now, you mangy mutt!' cackled Richard triumphantly.

Albert punched him in the face.

'Hey!' protested Andy. 'You can't do that. We've been chasing that dog for two days. He's dangerous!'

'He's my dog!' growled Albert, rubbing his bruised knuckles.

Richard was sprawled on the sand, his pole lost when he fell.

Ignoring them both, and with George's help, Albert got Rex free once more.

'What is going on?' Eliza snapped at the animal control idiots. 'What are you two clowns doing?'

'The wolf,' Richard mumbled through his fingers as he held his nose and wondered if it was about to start bleeding. 'It's on our most wanted list. We have to take it in.'

'Then what are you doing with Mr Smith's dog?' she demanded to know.

'Um, well,' Richard stammered as he attempted to find something to say. 'Well, the dog and the wolf have been seen together. They have been working in tandem to prevent us catching either one of them.'

Eliza gave the man a snort of derision. 'You're suggesting they are accomplices?' Her question got a ripple of laughter from those within earshot, but Albert interrupted.

'The wolf is sick. He needs urgent treatment. He isn't even conscious.'

'Very well,' Eliza pinned the two animal control idiots in place with a hard glare. 'Do your job. Get him back to your base and make sure a vet sees him as an urgent case.'

Quietly, and without arguing, Richard and Andy confirmed the wolf wasn't going to put up a fight and carried him back to their van in the blankets the police supplied.

Rex whined as they took his friend away, worried he might never see him again, and questioning if he would ever learn what had happened to him.

Eliza was quick to clear the beach. Getting her father and Albert out of their wet things and somewhere warm became a priority the moment Jimmy was declared stable and ready to be moved.

The coastguard arrived to deal with the cruiser, above them the pier had been evacuated until it could be inspected and proven safe, and the crowd of people who had gathered on the seafront were dispersed by Eliza's officers.

There was nothing more to see.

There was, however, something to hear.

At the police station, dressed in sweatpants and sweaters, and with steaming cups of tea in their hands, Albert and George regaled Eliza with the events of the day.

They explained about seeing Rex – Albert's sole driver for being involved in the first place – jump onto the back of the cruiser with the wolf, and how one thing led to another.

Twenty cops crammed in close to each other as they listened to the incredible tale the two retired cops had to tell.

Rex snoozed beneath Albert's legs, his head filled with doggy dreams about chases, boats, and sleeping rough.

Eliza was waiting for a full report from those involved, but knew she was in for a long night. The coastguard had been the first to locate the superyacht. It had drifted into British coastal waters, and was found to have no one at the wheel. The scene on board was a massacre, more than a dozen dead and more dying from their injuries.

The vessel itself was serviceable so was being sailed back to the nearest harbour able to accommodate a ship of its size. Some of the injured were being treated on board HMS Cutthroat, a Royal Navy frigate that was in the vicinity and called upon to give assistance. Among the survivors was a man described as a giant and a fat man who had to weigh at least four hundred pounds. Raymond 'Razor' Rutheridge had also survived and was recorded to be screaming blue murder at being taken into custody.

'What we lack is evidence of any wrongdoing,' Eliza lamented. 'There were guns on board, but it will be difficult to get any charges to stick unless we can pin individual deaths to ballistics and then fingerprints on weapons. Even then, it will be a fight with the lawyers who will claim self-defence. It will be a huge headache building a case that sees any of the big players serving the sentences they deserve. These are the biggest criminals operating in this area. We could cut crime by over fifty percent just by locking them up.'

Albert reached down to ruffle Rex's fur, scratching behind his ears before sliding a hand into his harness and pulling out the tiny tape recorder.

'What's that?' Eliza asked.

Rather than answer, Albert simply pressed play and picked up his mug of tea.

Requesting them to return the following morning so they could give a proper statement, Eliza saw no need to keep Albert or George at the station a moment longer than was necessary. They were obviously tired and had been through a lot in one day.

Heading out of the station where there were officers waiting to give each of them a lift to wherever they needed to go, Albert and George paused so they could talk.

'You will be heading home to Kent in the morning?' George asked.

'I must,' Albert remarked.

'This is to do with the Gastrothief case you were telling me about?'

'It is,' Albert admitted. 'But also, I feel a need to see my family. It has been many weeks since I held my grandchildren. It will do me good to be home for a few days.'

George understood the sentiment. He stuck out his hand for Albert to shake, the two old friends saying goodbye again.

'I'll see you in the morning for breakfast?' Albert enquired. 'We can eat and then come to the station to give our statements together?'

George smiled warmly. 'That's the best plan either one of us has come up with today.'

They shared a laugh, both thanking their lucky stars they had somehow come out of the adventure alive.

Albert walked down to the waiting squad car to discover it was Constable Gordon assigned to give him a ride. It was late now, approaching midnight, and Albert was keen to get into his bed. However, there was another place he needed to go first.

Rex lifted his head when the squad car stopped. The smell drifting into his nostrils was not the one he expected.

'You want me to wait, Sir?' Constable Gordon enquired.

'Is that okay?' Albert hadn't expected the gesture.

With the squad car parked outside, Albert let Rex lead him into the animal control centre.

A young woman behind the reception desk looked up as he approached, her wide-framed, round glasses distorting her eyes a little.

'Hello,' he waved. 'Can I enquire about the wolf you had brought in earlier this evening?'

Rex was listening to every word, and though he didn't understand them all, he caught the tone of his human's response and the sadness it contained.

'Can I speak to the vet?' Albert asked, keeping his tone polite but insistent.

'Um ... okay, I'll just need a second.' The young woman picked up the phone, dialling through the internal system to find the person she needed. It wasn't the vet she was speaking to but the vet's nurse.

She came out to see him, though it took a further fifteen minutes and three layers of bureaucracy before he got to talk to the person he wanted.

'He's scheduled for euthanasia,' the vet, a slender woman in her thirties, admitted. 'I have been attempting to revive him, but what he really needs is a blood transfusion. He has an injury on his chest; it must be a couple of days old now, but I pulled a piece of rotting wood from it. It looks like he either fell from a height or was hit with something. A large, filthy splinter embedded itself under his skin and left untreated it caused septicaemia. I'm not sure what I can do that I haven't already done.'

'You can't do the transfusion? Rex can give blood,' Albert offered, knowing Rex was fit and healthy enough to do so.

Rex wagged his tale at the mention of his name.

'I wish it were so simple,' the vet replied. 'Blood from a dog won't do it. I need some from a wolf. Preferably a Timber Wolf. Dog blood is close but giving the wolf that would be much the same as leaving the poisoned blood in his system.'

'How about local zoos?' Albert asked, clutching at straws.

What he hadn't realised, was that the vets working at the animal control centre were not used to thinking outside the box and looking for solutions. The organisation they worked for was not making profit and thus there was limited budget for any surgeries or treatments they carried out. The vet had not thought to contact a local zoo because she hadn't been looking for a way around her problem.

In less than ten minutes they had a vet from Blackpool Zoo packing a bag and racing to get out of his house.

Twenty minutes after that, Albert and Rex were staring through an observation window. On the other side of the glass was the surgery where the vet from the zoo was hanging a blood bag and administering an injection.

Three hours passed in which both Rex and Albert failed to fight their fatigue. When Albert awoke, it was with a sudden start that he instantly regretted. The jolt to his body as he twitched pulled at the numerous bruises and injuries he carried.

The two vets, the one from the zoo and his counterpart at the animal control centre were coming into the waiting room.

'He's awake,' the lady vet announced. 'Would you like to see him?'

Rex was on his feet and tugging at his lead to get Albert moving.

Wolf was still groggy, painkiller meds robbing him of his ability to stand, so he was lying on his side on a mat inside a cage in the centre's holding area.

Through the bars, Rex asked, 'How are you feeling?'

Wolf managed to focus his eyes just enough to see who it was.

'Oh, hey, Rex. I feel like I got run over by a car. No, several cars. I feel terrible. I guess that's better than feeling nothing at all though, right?'

While the dog and the wolf communicated with each other through the bars of the cage, Albert pressed a new question upon the vets.

'What will happen to him now?'

The zoo vet's face split into a broad smile.

'Would you believe our own alpha male died just three weeks ago. I have a pack with no leader. A strong wolf like this one will easily take over once he is well enough. I'll transfer him in the morning so we can care for him on site at the zoo. We are better equipped for it there. No offense,' he added quickly, not wanting to upset his female colleague, especially since she had given him her number half an hour ago.

'Oh, none taken,' she assured him.

'Did you hear that?' Rex asked his friend. 'You're going to the zoo. You're going to get your own pack to lead.'

Wolf lifted his head slightly, trying to work out what that meant.

'You mean like ... like lady wolves?'

If they had known how, the dog and the wolf would have high-fived through the bars of the cage.

Breakfast Goodbyes

Breakfast came and went, Albert and George feeling little need to speak during their meal. Rex popped his head up to table level several times, getting rewarded on each occasion with a piece of juicy sausage which Albert ordered as a special side plate, just for him.

Man and dog had finally found their way back to their room at almost four in the morning, so breakfast was a far later affair than initially intended. They were the last customers in the dining room when they folded their napkins and set their plates to be cleared.

'How are you getting home?' George asked. 'Train?'

Albert idly stroked the crown of Rex's head, happy to have his dog back at his side. He acknowledged a twinge of sadness that his best friend would never be able to explain why he had felt the need to run away and to help the wolf, or what had gone on when they were apart. Albert and Rex were back together, and that was going to have to be enough. He did, however, make a mental note to always have Rex clipped to his lead before opening the door if there were any further night time demands to go outside.

Rex had his eyes closed, luxuriating in the warm glow a belly full of sausage had produced and the affectionate touch of his human.

'My son is coming to fetch me,' Albert answered, his eyes still focused on his dog.

'Randall?'

Albert shook his head. 'Gary. He took the day off.'

'You said he's the one fronting the police investigation into that Gastrothief of yours?' George sought to confirm.

'Well, it's kind of off the books still. We haven't been able to come up with anything concrete enough to divert resources into an official investigation. Gary has been poking into things in his own time. Selina and Randall too, a bit.'

A waitress came to take away their plates. She confirmed they were finished with their meal and cleared the table.

Once they had allowed her time to retreat, the pensioners left the table. George waited in the hotel's reception until Albert returned from his room with his suitcase and backpack. All his things were in them. Rex's too for that matter.

George offered to carry the case, but Albert wouldn't let him. It was his burden to carry was the way he put it. Instead, he let George hold Rex's lead, suggesting he keep a strong grip.

Just in case.

Exiting the door, Albert paused to sniff the Blackpool air. Would he ever be back? He believed it to be unlikely, though not impossible. His desire to go other places and explore the world rather than his advancing years formed the basis for his feelings on the matter.

George and Rex were beneath him at pavement level where they waited patiently.

They needed to turn right to get to the police station, but a glance to his left as Albert stepped down to join his friend and his dog, caused a fast doubletake.

The sweetshop was open.

George followed Albert's eyes, curious to see what might have caused the expression on his friend's face.

Spotting exactly what caught Albert's attention, he choked out a surprised laugh.

'They didn't leave after all,' George remarked.

'And I never did buy that stick off Rock,' murmured Albert.

Lionel and Doris, despite their injuries, were in fine moods when the old men found them. They had heard all about the arrests and likely long-term incarcerations on a radio news bulletin in their car. It caused them to perform a swift U-turn - they had never really wanted to leave Blackpool.

Walking to the police station a little more than a mile away, Albert crunched and munched his way through a footlong stick of Blackpool Rock. Between bites he continued to tell George about the trail of the Gastrothief and about the young man who went missing in Arbroath.

Epilogue - Captives

'It's not hopeless,' Argyll insisted. 'We have to be ready, and we need to have a plan.'

Benny tutted. 'Is this about the old man again?' His tone of voice made it clear to the newcomers that he'd heard it all before and Argyll's rubbish wasn't worth heeding.

There were three new captives, for that was what they called themselves regardless of the barmy earl's assurances they were persons he had saved. Two women and a man, they were all wine specialists, kidnapped a few days ago. They were to grow and harvest grapes to keep the earl's wine cellar stocked.

The news that they were to spend the rest of their lives below ground in his gargantuan bunker had not been well received. However, their initial thoughts of escape had quickly been dashed when they met some of the other captives.

'I've been here two years,' grumbled Benny, a grain farmer employed to ensure a plentiful stock of wheat, rye, and barley graced the earl's larder each year. He wouldn't have thought growing underground was possible, but the intense light supplied by the earl's own power station actually made the grains grow faster and stronger. 'We ain't ever seeing the sun again, and you should all just accept it.'

'No,' snapped Argyll. 'There is always hope. We can find a chink in the guards' routine. We can arm ourselves, and if no one comes for us, we can fight our way out. There are ten times as many of us as there are of them.'

'Yes, but they are carrying guns,' Benny pointed out with a sad shake of his head. 'Attempting to escape will get you killed. I have seen others try and they are all dead now. They kill you if you don't do your job too, so don't think he'll let you go if he has no further use for you.'

The room fell silent.

They were captives, but they were well catered for. The earl had housing built to accommodate the many staff he needed to provide for him after the world ended. There were even leisure facilities, not that the earl could understand why people wanted to exercise when the time could be spent eating instead.

'What old man?' asked one of the new women. The couple who arrived with her were snivelling quietly, trying to come to terms with the sudden and manifest change to their lives.

'Oh, don't get him started,' whined Benny. 'It's all just a load of nonsense. His head is filled with clouds, that one.'

Ignoring him, Argyll met the new woman's gaze.

'I met him in Arbroath. He was there following a clue to a crime that he could barely explain. It was all to do with a master criminal who was stealing equipment and kidnapping people from the food industry.'

'Wait! That's us!' the woman blurted, the couple at his side instantly twisting around and shutting up so they could hear what else Argyll had to say.

Argyll nodded his agreement. 'He knew about it and had been following the trail of the earl's operatives for weeks. He will know I was kidnapped – we worked together to solve a case in Arbroath.' He explained about his father and the thirty-year-old murder the chief of police and a local politician had conspired to cover up. 'Albert Smith is tenacious in a way that I doubt many can ever understand. Against all odds and with no one at his side but his dog, he kept going until he found the evidence he needed to bring the whole pack of lies tumbling down.'

'You really think he can find us?' asked the new woman.

Argyll nodded his head again. 'I truly do. It could be tomorrow. It might be a month or two months from now, but that old bird ... he won't give up.' A memory surfaced, making Argyll smile. 'The Gastrothief, that was what he called the earl.'

Benny's voice dripped with derision when he echoed the words.

'The Gastrothief. What kind of daft name is that?'

Argyll was used to Benny's attitude and put it down to the stress of captivity.

'He needed a term of reference. He was talking to his children – they are all senior detectives in London, and had to call the person behind it all something. Besides, Gastrothief fits.'

'Yes,' agreed the woman, 'I suppose it does.'

Holding her gaze, Argyll reassured her one more time.

'He's coming for us. We just need to give him enough time to find the pieces, and we need to be ready.'

The concept of being ready generated a new line of discussion, one which took them all the way to lights out when the small settlement and its inhabitants were plunged into darkness at the flick of a switch.

The newcomers went to bed that night with a sense of hope. An old man was coming to rescue them. An old man and his dog.

The End

Author's Note

Hello, Dear Reader,

I hope you enjoyed this mystery tale. Occasionally, when I am writing, I find myself so engrossed in the story I am weaving that my heart starts racing. On even rarer occasions, I begin to feel tears forming from the emotion behind the words I am writing. Both things happened during the two weeks it took me to write this story.

I had some fun coming up with gangster names for Fat Bernhard's men. I wanted them to be entertaining, but not too ridiculous. I hope I got the balance right. Coming from a life in the army, I was used to people having nicknames. Some were given instantly based on a person's name. Anyone called Murphy gets called 'Spud'. Corporal White is going to spend his entire career getting called Chalky.

Hissing Sid, for those who do not know, comes from a song called Captain Beaky. It made it to number five in the UK charts in 1980 and for the nine-year-old author, became the first ever single in his collection. Hissing Sid was the snake who the other animals in the forest were trying to evade or catch – I genuinely do not remember which.

Cruelly, in the army, anyone with a lisp got called Hissing Sid. There were worse names for people with other afflictions.

I mention Brass Monkeys in the book. Albert and George are fighting against the cold of the late autumn weather when they are out at sea on the jet skis. Brass Monkeys is a naval term, specifically from the Royal Navy. The story goes that cannon balls used to be stored aboard naval vessels in piles, on a brass frame or tray called a 'monkey'. In very cold weather the brass would contract, spilling the cannonballs: hence very cold weather is 'cold enough to freeze the balls off a brass monkey.

Anyone who has ever been to Blackpool and most especially those who live there will be questioning whether I ever have. This is because I shifted the yacht club onto the seafront from its usual position several miles inland on the River Wyre. I'm going to hold my hand up and admit that I have never visited the seaside resort, but I put the shifting geography due to artistic license.

I needed there to be a sea chase and couldn't make the story work without everyone being in a position to witness some part of Fat Bernhard, Jimmy, Wolf, and Rex getting on the cruiser.

The pier and the tower really are close to each other though, so a vessel approaching the shore at great speed and using the tower as a landmark, might crash just as I described.

It's October now, a good portion of the year already behind us and somehow I cannot work out how many books I have written since the year started. Last year I kept a record, and I think I will have to do the same thing next year.

Tomorrow morning, I will start the editing process for this story and in a couple of days, I will be sinking my teeth into the next story on my list to be written.

Next up is a book called Terrible Secrets. It is the eighth book in my urban fantasy series, The Realm of False Gods. You're not interested in that though, you want to hear about the next Rex and Albert tale.

Check over the page to see what is coming next.

Take care.

Steve Higgs

History of the Dish

The earliest form of rock is believed to be sold at fair grounds in the 19th century and, though it was similar, it was not lettered or flamboyantly coloured like the Seaside rock we are acquainted with today.

Ben Bullock, an ex-miner from Burnley, began manufacturing sticks of brightly coloured, lettered candy at his Yorkshire-based confectionary factory in 1887, after conceiving the idea while holidaying in Blackpool. Bullock sent his first batch of lettered rock to retailers in Blackpool, where it was well received, and seaside rock was born.

Sticks of rock can now be bought in souvenir shops of most British seaside resorts including Blackpool, Brighton, Scarborough, and Weston-Super-Mare.

How seaside rock is made

It takes an incredible amount of skill for sticks of lettered rock to be created, skill that machines are still unable to master even in the 21st century. Practised craftsmen of seaside rock are called Sugar Boilers and, as the name suggests, they start the process by boiling sugar and glucose in a copper pan heated to three hundred degrees centigrade.

Once the sugar mixture reaches the ideal temperature, it is poured out onto a cooling table and separated into parts. The inner core part is aerated and flavoured (traditionally mint, though it can be a variety of fruit flavours), while the remaining outer layer and lettering sections are coloured. Getting the lettering correct is a skill that can take up to 10 years to master, as rock is often up to 6 feet long before it is cut.

The letters are made individually before they are stuck together in a line with white filler in between. Square-shaped letters (B, E, F, K) and triangle-shaped letters (A, V) are made first, while round-shaped letters (C, D, O, Q) are made last to prevent loss of shape before the rock sets.

The lettering, filling and core are rolled together before they are wrapped in the brightly coloured outer casing. The whole slab is then stretched into smaller, longer strips by machine before being cut and wrapped ready for sale.

No recipe to follow this time, sorry. Messing with liquid sugar is not for the faint-hearted, and this is a product that can only really be made in giant batches.

No recipe this time, boiling vast quantities of sugar is not something I wish to encourage homeowners to undertake.

What's Next for Rex and Albert

On the southeast coast of England, three wine growers have just gone missing and a fourth has been murdered. Could this be the work of the master criminal Albert Smith has been chasing all over the country?

You'd better believe it. Rushing back to his home county to see if he can pick up the trail again, Albert has no idea the perpetrators are still there.

They have other deadly tasks to complete, and they know to be on the lookout for the old man and his dog.

A FREE Rex and Albert Story

There is no catch. There is no cost. You won't even be asked for an email address. I have a FREE Rex and Albert short story for you to read simply because I think it is fun and you deserve a cherry on top. If you have not yet already indulged, please click the picture below and read the fun short story about Rex and Albert, a ring, and a Hellcat.

When a former police dog knows the cat is guilty, what must he do to prove his case to the human he lives with?

His human is missing a ring. The dog knows the cat is guilty. Is the cat smarter than the pair of them?

A home invader. A thief. A cat. Is that one being or three? The dog knows but can he make his human listen?

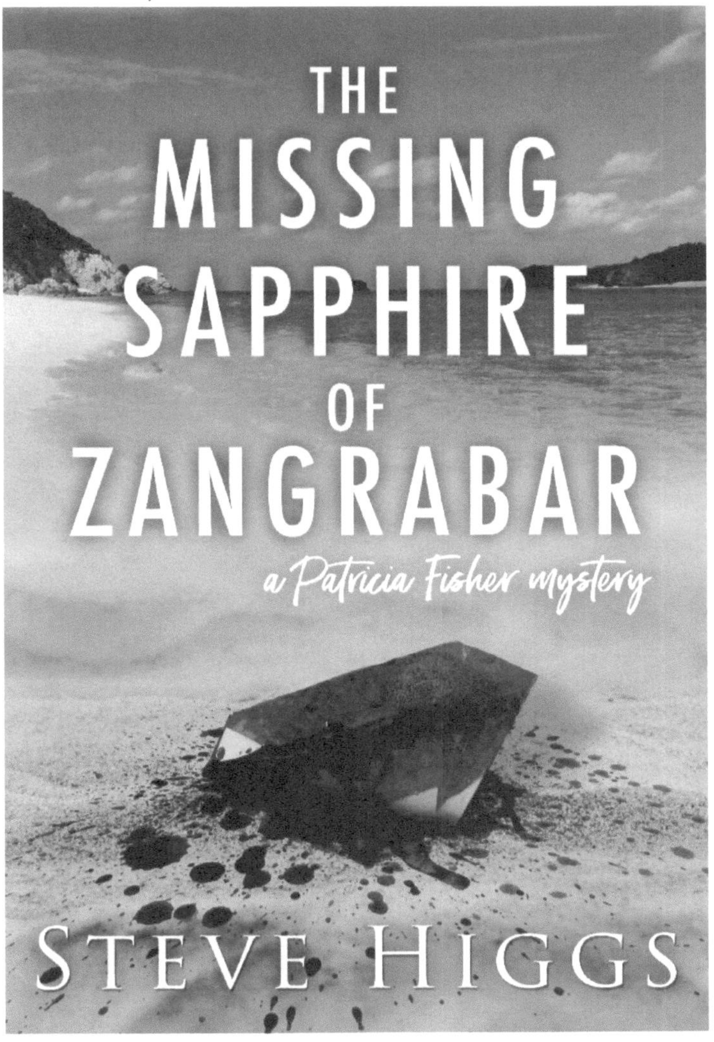

When life gives you lemons, empty your cheating husband's bank accounts and go on a cruise.

That's right, isn't it?

Fuelled by anger, and decision impaired by gin, Patricia boards the world's finest luxury cruise ship for a three-month tour of the world …

… and awakes to find herself embroiled in a thirty-year-old priceless jewel theft.

Less than twenty-four hours after setting sail, she's accused of murder and confined to her cabin. Thankfully, she is staying in the royal suite and that means she has a butler to help her. When he recruits his gym instructor BFF, Barbie, the trio turn detective to find the real killer.

But someone on board doesn't want them to succeed and when the next body is found in her kitchen, the team realise it's more than just her freedom at stake.

They'd better solve this fast or all three of them might be next.

The paranormal? It's all nonsense but proving it might just get them all killed.

When a master vampire starts killing people in his hometown, paranormal investigator, Tempest Michaels, takes it personally …

… and soon a race against time turns into a battle for his life.

He doesn't believe in the paranormal but has a steady stream of clients with cases too weird for the police to bother with. Mostly it's all nonsense, but when a third victim turns up with bite marks in her lifeless throat, can he really dismiss the possibility that this time the monster is real?

Joined by an ex-army buddy, a disillusioned cop, his friends from the pub, his dogs, and his mother (why are there no grandchildren, Tempest), our paranormal investigator is going to stop the murders if it kills him ...

... but when his probing draws the creature's attention, his family and friends become the hunted.

More Books by Steve Higgs

Blue Moon Investigations

Paranormal Nonsense

The Phantom of Barker Mill

Amanda Harper Paranormal Detective

The Klowns of Kent

Dead Pirates of Cawsand

In the Doodoo with Voodoo

The Witches of East Malling

Crop Circles, Cows and Crazy Aliens

Whispers in the Rigging

Bloodlust Blonde – a short story

Paws of the Yeti

Under a Blue Moon – A Paranormal Detective Origin Story

Night Work

Lord Hale's Monster

The Herne Bay Howlers

Undead Incorporated

The Ghoul of Christmas Past

The Sandman

Jailhouse Golem

Shadow in the Mine

Patricia Fisher Cruise Mysteries

The Missing Sapphire of Zangrabar

The Kidnapped Bride

The Director's Cut

The Couple in Cabin 2124

Doctor Death

Murder on the Dancefloor

Mission for the Maharaja

A Sleuth and her Dachshund in Athens

The Maltese Parrot

No Place Like Home

What Sam Knew

Solstice Goat

Recipe for Murder

A Banshee and a Bookshop

Diamonds, Dinner Jackets, and Death

Frozen Vengeance

Mug Shot

The Godmother

Murder is an Artform

Wonderful Weddings and Deadly Divorces

Dangerous Creatures

Patricia Fisher: Ship's Detective

Albert Smith Culinary Capers

Pork Pie Pandemonium

Bakewell Tart Bludgeoning

Stilton Slaughter

Bedfordshire Clanger Calamity

Death of a Yorkshire Pudding

Cumberland Sausage Shocker

Arbroath Smokie Slaying

Dundee Cake Dispatch

Lancashire Hotpot Peril

Blackpool Rock Bloodshed

Kent Coast Oyster Obliteration

Felicity Philips Investigates

To Love and to Perish

Real of False Gods

Free Books and More

Get sneak peaks, exclusive giveaways, behind the scenes content, and more. Plus, you'll be notified of Fan Pricing events when they occur and get exclusive offers from other authors because all UF writers are automatically friends.

Not only that, but you'll receive an exclusive FREE story staring Otto and Zachary and two free stories from the author's Blue Moon Investigations series.

Yes, please! Sign me up for lots of FREE stuff and bargains!

Want to follow me and keep up with what I am doing?

Facebook

Made in United States
Troutdale, OR
12/15/2024